a **lion** in your **number**

Also by **Kevin Klix**:

FICTION

Biflocka
A Lion in Your Number
Elevator Music
Skateboy
The Student
Wasp in the Opium Flowers

NON-FICTION

Beautiful Nihilism
What's Wrong With Millennials?

SELF-HELP

A Wellness Guide to Happiness
Stop Unreality

POETRY

*Why I F*cking Hate Poetry*

a **lion** in your **number**

a novel

kevin klix

k Publishing Co. | Est. 2012

for **Karen Newman**

This novel is the work of fiction. Any reference to real people, events, establishments, organizations or locales are intended only to give the fiction a sense of reality and authenticity and are used fictitiously. All other names, characters, and places and all dialogue and incidents portrayed in this book are the product of the author's imagination and are not to be construed as real.

"SILHOUETTES" / "SILHOUETTES: A POEM" by Thomaz Nadeau on page 125 was used with author's permission.

Drawings on pages 91, 92, 93, 94, 95, 96, 97, 100, 101, 108, 113, 115 are property of Alexander Harris-Murphy and used with permission from the artist.

A LION IN YOUR NUMBER. Copyright © 2014 by Kevin Klix. All rights reserved. Printed in the United States of America. No part of this publication may be reproduced, distributed, or transmitted in any form or by any means, or stored in a database or retrieval system, without the prior written permission from the author. For information about permission to reproduce sections from this book, email to Permissions, Kevin Klix, at kevinklix@yahoo.com.

Printed in the United States of America. This book is printed on acid-free recycled paper.

10TH ANNIVERSARY EDITION

Interior and Cover Design by Kevin Klix

Follow the author on X (formally Twitter) and instagram: @kevinklix

Text set in 10 pt. Hoefler Text, Chapter Titles set in 10.25 Helvetica Neue, Cover Title set in Helvetica Neue (with Beveled outline in post)

The e-book edition is available in Kindle, EPUB, and PDF formats.

Library of Congress Cataloguing-in-Publication Date is available upon request.

ISBN: 979-8-9907321-1-7 (paperback)
ASIN: B07CZ1WXMV (Kindle e-book)

14 13 12 11 10 / 10 9 8 7 6 5 4 3 2 1

If you purchased this book without a cover, you should be aware that this book is stolen property. It was reported as "unsold and destroyed" to the publisher, and neither the author nor the publisher has received any payment for this "stripped book."

"That's one thing Earthlings might learn to do, if they tried hard enough: Ignore the awful things, and concentrate on the good ones."
—KURT VONNEGUT, *Slaughterhouse-Five*

"Intelligence is one of the greatest human gifts. But all too often a search for knowledge drives out the search for love. This is something else I've discovered for myself very recently. I present it to you as a hypothesis: Intelligence without the ability to give and receive affection leads to mental and moral breakdown, to neurosis, and possibly even psychosis. And I say that the mind absorbed in and involved in itself as a self-centered end, to the exclusion of human relationships, can only lead to violence and pain." —DANIEL KEYES, *Flowers for Algernon*

A Note From the Author on the 10th Anniversary Edition

■ ■

It truly blows my mind that 10 whole years have gone by since making this novel, *A Lion in Your Number*. Over the years, messages from diverse readers have reminded me of the book's impact, which I wrote during a particularly dark period in my life. Revisiting it for this 10th anniversary edition, I now understand the comfort it provided to others, and perhaps to myself. I didn't know until I read it over again. And I think it makes sense.

Sally Fairfax is by far the most quirky character ever to come from my mind. I do very much hold her near and dear. She's the perfect unreliable narrator in the sense that the entire time you are reading the damn thing, you have to imagine that either she is full of crap or she simply doesn't understand what is objectively transpiring in her life. Oftentimes she gets it completely wrong. And in some cases it appears as though she *knows* it. It is the classic example of a youthful individual—young and dumb—traveling through the world of adulthood and trying to find their sense of identity, purpose, and where they fit.

It is fair to say that when I wrote this I truly was fighting demons that I have since overcome in my life—thanks to family, friends, and my own mind. I can honestly say that writing this book, in particular, helped me cope and keep a tiny sliver of sanity during my moments when I felt that my life was crumbling into darker and darker places. Images of the countless rat-race of paying rent, moving, and not fully digesting that my years of being a kid were coming to a screeching end. This mortality that I felt was the true crux of my insanity. I know that now.

It is easy to discount our youth and simply write them off as naïve or ignorant of life. The first thing that comes to mind is the image of a kid crying to his/her parents about something that is stressing them out or eating them up inside, and the parents passively laughing and saying to them, "*Pfft*, what kind of stress do *you* have? You are so young!" That lack of understanding is what drives one to complete and total alienation, especially from elders and those that we need help from the most. Not everyone has that luxury; not everyone can overcome what bothers them or what stresses them out, especially when it feels like you aren't in control over your own life—as you watch and compare it to others around you who seem hunky-dory. That in and of itself, combined with being young and not understanding how things are the way they are, can make anyone crack.

I think what Sally Fairfax was experiencing was that crack. It appears that her autism, lack of effective communication skills, her being young, and the sexualization of her attractive looks via "the male gaze" are the perfect recipe for the outlook on life that Sally harbors. Complete and total alienation. Nobody understands her—not even herself. And that, I think, was the overall theme of her story.

I've always been infatuated with stories from broken individuals. During the time that I wrote *Lion*, I was reading so many works from J.D. Salinger, Bret Easton Ellis, Chad Kultgen, Charles Bukowski, John Fante, Chuck Palahniuk, and so much more. . . . To me, those guys were the perfect creators of anti-heroes. And during my time with *Lion*, I wanted to write my interpretation of the perfect anti-hero. But as a young writer, it was very hard for me to find my voice. And with *Lion* being the second book that I wrote almost a year after my first book, I felt pressured to make something that I could be proud of—and probably at the same time cringe for, when it inevitably would be brought up later in life. . . .

Coworkers used to make fun of me for bringing my hardback copy of *The Catcher in the Rye* into work every single day, reading it cover-to-cover, over and over again, analyzing and trying to understand what it means to be alienated by society. That feeling is what I felt—and so many other readers felt, too. It's cliché to read Salinger in this way, as so many millions have, but I could not help myself. It was what led me into the genre of anti-heroes, or "Transgressive Fiction." Going through countless reading lists of the genre, I feel like, at the time, I had read nearly everything that even remotely found itself in said genre. Obsessively reading... and probably in an *un*healthy way. During that time I truly felt I had nobody to turn to, talk to, or comfort me. I turned to the books. And I turned to my characters. Sally was one of them.

To read Sally's words is like reading a jumbled mess of outlandish stream-of-consciousness. In some moments it feels like how completely disorienting William S. Burrough's *Naked Lunch* is. Some of the stuff I don't fully remember writing, which in a way makes it more disturbing for me personally to read now, as I feel like I have a solid foundation of myself and my reality. It sometimes feels like I'm reading something that I didn't even write. Which, I guess, is a good thing? I don't know. But it is eerie, in a strange way.

My mind would often be under extreme stress of work, money, and things that bothered me. I was coming to terms with my mortality and purpose as adulthood lurched its head full-swing at me. I felt—and probably was—completely unprepared for adulthood. I could blame my schooling (or lack thereof on my part), I could blame my parents or my upbringing, I could blame the chaos that my younger days were, I could blame my skateboarding in South Florida and realizing how cruel kids could become, I could blame my biological father not being around in critical moments in my life, and I could blame anxiety and depression... but the reality is that I have nothing and nobody to blame except me, myself, and I. The unpreparedness was because I was fearful of life, of pushing myself to my limitations, of failing, and of feeling something other than positive feelings.... Part of life, though, is failure, feeling the negative moments completely, learning from your mistakes, and living life, including the bad times.

It is what's going to make you stronger.

It is what's going to carve you out of hardwood.

But you know... the other curious thing about this book is the fact that even as a 22-year-old, it's surprisingly pushing the envelope with what

I could do as a writer. Typically, writers try their best to have good grammar, to have good diction, to spell correctly, to have no errors, and to be as concise as possible. The prose of *Lion* is definitely not that. The prose is riddled with errors, cross-outs, censorship black lines, random drawings throughout, and a splash of weird sentences that sometimes seem to end unexpectedly, as if the writer was too busy and left the paper mid-sentence. I realize that the writer was Yours Truly, but the real "writer" of this story is Sally Fairfax. Her journal is the book, the entries diving into the hellish world that she perceives—and that is the point, I think. As a writer, I wanted to make something that didn't have to be polished or perfect, in the same vein as Stephen Chbosky's *The Perks of Being a Wallflower*, a huge inspiration in my life at the time of writing *Lion*. Or the diction of *Catcher in the Rye*. Or the absolute whirlwind prose of Bret Ellis's *Less Than Zero*. Or the use of slang within Jay McInerney's *Bright Lights, Big City*. As a young writer, I wanted to push the envelope in the same way those guys did—but in my own way, of course. I have indeed seen prospective readers turn away from the book on the first few pages. I have heard that Sally is abrasive, condescending, and positively negative. I would hear their critiques and smile to myself because that is exactly how she is supposed to be in the book. In my mind, it's my story reading as completely authentic to the character of Sally Fairfax.

For the 10th Anniversary Edition of *Lion*, I wanted it to be something special, something that I could give to readers as a perfect product. I wanted something that was so Sally and so catchy that you just had to take it off the bookshelves and gander inside. . . . Late-2014 was when *Lion* was published, and a year afterward, my good friend Zach Birns was living in Los Angeles and doing various photography jobs to make ends meet. He and I, creatives at heart, always kept in touch with each other's work. In 2015, though, roughly in March of that year, Zach posted this photo that I could not take my eyes off of. His girlfriend at the time, the model in the photo, is an attractive woman, her back to us, nude and in the middle of a road within what appears to be a barren desert. . . .

When I first saw the photo, I had to use it. I mulled it over for a few months, which was a mistake on my part. I should have asked Zach about it sooner because when I finally had the courage to ask him about it for the cover of *Lion*, he had undergone issues with moving, issues with his computer, and work issues. This led him to lose the original raw file of the photo that is now the cover of the 10th Anniversary Edition of the book you now hold in your hand. Ten years later, in 2024, Zach and I are still friends. We got to talking about that photo, and surprisingly, he found the raw file by accident in his Dropbox login from years ago. I was very excited. But since then, he had lost touch with the model that was depicted in the photo. He reached out to her; she was very much on board. From there, the rest is history. I finalized the cover—and all within Amazon's content guidelines via strategic censorship whilst utilizing a note-like easter egg of Sally's handwriting. To me, it is the perfect cover. To me, this is the authentic product of *Lion* that I wanted years ago.

I truly hope you, the reader, enjoy this prose. It is something that I, again, hold near and dear. It is a part of me and a part of my writing career in a huge way. Some portions you may not get, may not understand, or may not believe, but that's exactly the point when it comes to Sally Fairfax. Take this book with a grain of salt. Take this book and just enjoy the ride. This is all I have ever wanted when it comes to *Lion*.

I hope this edition resonates with you, offering a glimpse into the complexities of human emotion and the beauty of overcoming adversity. *A Lion in Your Number* is more than just a book; it is a piece of my life, woven through the narrative of Sally Fairfax. Enjoy this journey into her world, and may it inspire you to navigate your own with courage and curiosity. Here's to embracing the full spectrum of life—challenges, triumphs, and all. . . .

Signed,
Kevin Klix
Tuesday, September 17th, 2024.
West Palm Beach, Florida.

a **lion** in your **number**

March, 13th, 3:30 a.m.

You opened my journal, silly! You don't have permission to do this (unless I told you in a *letter*), but hey! since you *have* already, I guess it's okay! Girl, I hope ~~your~~ you're some big-shot historian who's going to do some big-time "article" on *me,* Sally ~~F'ing~~ Fairfax! If you're a guy, though, you're probably going to do what all guys do and fall madly in love with me or some bullspit, but if you're a lady, you and ~~me~~ I *both* know there is one of two things you're going to think of me (we always do): You're either ~~gonna~~ going to think I'm a "bad b■ch" who you wouldn't mind to kick it with, take advice from, listen to, all that nonsense, or (in more realistic standards) you're just going to think I am simply a b■ch or w■re or s■t or s■nk[1], or a "bad" person if you're a goodie-two-shoes. Which is fine and dandy, I guess. Just dandy. Just peachy. We girls are always in some F'ing *lame* competition with ourselves, and guys, y'all just know all those times you hit on us, we got an ego boost from it. But also, yeah, you're the culprit in our little in*sane* minds! Yeah, I know, we worry like crazy, crazy, but who can blame us? *Right?* Right. I mean you got some chick who spends a majority of her time looking "cute" so she can think she's okay or whatever for this world. But then she comes home and wonders why she doesn't get this guy or that, not looking at the broad and only looking at the superficial. Honestly, though, you guys are mean douchebags, and you know it! I mean, really, all you mother-F'ers have to do is say what we wanna *hear*. That's it, and even *then* you F *that* up! Blimey! Do you know what we girls have to do? Do you know what we go through? ■ ■■ ■■

---

[1] — I just want to be clear, Mrs. Future Sally, that you blocked bullspit out because, well, you were writing with a friggin' pen! Jesus! and for this, mistakes happen. Block, block, block, why don't'cha!

Oh my. In*san*ity! We have to literally come out of our moms and be just all naturally pretty for you guys to even *like* us. And if we are not, mind you, then we have to be suckered into buying all this product crap that we obsess over, see. Gosh. All those calluses between my big toes and index toes from wearing those cute little pink sandals when I go to the beach that I bought at Target on sale for about, like, *twen*ty—F'ing—*doll*ars of my hard-earned *cash,* all ruined and worthless now next to the stupidity of trying to look good for the male species. So you know what? F it. But I've always felt that way. Nevertheless, ladies, hope you like me; and you men too, whatever *that's* worth.

I guess I'm required to paint a picture for you. Here goes nothin'! I'm lying down in my knickers here, they're white with pink poka-dots[2] (like my drawing!ature3]), and I have this light baby-blue over-sized shirt I got from my daddy about two years ago; out of a ▮▮ whim, ~~because it didn't fit him anymore~~. He's the one who encouraged me to go to college or whatever-spit—Okay, *stop!* I should never, ever curse. I have to cross things out when I make a mistake. I'm human, so bite me! I have to be lady-like, too. Taught better than that. Okay. Back to my daddy, now: He's a hardworking man, my dad, doing the construction mumbo-jumbo. He thinks I'm at college right now, but really I dropped out because it actually really bored the hell out of me. I'm not too into it. I went for about, eh, two months? and then got hella bored with it? Don't know. So I just went on in the one place of admissions and told them "I'm done." I don't think they cared, really, but it felt *good* anyway. Sometimes it feels good to tell people off. But anyway, I moved to an apartment and got a sweet azz deal with the lady down there. Her

---

[2] — My favorite!

[3] — *Not* my favorite.... Too crappy for words.

name is Bethany Rice. She's super nice. She offered me a job, but I couldn't see myself doing anything involving tours or anything. I guess call me lazy. . . . Oh, and guess what! I lied. Never been to college. I'll let you decide how it really was. Or is. *Ha,* ha! *Derf!*

Okay, yeah. I got the apartment and ▇▇, right now, I'm in my knickers and shirty shirt. It's comfy right now while I write this. Bought this weird pen to, you know, be able to write this down effortlessly. (It was twenty bucks—same as my damn sandals; same place, Target, bought from.) Sorry if my grammar is bad, or looks bad. I don't even mean it. I'm just pretty much talking how I talk in my head. Makes sense. Ha, *ha!* But anyway, I'm super into dice. Like black and white stuff. I don't know what it is. I just have dice hangin' all everywhere. Right now there's a plush die on my black dresser. My damn lamp is dice for-▇▇▇-F's sake. My hand sanitizer is in a dice-looking dispenser. It's coo-coo. People call it weird. But hey, keeps me happy. That's all we *all* want, right?

I'm in the food industry. Don't laugh. I know it's cliché as F of me to be all into that mess, but it pays the bills. I'm young. Twenty-two. I'm not going to be young forever, but hey, get it while the gettin' is *good,* as they say. I want to tell you about earlier today. Today I was working and jumping hoops through my ▇▇▇▇ A-hole. I had about eight, ten tables at the same time asking for refills of their dang Cokes. Which is pretty standard, but all of them wanted to chit-chat or some whatever-thingy. I have to play nice because these people are my little ducklings that I have to put a show on for.

Waitressing is like acting, in some ways. All I have to do is make your stay pleasant, savvy, smooth, and fast. Then you pay your measly little fifteen percent, and we both part ways. Sound good? Well, um, not *me!* All of these people see my face and all of a sudden they like to shoot me compliments: "*Aw,* I like your shoes!" "You have a pretty *smile!*" "I wish I had your hair!" All that. Which is cool—not saying I don't *like* it—but sometimes, *ugh!* it gets to be a routine. Sometimes I actually *know* what they're going to compliment on. Guys are so simple. I just now sighed. Now I'm laughing that I wrote *that*.

Getting off topic here. Okay. Eh-*hem!* Ten people needing drinks. I get to the ~~middle~~ *last* table asking for a refill and it's this really, really creepy old guy or something, and he goes:

"Hey honey, could ya do me a solid and refill this ri' here, sweetheart?"

He's so F'ing creepy he actually said "honey" and "sweetheart" in the same F'ing sentence.

"Yeah, sure," I said. Then I started to walk away.

God-dang index and middle fingers out, he stopped me by the arm. "Hey honey," he said, "got a boyfriend?"

Now, I could've done what most girls do and tell this A-hole that I do and let that be the end of it, but I was feeling sort of bored and I knew this guy would totally tip me more if I flaunted a little bit. So I was like, "No hun, *totally* single," and then I turned around and faced him straight-on. The cute smiles and high-pitch voices, ladies! Men like that kind of thing. You face them, they get all giddy and excited.

"That's a shame!" he said to me. "You're really a very pretty woman."

"Thanks." What more can you say to that when this is about the twentieth time you've heard it?

"Say, d'you ever consider an older guy?" His voice was F'in' country as hell ~~and super deep or whatever~~. It made me wince, almost. But I totally held it back, whatever.

But yeah, totally ignoring his question, I asked, "What you drinkin'? Sprite?" I ▇▇ knew better.

"Bud Light...."

Of course. So I said, "O'*course!* How silly of me! Be right back!" I actually would never say "How silly of me," but it makes it more interesting to talk pleasant like that. Tee-*hee!*

You may not get what kind of significance this has, the whole exchanging thingamabob, but I had to stop for this A-hole because he wanted to do and little of this and a little of that with the good ole chit-chat. What I don't get is this: what makes him think he can have me? It's weird. Sometimes I think guys think of us women as some kind of guard that is guarding a caged ▇▇ "P-word," and they have to get passed us in order to get to it. It's sad, really.

I went to the Coke dispenser and grabbed about, like I said, ten cups,

4

all red and crystaly-looking, and while I was pouring the third cup, Tessa walked up next to me.

"Hey, Sal. It's a good night, ay?"

"S'okay."

"How's about that table three." Her eyebrow raised and then she pointed on over to the table she was referring to.

I looked over and saw, of course, these really studdish football guys drinking beer and doing guy stuff: check a chick out; grab a few azzes; drink till you're giddy; drink till you're *burger,* even; football, football, football! *Seesh!* Male species. So predictable. *Ugh.*

"What about it?" I asked Tess.

"Sal, you're kidding. That guy over there has been totally checkin' you out."

"I gave that up. No more."

"You!" she laughed. "*You* gave the *D* up?"

I got irritated, kind of. I was pouring my seventh cup. "Don't you have something *better* to do, Tess?" I said. "Go to table three and work your magic."

"How much you wanna bet I get a Benjamin."

I turned to her. "Yeah *right!*"

She grinned. "Watch me."

We were so sly, are we not? I poured the cups and then grabbed a tray off the side.

"See ya," I told Tessa.

"Bye!"

I started handing out all the drinks to everyone, but then tables five and eight wanted their checks.

Money time! "Sure!" I always tell them. "One secon'."

As I walked over to the monitor to print out their spit (A.K.A. "S▓▓"), Mr. Creeper comes a-knockin' . . . again!

"Hey, Sally," he said, stopping me in the same way before with the same dang two fingers.

"How do you know my name?" I said.

He pointed at my name-tag. I pinched my shirt and looked down at it. "Oh," I pretty much said, sighing my dang heart out. This guy really *was* a creeper! I unfortunately looked back up at him. "Yes? What can I do'ya for?"

"Hey! Gotta take me out to dinner first 'fore I get into all *that,* lil' lady!"

He was flirting. Wow. Totally ran into *that* one, Sally.

I rolled my gosh-darn eyes and tried to put on a bullspit smile. "Oh shucks," I ~~said~~ whatever'd.

"I just need my check," he said . . . "Darlin'."

I really smiled! "Absolutely, sir!" Then I walked away.

Got all the checks printed and then handed them out, including Mr. Creeper's. He nodded and smiled. I walked away without caring or something. My other tables wanted their checks. Strangely no new hungry customers came in. It was kind of weird.

I gathered the tips. Ten dollars here, twenty there. Not bad. Then I got to Mr. Creeper's table. He was gone. No kidding. He left the receipt and one-hundred bucks! *and* his phone number with a note that read to "give me a call sometime, baby." *Gross!*

~~Ugh. Wow.~~ Roll my eyes. What a joke! Tessa was across the place, behind the bar, talking with Tony, her kind of sort of "fling." He's this bad~~ass~~ black boy, or something. He sells drugs and I totally think he's a scumbag, in a lot of ways. But that's neither here nor there.

Yeah, so . . .

I walked up to the bar and told Tessa, "Look." I flashed her the receipt. "See. *Booya!*"

She grimaced like a God-dang baby. "B■ch," she laughed, but she was only kidding, naturally. (Or was she?) "That group only gave me five bucks! Such a■holes!"

"I'm tellin' ya, Tess. Gotta hit up them creepies. They pay *big* time."

She learned a huge lesson from me and it's totally weird—I don't know. I may say a bunch of spit that doesn't even matter in this bullspit diary/book/journal, but whatever, you can go if you want. I guess just take

6

everything I say with a grain of salt. I'm not saying I'll *lie* to you—that's wrong, *duh!*—but I may beef spit up. I am a girl, a *good* girl, so be patient, have fun, and *bleh!*

If you're guy, that's difficult, since I'm a guard guarding my p▮sy. If you're a girl, I hope you'll know what I mean when I say the things ▮▮▮ I'm saying. Regardless, ~~I love you all.~~ I really like this diary thing. ~~I'm glad I started it.~~ Been wanting to for awhile now.

March, 14th, 10:21 p.m.

So, I don't want to tell you about why I wanted to write this. But I think I should. So, lately I've been hating guys. They seem to *all* be pigs, God-*dang-it!* I'm older now, so I can pretty much figure out their little tricks. Back in high school, though, it was *hell.* All hell. Everyone always thinks of us pretty girls as very extrovert and we don't have anything important to say, but frankly, we really do! But most guys don't like to really talk to me very much in a smart way. I mean, sure, they like to *say* they do, but they really, truly don't. I'm fairly sure that they, meaning the blubber-heads that roam this earth, just think about the inside of my undies. So fine, whatever. Sometimes, though, I let them. I really do. I just can't help to look at a cute guy. So maybe I'm the one that's the pig. It's all so very strange to me. It's like we want to have a naturally cute person for no reason.

I'm talking funny, sorry. ▮▮▮ ▮▮▮ ▮▮ ▮▮▮ ▮ ▮▮▮ ▮▮▮▮ ▮ ▮▮. What did I do today that was cool? Hm ... I called up Josh, if *that's* anything. He's my gay friend, ~~in case you right off the bat thought he was a huge crush once you saw his male-ish name.~~ He's really fa▮y as fork, and it's actually funny! Him and I always talk about who's cute or whatever. All those times we shop at the Mall, always a finger pointing across the room and little eyes wide, big, all that!

"Check him out!"—and probably a wave off, as if to say, *You aren't nothing to me!*

Josh always sees the muscle guys. You know the kind. Wife-beater shirts, Levi jeans. Tall, dark, handsome—the stereotypes of a young, youthful lad! ~~It's kind of what I'm into.~~ I'm a sucker for hipsters, though, to be quite frank. We did hit up the mall, though, but— Oh shoot, *wait!* I just did it again! I got off topic. I'm sorry! How lame of me. Let me go back: eh-*hem!* basically I'm writing because not only is it therapeutic (dare I say) but it can help basically consolidate my thoughts. Basically I started because there was this guy who really F'ed. Me. Over. Like really *bad*— let's just say that—to the point of caring about making scrawl on paper. But I just wanted you to know that—oh what*ever,* just continue on, you lame Sally-cakes:

Josh and I are in the food court or something, and Josh, his gay self with the tight skinny blue jeans, crop-top, an earring on his right side (the stereotype and all), pointed and shouted toward some guy: "Hey! Chicky baby!" He blew a kiss too: "*Muah!*"

It's funny because me and Josh were sitting down and his whole upper torso was whipped around. ~~So funny.~~ I just rolled my eyes and looked down. So <u>awkward</u>.

Josh turned back around and told me, "Agh, he was an as▓▓e. All these straight guys think I'm out to get them. I don't want you [referring to *them*]! So talk to the hand, sista cakes!" He was just mocking and messing around, I guess.

"You're weird," I said, my head still being down, but grinning at how funny he was. (Or still is.) Then I looked up. "What's that on your lip?"

"Huh?" said Joshy Josh. He had some kind of Chicken Chow Mien on his lip. He ordered it and everything with a soda pop. He was eating it, swear on it. Funny thing is that he says he's <u>vegan</u>. "Where?" he said. He kept touching and wiping his face, missing it every time, the thing on his lip.

"Oh, it's gone," I said. Totally lied to him. *Ha!* Sometimes I do that. Gots'ta keep ya guessin'! "So," I kept saying, going on and on and on, on a dang *roll,* "Josh, whatever happened to Terry?" Terry was Josh's boyfriend about some time ago. It was puppy love at first sight.

And not in a good way.

Josh went, "*Agh,* F him! He's so F'ing dirty!"

"Like hot dirty, or nasty dirty?" I asked. "Explain."

"Like he doesn't F'ing shower!"

I made a face. "*Ew* . . ."

"I know!" Josh said.

"Like this guy just didn't give a hoot? Like he just never showered?"

Hoot. What a funny word to say, right? Ha, *ha!*

"Okay, listen," Josh said, leaning in, "I would tell him, after he told me that he wanted to make love, that he hasta shower first before I'd even ever *consider* touching his privates. The guy refused! What kinda lame is that?"

~~Lame is that. Too funny. It didn't even make sense. Lame is a dang adjective.~~

"Lame," I said, laughing pretty passively. It's silly when you think about it. How can a guy have no self respect enough to date a lover and just simply not bathe? F'ing gross! "Wow," I said. ~~You'd probably would've said it too.~~

"I know!" Josh said. "And that F'ing F'er sleeps on the couch!"

Josh was totally getting heated, it was *so* funny! "Keep your voice *down,* Josh," I said. "Weren't you guys living together?"

"Still are."

"Wait a tick. You and him are broken up, done for, and you still have him staying with you?"

Josh nodded. "Yupp*erz.*"

Wowie. . . .

"Who pays the friggin' *bills?*" I said.

"I do," he said, ~~naturally.~~ Don't'cha just hate that? ~~Gosh. Guys. All low-lifes, I tell you.~~ How in the world would a God-dang guy just free-load like that?

"You goin' to college?" I asked Josh. He looked like he wasn't paying any friggin' attention, though. I was going to say "Hey!" but I decided I wanted peace and quiet.

"*Say!*" Josh said finally, "uh, let's f■king *do* something."

"I wanna just talk . . . or something," I said. ~~Honestly, fu■, I just wanted to sit and talk. I feel depressed a lot these days with spit.~~

9

So Josh said, " 'Bout what?" It's honestly lame when people omission their sentences in speech. But then again, I have to do it because it's normal . . . or something.

Whelp, I didn't want to come right out and tell him this, but I said anyway, "My therapist."

"You go see a therapist?" he asked. As *if!*

"Yeah," I said.

"WOAH. That's interesting. What happened?" he said.

"She thinks I'm, WELL . . . weird."

"You *are*, Sally!" Oh thanks, A-hole. Sometimes Josh never says what I wanna hear sometimes. *Sheesh.* Even gay men have straight men tendencies.

"Well I told her what I think of the world," I said. "And, um, it troubled her— Hey, can I have that fry?" I pointed down at it. It looked really good.

"Uh . . . Yeah? sure?" Josh said. "Knock yourself out." Such a common form of word. Knock yourself out. ~~Us humans are so predictable~~.

So I took it and ate it. Dry as fork. I didn't like it.

"So, uh, what's up with the shrink?" Josh asked.

So I go into some long monologue tangent, like for my therapist, and yeah, it kind of went like this:

"Basically, I'm depressed. Some people have reasons for being that way, but I really don't. I just hate the sensations of life. I hate going into this world. Like when I was born I came into this spit-hole without consent. I think it's strange to feel these senses of smell, sight, all that s██t. It's weird. I'm weird! But anyway, I told her—"

Josh totally interrupted me just then, the cheeky F'er. "Wait, wait. You're goin' way too fast, baby."

"Sorry," I said. I cleared my throat: "Ah-*hem.*" Then I straightened up and said, "Okay, so anyways, back to bull: I pretty much told her that I was depressed and that I look at life kind of like from an observer's point of view."

"Whatcha mean?" Josh said. His eyes were all squinty. He picked up his drink, sipped at the straw. It was empty so it made lots of noise or whatever, making me irritated.

I wish I could have told him more, but what's the use? If I told him what I thought, it's one ear and out the other. I just don't get it. Maybe it's better if I tell you what I said via just writing it down or whatever. I pretty much told him that I thought this world was completely a sensation, that it was only for the happy players of the world (whatever *that* meant). He didn't really understand. I told him that it was more about my thinking about nothingness and how I feel like I'm a little kid going from this—the nothingness—to this—life. It's like I'm depressed because I want to be. Sometimes I look at people and just see animals and their brains moving to the groove. If you're hungry, *bing!* your brain tells you to go and get food and drop everything else. It's like our bodies are predictable. Whatever. Lame as hell.

Of course, as I was explaining this, Josh was saying, "I need a cigarette." Then he pulled a pack out from his pocket and got one cig out, *bing!*

I told him, "You can't do that! We'll get in trouble!" but I said this with a loud whisper. The F'er always does his own thing! "You can just smoke straight up in a food court, hun," I said. I added the "Hun" part because I'm guessing it helps build rapport and make people "happy" or some whatever. Don't really know. It's a goofy way of looking at life, I guess.

"Do what?" said Joshy Josh.

"Never mind," I told him. It's not like *I* would have gotten into trouble. Let *him* take the wrap. Funny thing is that he probably just wanted a cigarette because his brain was thinking it needed nicotine.

After getting the cig up to his lips, lighting it, sucking in the smoke, blowing out with ease, Josh, his cutesy self, asked me, "Whatever happen to that fine piece of a■ Russell?"

Knew that was coming. Russell, as you could probably guess, was an ex-boyfriend. Let me tell you about him. I met him at a bar. *My* bar, the one I work at. I was doing pretty well. It was a cool Friday night, honestly. Everyone was sitting in rows and talking really lame and doing this or that. People always do this or that. Russell wasn't any different. He was sliding up next to me while I was leaning over the bar counter, about to get some drink orders, and he said to me, "Fine day," which I thought was cute! I have no idea why. Probably because he "looked" *cool.* Big whoop.

"Russell was controlling and wouldn't let me do anything and wouldn't give me freedom or responsibility and it made me quite mad!" I said to Josh. "So *ha!*"

I just now re-read that, and honestly, sounds nothing like the really real Sally F'ing Fairfax. I want to sound smarter. I'm going to try and research things online so I can speak better in this garbage. I'll read some novels or something. There's a couple on my list. I hope I'm not being lame or fake or holding-back-ish toward you. Then again, nobody is reading this. It's just me, Ms. Past-life Sally. But if you are, so be it!

"You go girl," Josh said to me, taking a puff on his cigarette. I don't know where I'm going with this entry. I guess I just wanted to tell you about Josh, my "sort of" best friend, and Russell, my, um, "nothing-ness." Or something sad like that.

— P.S.: We (meaning Josh and I) went shopping for clothes at Forever 21 and American Apparel and American Eagle; for there was a blow-out sale. Just kidding! Not really. But, oh *look!* A squirrel!

March 20th, 1:00 a.m.

Been awhile since I last wrote. Here goes nothing. Basically I have nothing to say; that's why I haven't been so cool, or *as* cool, with this word stuff. My head has been hurting. Aside from that, life's been pretty snazzy!

I bought this new shampoo that smells sort of funny. It's called "PinePeach." Pineapples and Peaches. It was pretty expensive but I got it on sale. So *ha!* I guess I could tell you how I get ready. I always wake up a hot mess. Always. Never fails. My hair is in my face, my ears are all crusty, my face is dry, my nose has boogers. It's gross. Basically, put it this way: you see me out in public, I'm me; but you see me in my house, about to wake up, for*get* it. No way. Can't. *Too* much for your eyes. *Ouch,* it burns! ▇▇▇. That's what it's like. I had this one time I woke up at 6 a.m., during high school ~~time~~ era, and I said "Oh spit oh spit oh spit I'm late I'm late!" real *loud,* as I was putting my pants on or whatever crap, and I looked out my window and could see my bus down the street. My house was close to the actual main roads or whatever. It was crazy. Picture a little yellow square speck and you see it stopping and going to the red and yellow and green lights. It's like a loading bar on your computer . . . but in real life. Anywho, it was coming down ▇▇▇ hella fast, so I put my pants the heck on quick. I bolted out of my house and passed my dad as he was making coffee. It smelled all ▇▇▇ coffee-y or whatever. Then, real quick▇, I said "I love you" to my dad and he was laughing, the little rascal. Then, faster than a jet, than a jack rabbit, I ran to the stop u▇r *across* the street. I made it! Holy smokes. It was just pulling up when I crossed. Some bum was sitting there. If he wasn't there, I'd've been a goner. I'd've had to literally walk back inside, explain to daddy I woke up late, and then tell him, with my cutest, most pouting face, to please give me a ride to school. He always fell for it. I'm his princess. I run s▇t. Honest. I do! But whatever, anyway, I got inside and the bum paid his seventy-five cents. It was my turn, then, to put some coins in the dispenser. The driver gave me this really, uh, creepy *sugges*tive look—I don't really know. So I was like, "F▇k. I have no money." The friggin' driver was all smiling and tells me, before I was about to dip, that it was fine and that I can ride for free. For free! What! Can you believe it? I call this Beauty Points . . . or perks. Happens a lot. Sometimes I actually forget I have them. So I told him, this fat, stinky bus-driver, "thanks," and then sat down, and dude, you'd've never guessed it but the next stop, this chick-hobo did the same thing I did, with the whole "don't have money to ride" bit, and the fat driver tells her to get lost. Wow! It's like he picks mercy for some and none for others. I guess it's just the way it is.

I got to school and then I totally realized it was daylight savings time. I didn't even look at my phone to know it—the f▇king *everyone* wasn't there. "Everyone" is a pronoun to me, so back off. Ta-*da*. Magic. Old, sweet magic. Maybe I'm a control freak. I'm actually laughing right now. Not because of ▇▇thing anything that's actually funny but because I sort of like you, Future Sal, in a weirdo way. Me and you could be pals. It's like I know what you're thinking before you think it. Like, don't think of elephants. Okay. You just did! Ta-*da*. Or maybe not. Oh well. I've actually been drinking tonight. I went to the liquor sto' and bought ▇▇ some Honey Jack and Vanilla Coke. So good. Friggin' *A*. You really have *no* clue. Drink that stuff like water. I do. Really! It's nuts! Try it sometime. I think you ▇▇ ▇ should ▇▇▇ ▇▇ ▇.

I wanna talk about something clever, but I don't know what. Lately I've been thinking about my dad. He's a sweetheart. He treated me right all throughout my years. Strict son-of-a-gun, though, I tell you *what*. From a young age I always had the boys looking at me. One time I was only about eight and my dad's business partner (at the time) came over for dinner with him and his wife. My mom and dad and them all had dinner or whatever. I remember this so clearly. My dad's business partner, his name was Ron Largo. He told me that I was very *special* to him, the nerve, and he kissed me on the dang lips. I couldn't F'ing believe it. He took me to the bathroom and everything. Not in a creeper way, though—I do remember that. He really liked me, a lot. My dad caught him, though, the second we walked out of the bathroom. My dad beat the living hell out of him. I screamed. It was pretty sad—the way it was handled, naturally. But I suppose that's creepy, the kissing, the guy doing that to me at that young of an age. But don't think I'm your typical girl who always suggests she was raped or something. Once or twice I've made up a story like that to a boy-toy. It always gains sympathy, but I really don't know why. Maybe it makes the boy feel sorry or something. Maybe we like to think that we're being intimate by confessing some dark secret that's being "clearly soaked" into the mind of a male . . . clearly. Me, I just think it's a load of S.

The boys probably think we're all crazy. <u>All girls are crazy, really. It just takes time for you to get us to confess a fake sob story for us to bond with you and be crazy for you</u>—that's all I'm sayin', sista.

So listen. I go into work, minding my own dang business, and my boss totally tells me that I haven't been writing down my tips. I definitely do, to some extent, but it's really none of his business. So I told him that and he kind of got into ~~the~~ a spiel about how I *need* to respect him, and how he's the boss of me, and how if I'm here I have to abide by his rules and blah blah blah. I tell you what, I quit. Just too much. These a■hole bosses always think they run s■■t. Like, just because they spent thirty F'ing years of their life in some business just to get a salary, they think it's justification to be a boss of me. Look at me. I'm kicka■■! I am! I make hella moo-la all damn day long. He doesn't need to know the actual amount. F tax.

So I started applying. One place took one look at me and said, "You're hired." It was really weird. I didn't take it because that's just *way* too needy, if you, like, ask *me*. Those jobs always end up having a boss that fires you for lying on your tips. That's the exact place they are. It's stupid as fork. So I kept applying today. I applied at this other bar and stuff, and it seemed okay. The guy that was there had a beard and he was really nice and nonchalant about my applying there. ~~I hope they call me back. I'd totally go for it.~~ Problem is that, with me, I'm, like, really weird about interviews. I'm super pleasant—not at all trying to tell you I don't have the ole charmy charms—but I always feel like we're robots. If I spent my whole life being serious—with all the "Goodmorning"s and "Hello"s and "You too"s—do you think I'd have a cool life? What if I just never really joked around and always was all about, like, business?

I left there and totally walked down Flagler Road like one of those swanky gals over there down in Miami. You know those runway models. I thought about doing it. It looks hella awesome. My friend Tessa, the one the other day, said I should get an agent, but I told her that I'm probably too short and have too big of breasts for all that mess. She said maybe I should do porn. Porn would be nice, but it seems like not a professional route to go. I know it's just like being an actor, with the lights, camera, and action, but it's sad to have the "Mattress Actress" title. I'd *hate* that. But anyway, some dudes in a Ferrari zoomed down the road and started yelling, "Damn! Look at the a▊ on *that* one!" It made me feel violated. Really. So I finally got to Lake Worth Road and decided to take the PalmTran down to Jog Road. I got on and, again, didn't pay the cents to get on. It was some Mexi-guy that paid. He said it's okay, lil' lady. I went through and sat close to the back. I thought of Rosa Parks for some reason, in regards to my getting on for free and also being the most good-looking on the bus or whatever. I guess that makes no sense. Maybe I'm just a b▊ch, I guess. Everyone there looked really, really bored and really, really tired with eyes droopy and clothes dirty. Gets shadier and shadier. I stood out like a sore thumb, like Rosa did. I stand for nothing, though. I guess I don't know.

This lady got on, pregnant. Holy . . . smokes . . . was she like a million months *in* or something! Her stomach was *out*. Like, really out. It's usually cute, to be honest, but hers, no way, José. That's just *too* much. I could *not*. But anyway, she came in and was all friendly, which never happens on the bus—or in Florida, for that matter. She actually came down and everyone widened and gave her room. Not because of courteousness but because they were sort of scared.

Then, not even joking, what she did, she sat down next to me. Right beside. *Dang it!* I had to scoot over. She had her purse at her feet on the ground. She turned to me and had one of those pleasant, friendly smiles on.

"Good afternoon!" Her voice was hella Spanish-sounding, something or other.

"Good afternoon," I said back.

Just then, no joke, this guy comes up and sits next to her. Oh my god! You wouldn't believe it. It was the guy that gave me the hundred dollar tip!

"This is my husband," the prego lady said. "His name is Jeff; my name is Sherry."

I said, "Hi, Sherry. Hi, Jeff," but tried not to look at Jeff.

"Hey . . ." he dully said, but he didn't look around his wife's big, big belly at me—thank Jesus.

"So . . ." commenced Sherry's small-talk, "lovely day, ain't it?" I absolutely hate that sh*t. All she was doing was filling in the day's gaps.

"S'okay, I guess," I said . . . "Better ones."

She nodded. "Yeah, I have to lug around this little guy all day." She rubbed her tummy. "I'm almost nine months in."

I tried to care. "Wow! Really?" I made my eyes purposefully wide—it's absolutely ridiculous slash F'ed up.

"Yeah!" she said. Excited as a witch.

Her husband, this guy, burps all of a sudden. It's funny how he was always showing his best self to *me* the times I was coming up to *him*. It's like he probably brushed himself off, cleared his throat, and then called me over, just so I could see his "best self." Men. Wowie F'ing zowie, the nerve!

"Honey!" Sherry said, looking over at Jeff. "Say excuse me."

" *'Cuse* me," he said, burping again.

I started to get anxiety for some reason. I don't know why. My perception was all strange-ish. I couldn't stand or bare it to be on the bus any longer. I totally stood up and then held onto one of the bus's bars. I was looking out the window, peeking for a next stop.

"Pardon my hubby, madam," Sherry said, turning to me, all close, "but he's got no home training."

"Uh-huh," I said. I didn't want to be around her anymore. She was just annoying me. No way was she helping with my anxiety.

"Got a hubby yourself?" she asked.

"Oh, heaven's no!" I said, with the fake, fake girly falsettos we all always do.

"Why?" she said. "You're beautiful. Why not? You could have, um, a stomach like me, lil' lady."

"I, uh, wouldn't want one of those, thank you—But, eh-*hem!*" (a cough, my anxiety was getting bad as heck, and I was starting to stand up) "I really gotta get goin'. Stop's here." I was looking out the window, not at her, all trying to see where the heck I was at. Where it was was at this, you know, place on L— W—— and M—————— T——, near John I. High School. You know the place, I bet. My friend lives there. She works at my job, Tessa—that simp chick.

"Oh okay, darling," Sherry said. "I hope you have a nice day." Then she turned to Jeff and tapped his shoulder. "Jeffrey Thomas, say good-bye to this nice young lady, huh?"

He looked up. Wow. You should've seen his face just then. He knew it was me from the bar. I was standing, all that. He was stuttering.

"Uh, uh, uh . . . Bye, lil' lady?" It came off as a question, I think.

I pulled the PalmTran string and there was a *bing* and a robotic woman on the speakers said, "Stop requested."

"My husband really is a nice guy," Sherry said, after the "Stop requested" lady, "I swear it. He and I aren't bad once you get to know us."

Little does she know that that prick totally flirted and tried to get some with a girl who obviously didn't even want him or give him the time of day. But I said to her anyway, "Yeah, sure, cool—have a day. Bye," and the bus was stopping. Have a day? Did I mean good or bad? Makes no sense. Oh well.

"Bye," Sherry said, then she nudged Jeff and he said bye, too.

I was holding my head and breathing hard. I'm not too sure why. I think I was getting nervous from just being around all the lames. I felt weird. Maybe I have a problem or something. I don't know. Don't take this the wrong way, if you're a lady like Yours Truly, but being pregnant looks like a drag. I feel like, as girls, we pretend to be happy when in reality we're just freaking out like our men do. I hope my kid ends up being planned out. I really hope. It's F'ed.

I was walking to Tessa's and I realized she probably wasn't home. I had no idea why I left the bus. I'm unemployed as heck. I go to look for work but then was walking to Tessa's. *Whelp!* guess it wasn't *so* bad. I just had to see if she was home, but she wasn't. People are never home when you come unannounced. I now know what a creeper feels like.

April, 1st, 8:56 p.m.

April fools! I'm still unemployed, but looking! I sort of miss the idea of people at a job making a big fuss over the insanity of playing tricks on people, the way ole Jeezy Jesus has led us to believe we're all equal in

God's eye. It's very opinionated that I think this way, but try to imagine my shoes. Go ahead. Go. You can't, can you? It's simply a matter of Whales and Catfish, you can't pick or choose the way they sway, only the way they look or weigh or swim to the lore, its bobber down below being bias and only choosing the littler over the larger bloated beast that is simply . . . impossible to get? I don't know where, or what, I'm getting at with this, but it's making me feel better, mind you.

Today, rather reluctantly, I rose from bed (is "rose" the correct word, or is that a flower?) and stretched my arms wide out, yawning like a little Sloth. Jesus Christ'ums on a bicycle, was I still exhausted! I always get the most poopy-est sleep you could ever imagine. Once upon a time, back in elementary school, I once sort of didn't wake up and Dad had to call the ambulance. I actually didn't or couldn't wake up. I was out for forty-eight solid hours in the dang ER room. They thought I was in some kind of coma. My sleep is horrible. Later—wouldn't you know it—they found out I had this weird sleep disorder called Circadian Rhythm Disorder or something. Basically I have no REM sleep, the sleep that actually matters. I mean, it *comes*—not saying it doesn't, fully—but it never is *act*ually fully, it's just brief. Most humans' REM starts about twenty minutes in, but mine starts three *hours* in. Crazy! My doctor told me out of all the twenty years he's worked at the hospital, he'd never see a true case of CRD; only in textbooks he has read in college.

Oh yeah, come to find out, that shampoo, the one called PinePeach, was a recall. They sent me a check when I gave my shampoo back. PinePeach is the one. Turns out it gives you migraines because I guess the stuff messes with your scalp and digs deep into your pores. So crazy. It was about a thousand dollar check for the recall. Four people died! *Sheesh!* The world is full of wild, exciting things, isn't it? I guess my check comes soon, I hope, for the sake of their a██es! I'll *sue!* Watch me. It's a good thing I'm getting this money, too, because I'm so close to running out. My complex people still think I have a job. I'm not really too sure if I'm suppose to tell them, but hey, it's all gravy!

I've been hyper lately, which is unusual. I think I always get excited when I write in this. It's all that gives me joy. Maybe that's why I'm writing, I guess. Jesus, though. What a hyper biscuit-eater. I'm very excited right now while I write this. It's good that I feel some relief. I think we all deserve it every now and again. Once, this one crappy day, I came home and was hyperventilating like crazy. I was punching the walls and not really doing any damage to them, only my hands. I was bleeding on my knuckles pretty dang bad. It was gruesome. I texted Tessa that I was thinking about killing myself and whatever, but she was mega worried. She told me to hang tight. I didn't know what she was gawkin' at with "hanging tight" because I had my dad's 9mm in my hands (that I stole) while I was texting her. That day was pretty scary. Actually, that night was the *only* scary part. I know now that that day wasn't even a biggie. Just when I put the gun up to my mouth and closed my eyes, cops started knocking on the door. My dad got up—his room was far away from mine. I know this because he was stumbling all over the place. It was a late shift—I was still working in food—and I had came home pretty dang late. About one o'clock. He answered the door, my dad, and I heard, because my room was right next to the door—I mean, really, *right* next to it—you couldn't miss it. He knocked on my bedroom's door a few moments later. I was bawling. He said from behind the door, "Honey, there's two policemen lookin' for you." His voice was very sweet, which surprised me. He seemed so damn *calm*. But maybe I'm not remembering correctly. It always seems like when there's a situation that traumatic, I always lose track of what is real and what is not. Not in an insane-person type of way, but more in the way of not knowing how things are moving. Things move a heck of a lot faster. But anyway, I saw the police and they asked me if I was suicidal. I said yes, obviously, because there's no use in lying when your bestie called these fellows here. They asked if I would go with them in their car. I said yes. I felt like a robber of some kind. Like I was a badass, in the back seat. They took me into the hospital, still bawling my eyes out. The nurses took vitals. I didn't know why they did, but they did. I told them I didn't need it. Then, about two hours of waiting, a therapist came in and let me talk for about one hour. She didn't say anything. She was a noobie—just straight out of college. I hate those beezies. She told me I shouldn't fret and that I was beautiful and I shouldn't do it, the killing of oneself and all that bull. I told her my reasons, but she didn't understand. Nobody never, ever understands anything. I F'ing hate it. Afterward, she gave me a list of other doctors that could help. The funny thing is that I kept Dad's gun, even now, and he never said anything about it.

But where I want to start getting at, anyway, is this place near the hospital. I actually looked at the list, the "help" list— Well . . . no. Not exactly. I *kept* the list, I should say. This whole suicidal meltdown was actually quite a long time ago, about nine months or so ago. But I kept the list that doctor chick gave me. One of them had this therapist on there, and the doctor put a gold sticky star next to his name, like I was a kid or something. I mean, I sort of *act* like it, but still, it's whatever. I can prove it. Why, if I'm looking around the area, even, and I see a squirrel, his tail going all over the place, I'd totally get on my "hind" legs, arms forward like a T-rex, and start hopping up and down like a bunny rabbit. Total kid-status. But I kept the list, so I called up there yesterday. This really, really deep voice answered—it was totally, like, *hot!* His name was John. He was a male receptionist. He told me the "no problem"s and "how are you"s and all that stuff. He was nice, but *gosh!* I wanted to see him! He just sounded so professional that I couldn't hardly stand it. But anyway, enough of that. I scheduled an appointment, via Johnny-boy, the little devil that he is (or was), and he said, "Great! See you then, hun."

Hun. Oh . . . my . . . gah-*lee!* So sexy. So the next day—to*day* in fact—I went!

Woo-*hoo!*

The office was hard to find. I had to call John up and ask him for directions. He was all cool with it, which makes *no* sense and made me think that he wasn't that busy or whatever. So, yeah—going, going, going, in my car, I was going back and forth on this street I never even heard the name of. Something sounding like Jefferson or something. I still don't know it, really, to be honest with you. I called sexy Johnny-boy up again when I parked at some Red Cross I found. He told me the doctor's office is across the street and I can't miss it. I was being overly nice or whatever and I felt extra weird. I was only doing it because he sounded sexy, and I think it's rather weird. But anyways, I hung up on him and drove right the F on over. The place looked swanky as fork. I was pretty dang nervous, to say the least. I parked, did all that, and started walking up and checking the place out. It seemed really peaceful, come to think of it. I just don't know, but I walked on in.

The first thing I saw was this tiny black girl. She was jump-roping in the waiting room. Her rope was making a tic-tac noise with every jump she did. There wasn't anyone else, just the black girl. I walked up to the help desk, it having a tinted, slide-back window, and I vaguely saw the black girl in the reflection. She had that crappy thing or whatever. Down-syndrome or something. Gosh, you have no idea how bad I felt. But you can't feel too bad for them, just in the way that, um, they are helpless or something. Don't feel bad for them. That's the *last* thing a person would want. She looked happy, though. Honest.

John totally slid back the window and smiled. Gosh he was so perfect. He was tall, he was so excited, it seemed like. I almost felt inferior to him because he knew why I was there—for the insanity thing or whatever—I told him, when setting up the appointment or whatever. Story of my life. Take a hot guy—one I like—and let me "blow it." Not in the good way, you scallawag! "Hey there!" said Johnny-boy. "Goodmorning. You Sally?"

"Yes, sir," I said. Gosh. I~~ was being super timid.~~ His voice was so frickin' deep, in person, I swear it. "Um, I have an appointment," I said.

"Right," John said. "Uh, fill out these bits of paperwork. Your counselor'll be with you shortly."

"What time is it, hun?" My scheduled time was for ten o'clock and I had to make sure I wasn't actually late or something.

"It's just nine forty. You're fine," John said. Then he smiled. "Just wait, fill these out, and she'll be right with you, darling."

Darling. Gosh. Such a stud. Then he started handing me the clipboard with the paperwork and—Oh my. Worst thing, ever! He had a gold band. A ring! He was married! *Frick!* Sucked so bad. "Thanks," I said to him.

"Mhm," and then he shut the window.

I sat down with the clipboard. There was the usual bull about checking my "family's history" or some bull. I just checked no for everything. But yeah, as I was doing that, I heard, sort of on my right side, a bum splat down three chairs to my right. I turned my head and saw the black girl. She was staring straight at me. I hate when people do that, and then, get this: she smiled. I hate that so much. How can people smile? Like really. *How?*

Never mind. I just looked away from her and kept check-marking stuff and signing disclosures and blah blah blah. I looked up, sort of after that, and saw the clock next to the TV. It was nine fifty eight. I got up and went over back to Johnny-boy, his sexy self.

Slide-back goes the window! "Hello," John said to me. "Need help?"

"No, John. Here." I handed him the filled-out sheets. "Much longer 'til she's ready?"

"Not much. A lil' bit more. I apologize. Just relax."

"Okay."

He took the clipboard and slid the window shut.

I walked back to the seat, furthest away from the creepy black girl. Above, on the TV, there was something about houses getting remodeled. I didn't really get it, and to be honest, I don't remember what they were talking about. Something about counters being able to come off easier with a specific tool of some kind, whatever.

Finally, these two people came around the corner, near the wall next to me, crying. Boy, oh boy. Criers. More my turf. They were both black and holding hands. The black girl sprinted up to them and hugged them both.

"Thank you, Dora," the black lady said, sort of turning around and looking down the hall.

Then, get this: "Dora" come out from the hall, sort of following behind them, and she says the Dora the Explora song! No! *Ha!* Just kiddin' ya. She really said, "All see y'all next week." I thought she said "All," at first, but it was probably "I'll."

"Thanks," the black lady said. She held her husband's hand and also had the little black girl still hugging her. They walked out the office, together. It was so sweet. I thought about what was said in their session. I wish you were there to see. But you're Future Sally and probably don't remember.

"Sally? You ready?" Dora said.

I looked up at her . . . and . . . she was . . . smi-, um . . . <u>smiling</u>. Wowie! "Yeah. Ready," I said. I got up, and yeah.

She started walking back down the hall, and I followed. She opened the door for me and I walked in and then she closed the dang door behind us.

"Have a seat, make yourself comfortable," she said.

I looked around the room and it was so classic Doctor-status. Small but cozy, whatever. I saw the sofa and Dora's desk and her chair. I thought about sitting in her chair, as a joke, but then I thought it probably would be beneficial to be normal and sit in the sofa, like a normal human being. But yeah, I looked down at the sofa and saw a box of tissues. I grinned, then made a rather dumb comment.

"Wow. Gets emotional in here, huh?"

Dora didn't take it as dumb, though. She actually laughed. "Eh, sometimes," she said after. "Just sit and we'll get started."

So I did. It was really comfy. Super comfy, in fact. I crossed my legs and propped my chin up with my arm. I guess you could say I was looking rather bored, like a total D-bag, whatever.

Anyway, it was pretty awkward. We both were looking at each other and stuff. So finally I said, "Um, I don't really know how to start this off . . ."

"That's okay," Dora said. "How are you feeling?"

"Stressed."

"Why's that?"

"I lost my job," I said. Then I uncrossed my legs and crossed the other way. It's a nervous habit, I guess.

"Hmmmmm," Dora said. "Interesting." Wow. She did it. She really did. The classic "Hm . . . Interesting" spit shrinks always say. Then she asked me, "Do you want to talk about it?"

To discuss such a monotonous thingy thing (yes, I know the word "Monotonous," thank you very much) would take days, months, maybe even *years* to accom-com-*com*-plish. But I tried.

"Well, Dora, let me see. Hmmm. It's all so fuzzy. Basically my past life is so, well . . . consuming. Know what I mean? [She nodded.] And yeah, to say I don't think about it would be a lie. I lost my job because I wanted something new. Something new is always consuming me. Maybe for others it's easy to just swim on by, in life, but I really don't care to do that.

"Example: I woke up this morning and stared up at the ceiling and thought, 'What the hell am I doing today?' Obviously seein' you, of course, but I mean, besides that. Guess you could say I am pessimistic." I crossed over to my other leg, to maybe get more comfortable.

"Why do you, ah"—finger waving, searching for the right thing to say—"feel this way?" Dora asked me.

"I guess for a long time I've tried to pin-point why. It's the golden question. Sometimes I wonder why we even ask why. Is it to continue? Is it to grasp? Is it to learn ourselves? Why would you need to learn yourself.

"*Ump!* There I go again, see. Asking why again. I'm a mess," I said. Then I un-propped my chin and I uncrossed my legs and leaned forward and sort of leaned my forehead in my hands or something.

"Hm. You seem tense," Dora said. I didn't want to look up. For some reason I thought of her as my mom, see. It's really crazy. She's crazy in the head, Dora, but I think she helped me. "You think an awful lot," she said. "Tell me more, Sally."

"Call me 'Sal,' " I said, "and yes, an awful lot, my thinking. Jesus. I think so dang much."

"Why, though, Sal?"

"Because . . . Well, let me put it like this: say you have . . . uh, an infant. Okay?"

Dora nodded.

"Okay," I coughed for a second, "and this child is in its little cocoon. Then you push it up into the world and, *voilà!* the child is struck by all these crazy things."

"Crazy things?" Dora asked. "How you mean? Sorry I'm asking so much. Just trying to get a better picture of you."

"It's okay. Basically what I mean is that, for me, it's like being a child and going into this bizarre world of chaos. I just don't get how us humans function. I just hate it so darn much. Just with not knowing. I don't know. I guess I just mean that it's too much senses for me. Like too loud."

"Too loud?"

"Too, too loud," I said. "Like you go here, this place full of nothingness and no senses and no anything, then you go here, this place full of colors, cars, sounds, money, places, beings, et cetera, and you have to live with it all. Know what I mean?"

"I think you, um . . ." Dora said, looking for something to say, it seemed like. I mean, she looked like she was struggling.

"Spit it out," I said. Didn't mean to be rude, though. So I laughed to make it seem joking.

Dora smiled. "What you're describing, Sal, is Aspergers."

That's when it hit me. "What?"

"Aspergers. It's a form of Autism."

I pointed at myself. "Me? *Au*tism?" I said. Then, like a rude hobgoblin or something, I laughed. "No way! I mean, gosh, I do have problems with social skills, I guess—but not like that!"

I'd love to say more but this entry is already too fat as it is. Basically I explained that the world is strange to me, is all a joke sometimes, and how I see people as robots. You know, like if you slap a person, what happens is that it sends the nerves on the cheek bones into a frenzy and jolts signals to the brain. Then the brain references back to being hit in the past and how it brings up feelings of unpleasantness. Then the person gets super heated and probably slaps you back. Full circle. It's just weird. I was getting anxiety or something just explaining these things to her, but I didn't tell her. Why, if you tell someone, even, about your anxiety, or your feelings of un-comfort you're having, they frickin' blame it on <u>themselves</u>, because they think it's *their* fault, and I didn't want that, not one teeny tiny bit. I just met Dora, for Lord's sake. *Eek!* That's one thing I know for *sure* people do, and that is "being selfish." I think everyone is. It's always "How can I get mine?" crap. Don't let anyone tell you different.

Anyway, though, I left there and Dora told me to schedule another appointment with John. So I did. I picked two weeks from then, because thirty dollars for a co-pay is a lot of money, considering I'm broke and PeachPine money won't last very long. Not to mention I think my insurance is going to expire soon.

John asked me something rather odd, though—but super great on my end!

"Want my number, Sally?"

Patients and receptionists can have fun, right? *Ha!* Just kidding. I totally gave him my number. I told him that he was the man in this, and he has to take initiative. Thank God Dora wasn't there. She probably would've fired Johnny-boy. . . . So scandalous, though, right? Gosh. Girl, I need to find me a dang job! I hate being unemployed.

April, 12th, 10:16 a.m.

So I slept with John last night. Started texting me like nonstop these past couple days. Never again, though. He has two kids. *Gross!* He lives life on the hog, though. Mansion and all. Has some big-shot wife in stocks or something. He was one of those guys who looks like one of those lions on Animal Planet when he makes love. You know the ones. With the grunting and sweating over you. I faked an orgasm. I had to! Not to be a total b██ch or anything, but um, yeah, he just wasn't *that* good. I just don't get it! These hot guys never know what's going on, or what they're doing. I mean, he was so bad that his looks weren't nearly as worth it. Gosh, I hope I didn't get pregnant. I let him cum inside me. I know, I know. Sl██. I know. But hey, I didn't have a good time. I let him do it, the cumming, mostly because I just didn't want him to do the ole, "Baby, let me cum on your face," and I'm all like, "Sure," pretending to be sexy. I hate that s██t. I let him. He had a lot. *Frick!* That crap is gross. This one time, this guy, Pete, God rest his soul, came on my stomach and then coughed while he did it. His abs or something, these cut ones, had this fat bulge or something. He found out he had a "hernia" (or whatever you call it) and had to go to the doctor afterward the next day. Anyway. This, the guys and their little masculine-ness that clouds their own perception of women, this is what makes me sort of sick to my stomach, girl. It's all gravy, baby, anyway.

Anyway, I'm not really doing anything special today. Tessa is inviting me out to some place. This really country breakfast place. She says the skillets are absolutely to die for. So silly. I love her. She's really, like, excited about things. I should tell you about this one time, in elementary school, her and I, like, liked this boy named Jerry, and Tessa and I hated each other because of it. Girl, did we hate each other. She told this teacher, Mr. Nordwall, about it, and Nordwall sat us down and told us to cool it. The funny thing is that we both hated this girl, who was also named Sally, like Yours Truly, and she, Sally, hated us back or whatever. I ended up being friends with Sally later. I think it was because she was more popular or something. We were eight or something like that, I and Tess, but anyway, Sally and Jerry had a secret thing the whole time Mr. Nordwall was telling us to cool it. We found out, me and Tessa, by some out-of-the-blue situation where I and her were hall patrols and we saw Sally and Jerry kiss behind one of the portables. So we announced it to the entire school, and I don't mean like gossip or drama or word-of-mouth, I mean, like, Mr. Nordwall did the morning announcements and we asked him if we could be on it. He said certainly. So we did this announcement and told everyone about it. The funny thing, though, nobody cared, it seemed like. Nordwall got pissed, though! Too, too funny. It was really only for Tess and I's satisfaction. We were friends ever since. Since elementary school, baby! Now *that's* dedication!

So yeah, besides that, I have to get ready soon. I don't exactly know what I'm going to wear but I want it to be something casual. You dress too flashy, people stare. It's like, hey, look at her; she's better than us, or *I*. GET HER! That's just how I feel on the matter. People scare me, to be honest. I never know what their intentions are. I sometimes wonder if they really even care at all. I know *I* don't. I try to pretend, but that's fake of me. All I know is, while I write this, I'm feeling some weird jelly-like thingy on my foot, and I don't want to look down and see. But I have to. Hold on. . . . Oh my lordy! You won't be*lieve* this! John wore a condom. It was at my footsies! No bulls■t! I'm so happy! He was considerate enough to wrap up. I know I'm a home-wrecker, but yeah, I'm happy! He seems really sweet now. He left around five-ish this morning. His cute booty in those blue Levis. So *hot!* I might text him later. We'll see, ay? But anyway, I have to get ready and go meet up with Tessa. Bye-bye. Ta-*ta* for now!

April, 15th, 5:34 a.m.

Today's session was not bad at all today. I saw John, though, at the help desk. He was smiling at me as if nothing had happened, as if the cat wasn't out of the bag. Heys and hellos were said. The problem is, though, is that I'm wondering if he knows I didn't like it, the whole him not being good at sex crapper thingy. Maybe. I don't know. But I *did* tell Dora about the "guy" I slept with three days ago—I didn't say it was Johnny-boy, for Pete's (or John's) sake. I'd hate to have another unemployed simp roaming this earth. But yeah, Dora asked if I am promiscuous, and I asked her, "Who isn't?" She laughed, I didn't. In the simple fact of sex, simple is not totally there with me. Let's just say, I don't have a way with words. I don't really feel romance with people. In fact, I don't think I've ever known what love is. This one time, at this arcade called "Fun Depot," I and this guy, Cory (or was is Cody?), went and had oodles of fun. Girl, was is cray cray! We totally killed it at some Nascar, and totally killed it in the Jurassic Park shooter game thingamabob. We had *loads* of fun. I actually somewhat came out of my shell, to tell you the truth. It was great to have a breath of fresh air, for once. The thing is, though, is that this guy was kind of a geek. Okay, okay, so he. Came. Up. To. Me! Guys never do that! I mean, they do, but never the *nerdy* guys. Aww, he was *too* adorable! He was all nervous and stuff and was looking at the ground. It was sweet. He had his little hands behind and back and then he was rubbing his neck when he asked me, "Hey, uh . . . What are you, uh, doing this weekend, Sally?" Of course I told him I was doing nothing, it was too cute! What's crazy is he knew my name and I had never talked to him before. We have a *spy* in the building! He was a hipster. That's how I started to like the nerdy-types. They're so cute! Anyway, he told me to go to Fun Depot, so I went. Blah, blah, blah, whatever. I kissed him when my dad picked me up. My dad is pretty cool about that sort of thing. He's not all protective or whatever, unless it's of course a co-worker trying to score with your eight-year-old daughter, then yeah, you're getting socked in the face. You bet your A you will!

After John, Dora the Lovey said to me, from her office, her head peeking all out and stuff, "Come here, Sal. You ready?" She really remembered to call me by my nickname. Big whoop. It's just to build rapport or some kind of something.

Funny thing was, though, was that when I sat down, waiting for her, Dora the Lovey Dove, before I came in to the office, I was crossing my legs, sort of fidgeting, in the waiting room, and she came on in through the door and I looked up. Our eyes met and and she said "How are you?" and I said it back, too, exchanging the waves and fake smiles and yeah. Anyway, what I'm getting at is, well, I told her about this exchange, in our session, and how weird it was to me. She didn't get it. She told me this story of how she picks up her morning milkshake or coffee or something from Dunkin' Donuts and how she always says "How are you?" to the workers, and they remember her. She said they never, ever miss her order, ever. She was shaking her dang head about it. I asked her what her point was. I guess you could say I was being a b■ch. Hate doing it, but hey, <u>a girl's gotta do what a girl's gotta do</u>, to get some kind of validation, I suppose.

I don't know exactly where to go with this entry, girlie, to be quite frank with you, but I did leave that office feeling a heck of a lot better. I don't really know why, exactly, but I did. Why, if Dora and I get into it, even, doing all that mumbo about life and this or that, we can conquer the dang world, girl! That's how I feel about my gay friend, Josh.

Speaking of him, he and I hanged after Dora and I's meet. What's crazy, after I left the office, I sort of was thinking about work, because I normally would've had to hustle and bustle and go in afterward, like a lame-O, but I'm unemployed, so frankly, I got pretty bummed after coming back to reality. I drove over to Josh's. *Knock, knock.* He answered.

"What the heck, chicky baby?"

He's always got some kind of weirdo thing he says. Always. Never fails, girlie.

"Can I hang with you a second?" I told him. "It's important."

"Yeah, sure. Come in, sista cakes."

Josh's house is, well, neat, but also kind of shady, you know what I mean? Like, ever have a friend, you know, that is messy but also kind of neat? Say you got clothes everywhere, but you separate the colors and the whites. Like, what the heck? *Why?* Makes *no* sense to me. That's how Josh is. He actually isn't a loser, really. One time, long back, he said he wanted to sell drugs and play video games all day. So guess what, he did that very thing. Happiness! Instant F'ing happiness, girl. I envy him. I really do.

Going into his kitchen, I told Josh, "I wanna get high."

"Righto, cowgirl." Always saying weird shizz. I swear.

He went into the fridge and got some pizza poppers out of it. Jesus Christ'ums on a bicycle, wow. Pothead.

"Want some?" he asked me.

"Yes!"

What can I say? No? F you, then, sister.

"Go to the living room and get my bowl, will ya?" Josh said. "I'll pop these things in the microwave."

I nodded. "Sure. Yeah."

I sort of felt depressed for some reason, even though the meet was great and I felt a little better after. It's just one of those things, I guess. I don't know what I'm saying.

Walk over to the coffee table in the living room, grab pipe, bang it against my palm, get the black crap out, whatever. It was all dull. But I heard the shut and beep of the microwave. Jesus, was it amazing. Just awesome.

Then Josh came back and sat beside me.

"Sal, seen my new stuff?"

"No."

"Check it out."

He pulled out this baggie from his front pocket and yeah, untwisted it and stuff. The nuggets were okay, they weren't anything special. Probably reggie.

"This is Chronic," Josh told me.

Bull. Just complete bull.

"Oh, okay," I said. "Pack it." I was sort of getting annoyed. People always talk about their weed in some magical way. Someone's weed is always better than the person before him. Heck, even better than before their past selves.

He packed it all right. Packed. Full. It was epic. Fat, fully fat bowl.

Giddy alert! *Woo!* We smoked it like crazy. Kind of had it hit my stomach a little bit, coughing and yeah, whatever, life goes on.

Josh put the TV on, girl. He always puts it to the golf channel. He says the guys on there are hot. Remember Happy Gilmore? Well, Josh says that when Happy talks about golfers having a huge "a▮," it's really true. I just think it's a bunch of old guys, to be pretty realistic with you. But anyway, I came out and said it.

"It's just a bunch of old guys, girlie."

"No, Sal. These guys are, like, *soooo* sexy. Look and him, and *him*. Jesus! Look at her. Hey! Want some more reefer?" Always giddy, he is—hate it so much. I hate people smiling.

"Sure," I told him. "Why not?" I got the bowl and did another hit. Basically I was already feeling zonked out or something.

What happened next, basically I laid back and sort of passed out. It was really weird. I had such weird dreams. I thought about journal entries, to be honest, and it was scary. Like, I'm foreal. I could go on and on with this. I basically saw a bunch of pages. The pages were sort of taped to people's foreheads and everyone was able to read my stuff. I was sort of embarrassed, but I wanted them to read it, even though I was indeed embarrassed. I just felt like I was zooming. The people with hoopty-hoops around their waists and they were twirling around and stuff. Pages on foreheads. I'm psycho, honestly. Then I was inside Josh's house and stuff, in the dream, walking around like Frankenstein, and Josh was laughing hella hard. He kept asking what I was doing. I kept sort of touching myself. It was weird. I'm in this dream and basically feeling like I'm in some kind of dark forest seeing big elves or devils or something.

Gosh, I was out of it, girl. But then I woke up and I wasn't on the couch anymore. Josh basically told me what I did and what was the scoop.

"You were hallucinating! It was *hilar*ious!"

He told me I kept touching my tummy and face and my eyes were super wide and I kept saying I didn't know what was real and what was not. <u>It was the scariest thing</u>. I started to breathe really hard, then. I really did. Gosh. Hated it. The feeling of losing control is unbelievable. I couldn't really remember jack squat.

After coming back to "Now-land," I decided, sort of, to leave Josh's. It was too sudden, the realization of psychosis and yeah. Too, too wild. I left. Josh wanted me to stay—he was laughing and thought this whole thing was funny. I was embarrassed. A girl like me isn't like that, the druggie-type. So what he did, Josh, he friggin' got pissed and pulled the ole card out that hits deep.

"Fine. Go. Find a job while you're at it."

<u>When people are pissed, or let down, or feeling unpleasant, you sometimes wonder if their real side is coming out, or if they are only upset</u>. It may be a little bit of both, to be realistic with you, but then I think, after coming back, if really it's *you* that's the real one coming out when you disappoint. It's always who is on top in this world, and I hate it. I was embarrassed. He wanted to have fun, little Joshy-Josh, but I *had* to go. Can you blame me? I'm ranting now, sorry.

April, 16th, 2:13 a.m.

It's late. I'll try to stay up long enough to write this. I don't really have anything that was cool going on in my life since the last I wrote. I do want to vent here and little bit. Basically I, um, am surrounded—surrounded by distances. Let me tell you. Distance. Okay, you got the future, right? This black, dull, unknown future ahead, and then you have to make something of it, trying to make yourself better. Right? You following? Okay, so—this distance is ahead, and it looks so great and wonderful. Like it looks like it could be better than where you stand. So you run toward it, but in the way of it is Lions and Tigers and Bears. They growl and get in the way. The Tiger is in the river or something, chasing you, then goes away. The Bear is in the woods, and chases you, too. The Lion, though, the Lion is in your Number. Let me explain. I had this dream just now, where this little girl was playing hopscotch with a friend of hers. I got up to write this, literally. Anyway, the friend kept drawing animals in the number boxes with chalk. Foxes, Monkeys, Lions, Bears, Birds, et cetera. And this girl is drawing whilst her friend is playing hopscotch with herself. The friend goes back and forth, back and forth, and finally, she says something: "Hey!

There's a Lion in my Number! Number one! Get it away, now!" and it was too adorable. She didn't want her to draw in *that* specific one. Too, too funny! She thinks she's number one, and she doesn't want this Lion in her Number, all being in the way of it and yeah, whatever. My point is this: want to be number one? Well, you may have to have a few Lions and Tigers and Bears in front of you. People just don't get it. The number one is an opinion. It's pursuit, I guess. Anything you want, there's bumps in the road that'll stop you. Part of life. Being a girl—a beautiful one, at that —yeah, I do feel good about it sometimes, when I dress up and look absolutely dazzling in the ole mirror thingy, but hey, I have my own Lions in my Numbers. We all are going to suffer, so why fight it? Embrace it! End of rant. Goodnight. Oh yeah, and one more thing: <u>I am beginning to see that becoming a successful adult requires you to be as fake as you can possibly be to get what you desire most.</u> Am I right? Preach it! End. Now.

April, 18th, 6:31 a.m.

It's really, really early, girlie, and super crazy of me to be up this late; but whatever, decided to write. I can hear the birds chirping outside. It's not calming, it's annoying. Hate it. Wow. Anywho, though, I want to tell you basically about "yesterday." I put quotes because it now's the tomorrow of yesterday, if that makes any lick of sense. But yeah, me and Josh went to the mall. He called me and woke me up. I had the whole bedsheets and everything over me and I was looking like pure a■. Jesus. He kept saying, "Get up, Sal! It's a lovely day!" I sighed, like I always do, the weirdo that I am, and looked over at my alarm clock. It was about one o'clock! I overslept like crazy. I guess it was because unemployed people get the privilege of not doing anything important. So yeah, Joshy Josh called me up and told me to go to the mall with him. He even told me, too, that he would pay for one piece of clothing. Drug money is gold, girl—tellin' you! I said sure, of course, and went. Jesus Christ'ums, I got ready quick. It took about forty minutes! I mean, really, that quick!

In Florida, in case you don't know, the PalmTran is really convenient. I'm not F'ing kidding your gorgeous little self. It's cheap and those suckers get you *anywhere* in town. Crazy people on them, though, but I think you already knew that, from just what I put in some other entry, or whatever. Josh and me were not really talking much when we met up on the bus. It was eerie, to be frank. Like, really. Not a word! In fact, we were really the only people on that dang bus. We sat in the back, not like Rosa Parks (Ha!), and I was hearing the huge AC unit bubble and *rum-rum* or whatever. I could feel it vibrate. I sort of felt my jaw chitter-chatter from the unit. Still, Josh and I didn't speak bullspit. I think if you have nothing to say, people don't say it. It's not on their minds to say. I like to speak my mind, but you already probably know that. People think I'm weird for it. This one time . . . at Band Camp . . . *Ha!* Just kiddin' ya! Not going to start that way with the ole American Pie mumbo-jumbo. But really, this one time, I'll tell you. Okay. Me and my friend, Sally (yes, also named it), were being approached by these two guys. I mean—don't let me front—these were not your high-on-the-hog type of boys. They were geeks. Not the type that are cute and hipster-y. I mean the pimple kind. You know the kind. Know-it-alls. Doing the Star Wars stuff. Anyway, they came up to me and Sally, and they were trying to spit "game." I was having a crazy hectic day with finals. It was finals week. We were at this coffee shop to study, Sally and I. These geekers middle-fingered their glasses into place and asked us of they could buy us something. We were out of money, so yeah, of course us girls are always going to say yes. Well, Sally did. They did, the geekers, and brought them over. Big crap, too! We started drinking them and saying thanks. Then—the nerve of them—then they asked us *both* out like we were so simple to get that all you had to do was buy a little drinkie for us and ask a female dog out! *Bonanza!* Wow! Told the kid off. *Really* off. ~~You're~~ Your dang skippy I did. They beat it, naturally. Sally told me that you can't reject people that fast. I just didn't get it. Like, really. People never speak their minds. Why be pleasant for the sake of it all? Is it really necessary? Is my saying something sweet to make you scram really going to make your life better? Then again, I probably F'ed those kids up in the head. I never saw them again. They did go to my school, at the time, but they just disappeared. I don't know.

Getting off topic. Hate it. To get back on, me and Josh got off at the mall's stop. Hella hobos everywhere! All colors. Big and small, really, and really uuuuu*gly!* Not every person can have it totally made, but whatever, life goes on for them, I guess. No bother. I'm a b■ch. To get back off, I sometimes think about maybe writing letters to all my friends, stacking them, addressing them, and then, when all said and frankly done, mailing them out to everyone, incohesive-ly, I guess, by giving them everything I've always wanted to say to their righteous little minds. Then I would drain my bank account and give it all to my father, along with the title to my Acura that "doesn't work." Homeless life after that! I mean, more in the sense of backpacking it and going away to wherever, like hiking it over to other states or countries and not caring at all where the hell I'm going to next! And if I'm ever hungry, which I will be, of F'ing course, I'll just eat whatever. I'm tired of being around everyone. They all make me sort of sick, if you truly care to know. I guess I sort of envy those homeless people. Then again, they are probably being homeless for an entirely different reason than I am mentioning.

Okay, so me and Josh go into this place, the mally world, and we're being like, I don't know, struttin' b■ches or w■res, I guess. It was like a loud carnival or something. Lights, camera, and action! Stands everywhere! Higher prices on candies and drinks at convenient-er lines—that sort of thing. We were passing this stand, Josh and I, and this really weird gay guy was stopping us, trying to sell weaves.

"Hey, ladieeees! Wants to buy a weaves?" he said. *Hayyyy, lay-deezzz. Wanths tu bi a weavths?*

"No thanks. F■got," Josh said. Which was pretty funny, considering he's a dang fruit. He even waved him away. "We're busy. Get lost."

"B■ches," the guy said, and he turned away.

I laughed. It was really great to see people bicker. If you notice, people are only genuine and pleasant if you are it back. Makes sense, but then look at electric signals in the brain communicating negative and positive. Trips me out!

I'm a F'ing fashionista! I love clothes, clothes, CLOTHES! I just love SHOES! Passed everything else, in regards to life, liberty, and the pursuit of happiness, I absolutely, undoubtedly love shoes!

As we were passing some weird store I can't think the name of at this point in time, I turned to Josh and said, "Shoes."

He knew what I meant. "Let's kick it, girl."

We tried on everything. From Chucks to Nikes to weird skaters shoes. Tried it all— *Oh!* I remember it now. Journey's. That's the dang place. We didn't buy anything there. It wasn't all that great. There's nothing like a good thing of shoe-shopping.

We kept on walking. I sort of came up with this weird idea.

"Hey, I have this idea," I said. "These people are sort of institutionalized, in a way."

"How you figure?" Josh said, sort of laughing a little bit.

"Because the people are—"

"Institutionalized is a jail, stupid."

"I said 'sort of,' estúpido."

Josh laughed. "You make *no* sense," he said. It was times like that where people never understood me. Then Josh was all looking along his right, or something. "Sal, let's check out Toys-R-Us," he said. "Been a long while."

"Too long." I really meant it, too, no doubt. It had been about, like, twelve—count 'em—*twelve* years since I'd been to Toys-R-Us. Hella gadgets and gizmos in every place. Loved it, once upon a time, back when I didn't know a thing and never thought about us being institutionalized —that sort of thing.

We went on in, right smack dab in the middle of the place, near the registers.

"Good afternoon!" an associate said. "My name is . . ." I actually forgot her name, come to think of it. Anyway, it was a she, and *she* was seriously *all* about her little jobbie job. "Just call me if you need me!" she said. "Sale on Teddy Bears."

"Oh, cool! Thanks," Josh said. Then he muttered, "B■ch."

"What was that?" the associate said, really, really quick, her hand being all up to her ear. "Didn't catch that. Say again. Need help?"

Josh just laughed. "No. We're fine."

"Hm . . ." the associate said. You could tell she heard him, even though he said it real soft. "If ya need anything, just holler. Again, Sale.

Teddies. Aisle four. Think about it." Let her leech our money, why don't'cha? Gosh. Hate things like that. I just darn *hate* them.

Josh and I kept on a-steppin', straight into this display that had these little dogs that yapped when you wound them up. They were super tiny and kept going in little circles.

"These things are boring. I used to think they were hella cool when I was a kid," Josh said. (I totally did, too, but didn't say anything.) "—Hey, Sal! look!" He pointed. "The Teddies the b▆ch was talking about. Over there." Josh sort of started tugging me along.

Turned my head, sort of around, real fast, and saw the sales associate. She was shaking her head and looking at us. Probably heard Josh call her a b▆ch, yet again. Josh is the most inconsiderate person I've ever met, to be quite honest. But I love him. ~~I love him to death.~~

We were walking down the aisle and this little boy ran past us. Kids are always running in toy stores, I'm thinking. <u>Not much different from adults</u>. The kid's mom was saying, "Stop running, Ralph. My little Ralphie, stop running, sweetie." Sorry, little Ralphie. There's a Lion in your Number. The mom said excuse me as she passed I and Josh.

"These bears are so cute!" Josh said. Then he turned to me. "—Oh my god, Sal! I have to *totally* tell you about Becky." Her name really wasn't "Becky," but it sounds funnier in my head. Picture a really flamboyant male saying it, girlie. Too, too funny! "Oh my god, she and this guy are together now! But the guy is also talking to her sister."

"No bull?" I said.

"Mhm," Josh nodded.

"Scandalous." Gossip really isn't my forté, none the slightest, but hey, it makes little Joshy-boy hap-hap-happy when I, like, participate in his little shenanigans, or whatever.

"Did you hear about Ashley?" he said. "You know. Ashley. Lives in Palm Beach?"

I nodded.

"Well, anyway. She was talking to this guy or something, and she told me that he turned down sex from her!"

"No bull?" I said.

"Yeah, Sal—*no* bull. We were laughing about it or whatever." Then Josh started looking at this little pink bear on the shelf. "This one is cute." He grabbed it. "I like that he has a tail like a bunny, all poofy. I like it."

"Why are you acting so weird?" I asked. It wasn't like him to be all, like, giddy or whatever.

"No reason. I like kid stores."

"You never told me this."

"Never asked!"

He really never did tell me, the joker. Whatever. It's all water under the bridge4. "I wanna go to Hot Topic," I said. I was feeling gothic as all fork, for a weird reason.

"Go to it," Josh said. "I wanna kick it here." He kneeled down. "Gosh, look at *this* one." He grabbed it. "It's orange as heck! It's like highlighter-orange!"

"Jesus Mary-ann Joseph5, Josh. You act like you've never seen the color *orange* before!" I was getting mad. Stuff like that irritates me like you wouldn't be*lieve*. "I'm going to Hot Topic. Text me if you need me," I said, and then I turned around and walked away.

"Sal! You totally gotta check *this* one out! It's——" I walked too far away to hear anything else he was saying. I just didn't want to be around him when he was all overly happy like that. It makes me feel too funny inside. Inside, though, Josh is kind of a kid. I should say that I, um, basically am the olden one. Let me explain. Basically, there's me, a twenty-two-year-old, and then there's Joshy Josh, a nineteen-year-old. This said, he knows a lot more high-schoolers than adults around, like, my age. Ashley is about eighteen. "Becky" is around, eh, maybe seventeen? Don't really F'ing know. Never met the b■ch. I don't particularly like teenagers. I hang with Josh because he's hilarious in so many insanely *yuk-yuk* ways! How can I say. Knocks your socks off. Like that. I just love him, *adore* him, even. If I was a dude and gay—something like that—I'd try him on for size, in a magnificent heartbeat, you bet.

---

4 — Whatever *that* means.

5 — I think I got this saying from that one movie "Bad Santa." I could be wrong, though.

Coasting along in style, struttin' my stuff, I was walking by myself, minding bizz-nat, girlie, and I saw this HUGE playground—or, rather I should say, courtyard—full of children, ages three to infinity. Miraculous! Their laughs were echoing all around me, in that way. I wish you could've seen it. Once in a blue moon, I like to watch kids play. Not weird-like or creeper-like, in any way—I'm a girl, and totally not like that—but more in the way of feeling some kind of nostalgia. I like to "go back in time," in that way. The kids sort of running around in aimless circles with blue, yellow, or red balloons, and carrying cotton-candy, and laughing, and chasing one another. Why, I can remember so vividly having crushes on cute boys. We all were so ~~nieeve~~ naive, so innocent, so free from worries, that we had no *idea* what in the world we blasted had. I felt poetic. So I sat there, on a bench off on the sidelines, crossing my legs, and just watched. For a second I sort of looked up at the ceiling and closed my eyes and heard all the parents yelling for kids to not rough-house or horse around or kid, and I heard laughter, simultaneous and enchanting to this, telling the parents, NO, I do not want to do THAT! You're not the BOSS of me! and the parents get up and hold wrists and give time-outs and blah blah blah. I was happy to go back in time. Life just seemed more simple. There was no bills, no stress, no worries. But what's crazy is that even back in those days I still was pretty much a depressive. I couldn't talk very well and I couldn't understand people's emotions. I guess not much has changed. I still don't really know. I guess when I was a kid I just didn't understand humans. I didn't get how to play, or to be simple, or to listen, like I sort of do now. I guess that's why I'm writing this. I don't know. Maybe I'm speaking nonsense.

It's like watching cars. You know how people move back and forth, in a alert, focus ways, all trying to get to a destination. It's like that. Trying not to bump into each other. Screaming and playful yelling, invisible sword fighting. Gosh, how I wish to be them and go back in time. I wouldn't have to be around this bullspit of the world. By "them" I mean the kids. Outside the playground, it's a whole new ballgame: advertisements, stereos, TVs, clothes, cars, money, jobs, sports, beer, alcohol—all great things, mostly in the "adult world," but come with a price: energy. I swear to hell people are selfish. They really and truly are. All those people selling you things try to make you think you need them for *your* life. "What's in it for me?" kind of way. That's all sales really is. You take a person, one miserable as fork, and you promise them, qoute un-qoute, "un-misery," they may just fork over their hard-earned cash they slaved over that you now possess. It's F'ed, when you sit down on a bench and honestly think about it.

But let me tell you, once I was thinking all this, a kid, about, eh, four years old, came up to Yours Truly, and struck up a conversation with Yours Truly, an *act*ual one at that. It was actually a good one. She had a real knack for words. Smart as a tack, girl! Her voice was really, really sweet.

"Hey, misses! What's *your* name?"

I wanted to pinch her from head to toe, she was so gosh-darn cute! "Sally!" I said, smiling for once. "And yours?"

"Sam." And she smiled, too! "Say, why's you sitting *alone?* Don't you have anyones to pway wiff?" So dang stickin' cute!

"I don't know," I said. "I like to watch *other* kids play. Where's your friends?"

Sam frowned. "Kids laugh at me*hhh*——" She coughed.

"Oh gosh, my goodness. You okay? But yeah, I can relate, Sam—why do they, you think?"

"*Wellll*——they think I'm a weird." She started sucking her thumb.

A weird. Too cute.

"How you figure?" I asked her.

"I don't like to play with kids. They are too hard!"

"What do you mean by 'too hard'?" I said.

I didn't really know what she meant. "Like, hard as in difficult?"

Sam un-sucked her thumb and spread her arms wide out. "Yeah! Yeah, yeah!"

"Oooohh! *Now* I get'cha!" I said. Sam was really adorable, I have to say. She reminded me of myself, if that doesn't sound too cliché. But then I thought of something. "Hey. Where's your mom? She around?" I was genuinely worried.

"Oh!" Sam said. "She's . . ." She started sort of looking around, head spinning or whatever. "Actually, um, I don't know." I started laughing, and I don't know why. It was just too funny and too cute! I guess kids really knock my socks off. They're so oblivious, it's awesome.

"That's really not good, Sam," I said. "—But *hey*, want to do something *fun?*"

Her eyes really lit up, girl! "YES! What?"

"Okay, okay. It's called 'The Helicopter.' Want to play it?"

"Yes!"

"Okay! Here's what we do [gosh, I thought this was sooo stickin' *cute*], we basically—well, *I* basically grab your hands and lean back and spin. You're the helicopter blades. So you'll feel like you're flying! How's that sound? *Huh?*"

Sam started clapping. "Sounds great! Show me! Show *me!* Please! I'll be *good.*"

"Let's kick it," I said. Then I stood up. Sam was super tiny; about three feet tall. A little whipper-snapper[6]! I stood over her and, girl, she was *griii*nin'! I tell you what! Her eyes were so big, too. I grabbed both her hands and started to say, "Okay . . . One, two . . ." then, "THREE!" and I lifted her up and spun her! Round and round we went, girlie! She was giggling like crazy and yelling "Woo!" at the top of her lungs. Having a terrific blast! I was laughing my butt off, too, like her. It was *so* dang cute! That's all I can say. Cute.

I stopped and then put her down. We were both insanely dizzy—I was having major vertigo, she was laughing. "That was fun!" she said, toppling around and stuff. "Do it again, please!" She was so gosh-darn cute. "I want you go, uh, faster. I want you to——" She stopped.

"What?" I said. "We can if you want. It's okay. Really."

She looked behind her—all around, really—and then she said, "Mom! Dad! New baby sister!"

I looked up and, sure enough, a mom and pop came up. You really won't believe it. It was Sherry and Jeff. Thing is, South Florida isn't even

---

[6] — I was going to cross this out with my pen, but hey, it seems legit. I don't ever say "whipper-snapper," not even closely, and for this I hope you understand my footnote here. Crap. I talk nothing like how I write, I'm starting to gather.

small, none the slightest. West Palm Beach is actually really large. 13 million people. Everything is condensed to make room. I didn't get how it was possible to see them . . . Or run into them, rather.

"Sam!" Sherry said. "I was worried sick! Don't you ever run away from—" She broke off, then stared directly at me. "Sally? Oh *my!* What a pleasant surprise! How are ya?" You take this chick, you only met her once, at a dang bus, and she'll treat you like some *huge* F'ing friend. Don't get it, really.

"Mom, she showed me the helicopter!" said little Sammy. "Watch." Then Sam turned around and stood in front of me with her arms up. "Helicopter! *Heli*copter!"

"*Sheesh!* Okay, okay. Let's do it," I said. So I grabbed her hands and spun her around and around, faster and faster. She was laughing so hard! Giggling, in fact. Hella adorable.

Then I stopped.

"Gimme high-five!" I said, kneeling down to Sam's level, and she totally, like, spanked it, hard. Kinda hurt a bit. <u>Kids are strong without you even knowing</u>.

Sam was smiling as she ran over to Sherry. Sam hugged her. "Mom! Cou' I pway with Sally? Pwease!" she said, clenching Sherry's waist. Sam looked up. "*Please*, Mommy!"

Mama Sherry just laughed. "May*be,* sweetheart." Then she looked at me. "How are ya? You two seem to be just peachy."

I held out my hand for a shake. "I'm doin' okay, Sherry." We shook. It was friendly. Then I held my hand out to Jeff. "How are you?" I asked him.

"Good." He shook my hand. "Just good."

I don't want to be rude or sound like a b▪ch, but I wanted to leave right then and there.

Then came the awkward silence.

"Sooo," Sherry said, breaking it, "were you sick when you got off the bus? We were worried"—she turned to Jeff—"weren't we?" and then she nudged him.

He snapped out of his little trance. "Oh! Yes, yes. Worried." (Sherry sighed briefly after that.)

"Yeah, I was sick," I said; "super sick, in fact. Had to go, so I just left. I'm sorry, guys—I have to go, now. My friend's waiting for me. Havta go."

"Oh. No worries—I, *we* understand," Sherry said. "Catch you on the flip side." She smiled.

I hate smiles.

I kneeled down and said to Sam, "Hey, stinker. Come and give me some lovin'."

She was sooo happy when I said that. She un-hugged Sherr-bear and ran over to me. I had my arms forward and she ran into me, hugged me, and giggled. "Woah, easy now, sista," I said. Then I looked at her. Heck of a kid. "I had a swell time with you, Sam. Another high-five?" I had my hand sort of up, she spanked it, hard, again. *Ouchie!*

Sam kind of looked sad. "I'll miss you, Sal," she said. Then she walked back to Sherry and Jeff.

"See ya," Sherry said, and she and Jeff waved. They stopped. "Come on," Sherry said to Sam, looking down at her. "Let's go." She held Sam's hand. I watched them all three walk away. It made me hella sad—*too* sad, in fact. But I guess I was the one that ended the interaction prematurely. Sam was looking over her shoulder, at me. I felt really bad. Sam was so gosh-darn cute. I usually hate kids. But I know their happiness is real and perfectly perfect. I miss being that young, to be completely truthful with you. Why am I depressed all the time? I don't really know anymore.

So I walked back to Toys-R-Us. I saw Josh again, and he was talking with the associate, go figure. They were laughing and stuff. Later, Josh told me her name and that she was cool and stuff. I didn't care. She invited us both to some party when Josh and I were about to leave. I declined, Josh hadn't. I always decline positive things. It's in my nature. Oh yeah, and by the way, Josh never bought me that one piece of clothing, the jerk. Oh well.

Evening.

I want a word that describes what I'm feeling inside. This writing thing is really very *bleh*. I guess that's the word. "Bleh." Writing isn't even like it's what you're thinking, I'm getting at. I think it's more just my brain telling me what's going on inside of it. Like mush. I want to tell you there's some secret thing I'm doing here, but really, there isn't, not even slightly, or boldly, if you will. I'm just here talking. Really I hate the life I live. Most of the time nobody understands me. I know, I know. Writers always say some cliché bull like that, but it's true! Nobody really does. Sometimes I talk to people and it's in one ear and out the friggin' other. I feel like I'm going insane in the membrane sometimes.

Evening. (Even Later.)

~~For you, in one ear, out the other. For me, in one temple, out the other. F you. Bye.~~

April, 20th, 4:05 a.m.

Josh told me about Tina. Tina is the girl at Toys-R-Us. Josh says she's a total "beef cake," whatever in the world *that* means. I think she's riffraff, personally speaking. I don't like her. She's just got this . . . *look*. You know? I don't know how to describe it. Like she's being your friend but not—all at the same time. Like, she would be all smiley and giddy with Josh, and then with me, but then she would have this look. This really distant, conniving, egotistical, lost look in her eyes, like she was hiding something, or keeping something, from us, or everyone for that matter. I really hate basic b■ches, I'm sorry—I just F'ing do. I hate these girls that try to come in under the radar or whatever. Gosh-darn hate it. What I'll end up doing, probably, is end up fist-fighting the b■ch and pulling hair and digging graves. You just wait and see. But anyway, how I found this all out is by being invited over Josh's. He invited me on a whim. Told me it'd be epic and fun. He didn't tell me *she'd* be there, the A-hole, but hey, I digress. (I also want to note, here, that I'm getting high on a fat jay.)

The party was pretty wild. I don't remember much, though, because it was yesterday—but I'm sure as horse spit'll try. Okay, so—Eh-*hem*. Basically it started out with me going in there—minding my own dang business, naturally—with Josh, and yeah, this was all at Tina's house. Her parents are super rich. I mean, holy smokes, insane. Truck loads. They have a jacuzzi within a pool. That rich. But yeah, so we, meaning Josh and I, came in there and it wasn't Tina the Great answering the door. Nobody did. We rang and rang but nobody bothered answering. The music was loud. It hurt my dang ears. We went in, though, and I started to feel really weird. I wanted to sit down, shut up, and breathe. Josh knew somebody and stopped and started talking about this one time he and them went camping at some boy scout's parade. *Ugh*. Boy scouts. What a load of potatoes. But anyway, I was all alone, sitting near this conversation just happening.

Then, holy smokes! You won't believe the *nerve!* This guy, some jock-f■k (excuse my language), came up to me and started hitting on me. It was like he didn't even care I was nervous to be around there. I had my arms crossed and everything. I don't even want to put the conversation in here because I would actually vomit. He kept talking about how he never seen me around, and what college I go to, and what would I like to drink, and he liked my dress, and he thought I was cute, and blah blah blah. What . . . a . . . *tool!* I was nice about it, though—don't get it twisted—but I was giving the obvious signs. You know them. The signs for a guy to beat it. You basically say "yeah" a bunch of times, look away from them a bunch of times, change subjects a bunch of times (mostly something like leaving or going to see another friend somewhere off in Africa), and you never laugh, ever. Like normal and always, he didn't catch on. Guys never catch on to the signs, ladies.

I want to tell you that I told this guy scram and shoo, but I really didn't (leaving, to some standard, wasn't in mine, or his, body of language; more in the setting of one's party), given the situation; and then, too, I really did proceed to the kitchen, where cohorts, Josh and Tina, coaxed me into a lovely Jack 'n' Coke, which, *duh,* I gladly accepted. I didn't know the guy's name, this jock, but he left me with Tina and Josh. Oh yeah, Josh left the conversation of boy scouts, mainly because, well, it was the wrong person he thought, I guess. Don't you hate that? When you're talking to someone, one rather enjoyable and that entails the lavish finer things in life from one's past encounters, and at the end of the conversation you find it wasn't the person you originally had in mind? Happens all the time. Nevertheless, what's more, we fiesta-ed. A bunch if I-ness and you-ness comes together in this setting, the party-life setting. All around were little ants and their drinks and this and that. I feel like I'm talking, be that as it may, but the words compute in a different realm somewhere; and then, as explaining this very feature of speech, the people around me, namely Tina the Great, were telling me they didn't get what I was saying, further proving this thought-process. I gain nothing for this, but whatever, it's all gravy.

Total Zen Master. This is what I was thinking while I was there. This bald chap—his name was something very Eastern—was in the backyard, by the pool, slurping away at—you wouldn't friggin' believe it—water! Anyway, total Zen Master. That's what he called me; when I ran from this mayhem of a fiesta, passed the bloody Americans and their American Corona, made in—*duh!*—America, and I went to the poolside, where, too, I saw the bald man, churning away at this thought-process I told you about. He knew what I was saying; but then again, he, too, had Aspergers, like The One and Only, your lovely and great Sally Fairfax. I had this really strange feeling of him. He had this great complexion. You know the bald guys like Mr. Clean? Super, well, clean-ness? He was like that. Totally clear-skinned and tan and, I don't know, no zits to his name. Him and I discussed the weirdest thing: Buddhism. He told me that he meditates every day before he does anything. He told me that the mind is often off in some other place and is never with the body and soul. He told me two things: "By putting your body in the sit-position, breathing in and out, you give yourself one-ness." The other thing was—". . . and by clearing one's mind from all its trials and tribulation, you <u>gain a sense of peace and come back to 'the now'</u> . . ." as he put it (though I have my own wasteful and gainable thoughts in regards to coming to grips with waking-life's desires)—really a total charm, be it as you take.

My brain works like a powerhouse. Talks about one thing and switches to another. This party became basically a place where I met a man that had real intelligence. I can be intelligent, too, when I want to be—don't think I ever can't. But I always keep it inside because people often never understand. I guess that's what Zen Master was explaining: The mind often wants to leave the body and soul—that's what I took from it. (But this is all such a contradiction, and has lead me to believe that I'm not living life to my fullest potential.) Being told you're nothing is scary. Now, being told you're smart, it's completely another. Basically up until that point I was told that I was nothing—and pretty content about it, too, I must say. I guess I almost enjoy negativity. I haven't ever had a lick of positive in my life. Well, I have, but I haven't recognized it, if that makes any sense. Take this party, for example: Most people would think this is an extravaganza that should be taken as a blessing, but I take it as a bunch of heathens looking for a good time. It makes me sick to my stomach. Take this: F you.

Sorry. Where was I? Oh yeah. So me and Josh weren't even around each other. Luckily for me I dipped out of there. I wasn't drunk or tipsy or anything like that, no—I was more euphoric. I just wanted to get out of there, stat. It felt like a burden, in a way. So I walked down the street, and I saw this really weird thing in the road. It was a dead bird. I mean, really. Dead. Completely *dead*. Very, very sad. I looked down at it and thought of this thing as something that other animals—like maggots, roaches, things like that—are going to take advantage of and use as a resource. But I had a curious thought in my head. Hmmmmmmm. I thought about this world being as one, see. I thought the universe is one big life-form. It's like God. We're all God, see. Time is really an illusion. There isn't a past, present, or future. It's all a made-up scam! Basically all what we are is together-ness. Without Death there wouldn't be Life. There wouldn't be the beautiful birth of a baby. Maybe that bird could cause a chain-reaction for your child to be born. You never know. That's the thing, though. That's the trouble: it's all completely random. That's the beauty of it all! We are just One. Maybe you don't get it, but the Zen Master got it, fully. He told me I was wiser than he was. Or is. I thought, or still think, it's a load of crock.

Up, up, up the dang street, the sky blue as blueberries, the cars nonexistent, I came up to the Help Desk—or the Main Office, if you will

—of my apartment complex, dazed and confused, beyond a kick of a doubt. Bethany Rice, the lady that got me a sweet a⬛ deal on my apartment (remember?), well, she was at the desk, naturally. "Hey!" she said. "How's it goin'?" The usual bull. "Fine," I said. "My mail in, by any chance?" "Yeah. Some guy came by and dropped it all off," she said. I said, "Swell. Thanks," and I turned around to leave. "—Wait!" Bethany exclaimed. "Word around the grapevine says you need a job." "Yeah, I do —*bad*," I said. "Got one?" "Oh yeah. You could be our tour guide," she said. I said, "I don't know about this. Sounds like I can't hang. Would you train me?" "Of course I'd train you, silly willie!" she said. "Of course! I have to. Takes practice, just FYI." (I nodded.) Pause. "Say, Sal." "Yeah?" "Start tomorrow?" "Can I next week?" "Ummm . . . *sure!* Why not?" "Cool. Cya." "Cya. Hope you're doin' okay . . ." and I then left and went on home; home being literally twenty feet away. Hello, next jobbie! *That* easy, sista cakes!

Evening.

Telling someone your problems is never easy; but you do anyway, you guess, for the sake of telling. That's how I feel, and how my take is, on the subject. Most of the time, even, what I want to do, though it feels like I can't sometimes, even in a state of safety, I ask someone for help. Sometimes my head hurts so much that I get, like, frustrated. You know, like, agitated and frustrated? Yeah. That. Well, uh, anyway, this one time I was so much on the verge of insanity, I, like, was seeing things: a bunch of fuzzies here and there; people laughing at my face; children laughing; busses whizzing on, all by, or near, supermarkets; money falling from the sky; and (the most scary, I should tell you) staying in a perpetual state of high-ness. Sounds like being high all the time would be fun, right? *Wrong.* It's not. By God it's not. Imagine losing track of yourself. It's very easy to do. People don't realize how easily your consciousness can be bent. Time moves very oddly; heck yes it does. So really, mind you, there's multiple places you could be in. "High" is a synonym of "psychosis," in a plain way. I'm high all the time, see. I'm high, like you are conscious, all the damn time. Everything I see bugs me. I could go nuts, girl. Take this: lay in bed, turn lights off, close eyes, do a pound of shrooms, and just stare. You'll see some crazy spit, girl. Honest. No lie. I want to tell you about anxiety, too. I feel this quite often, in moments of psychosis. Okay, so. I need comfort. *Right?* Right. I usually call my most trusted person: my dad. Back after I graduated, something like four years ago, my dad told me something that was super insane: "Sal, you have a form of Autism called Aspergers." I didn't know how to take it, really. Aspergers? No! No way, José. No, no, no. Never. Not me. That's just how it was. He said he took me to a place, my dad. He said he took me sort of to this place where the doc said I was a classic case. On the outside, no; of course not, I'm a hottie, I guess. On the inside, pure Autism. I'm not a real b■ch. I just act like it, sometimes. I don't know. Maybe I'm pessimistic. But that's just how my dad is, that's just how my life is: Autism. My dad told me he didn't tell me about the test, when I took it around my Sophomore year in high school, because he didn't want people to pick on me, set standards, and have me end up being unhappy. It all backfired. I *am* depressed. He tells me I can get help. Now look at me: twenty-two, alone, and going to therapy. But hey, who's the a■hole? End of rant. Bye.

April, 26th, 4:05 a.m.

Nothing super epic happened today. I started that jobbie. It was . . . okay —but weird! It's all about "What's In It For Me"s; A.K.A. "WIIFMs." Apparently, if you want to sell something, the only thing you have to do is give the consumer reasons to buy that'll ultimately lead them into deciding that it's a better choice for their life. Or their family's. For example: selling toilet paper. What makes you different from the rest? Well, you firstly have to have attributes of the product that are (1) Healthy for the environment (because that sells), (2) Functions so the product is "beneficial" and "practical" to the consumer (because, *duh!*— people, people, *people!*—it's obvious), and (3)—and probably the biggest thing—Make sure the price matches the demand, or potential demand, of the product in question. There's more things that can happen—I do understand that, girlie—but these are the main points, so bite me! Toilet paper is just toilet paper, right? Yours is better. Is that poo on your bum? Well, use this. You need it to feel comfortable, and oh yeah, it's also the softest on the market. The softest? *Woah!* No way! Yes, sir or ma'am, it really is! Ten dollars for five rolls. Then you wait. They say things like "oh"s and "um"s, but that just means they are on the fence and don't trust you. Throw in friends you have connected with to do your dirty work. Friends sell. Friends can really give you the kind cash flow you potentially want, but that means you have to win over the friends, too, which is tricky. It's all so interesting. But anyway, this is basically what Beth told me. I no longer call her "Bethany," on account of she really doesn't really like her full name. Women. Gosh. We always knit-pick things. We always want shorter names.

Anywho, I went there in the front office, dressed to impress, like the beezy that I am—just kidding!—and Beth was totally at her desk, her red, rosy red lipstick on, her business-like shirt and skirt, and she told me, "Well, hey! Mornin'. You ready for a fun-filled day?"

"O'course!" I really wasn't, but it seemed like that was the right thing to tell a new boss. Your being all right, I mean. Not being fake. Reason I say that is because you won't be*lieve* what Beth said.

"You don't have to lie." She paused. "Fake it 'til you make it."

I laughed; she did too.

"You're lookin' good," she told me. "Is that from Macy's?" She was talking about my top.

"No. Walmart," I said. "Strange thing is, they have fan*tast*ic sales."

"Yeah?"

"Oh yeah, and—Oh! Crazy thing. Their shirts from the generic brand and from the Target brand are, uh, actually bought from the same distributor, but Target is a hell of a lot more expensive. It's like about—"

Beth held her hands out in front of her, just then. "Woah, woah, *woah,*" she said. Then she got up from her desk and was walking around it. "Jesus! I said you look *good*. Didn't want a whole thing about shirts or anything."

I said, "Sorry," and then sort of put my head down.

"Just messin' with ya!" lil' Bethy Beth said. "Take a joke why don'tcha." Then she sort of nudged my shoulder. I just don't get it, frankly. People really are weird to me. "Let's get started, shall we?" Beth said. "I'll give you the tour."

And she really did. Hella did. I mean, yeah, it was my neighborhood and all, but come on! she showed me everything: the steam room to the pool; the inside of her desk; the outside of this and that; even the dang laundry room for the employees. Believe me, huge deal. They over*due* it, the employees. It reminded me of my mom, for a weird reason. I know I haven't talked about her, but it's mainly because I barely know her. She left with some lame-O about when I was twelve or something. My dad was heartbroken, but whatever, life goes on. But anyway, it, the laundry room, reminded me about my mom because I remember she tried to dry about ten, fifteen loads of clothes in the dryer we had, and then, get this: she didn't take the lint out of the slider thingy. Can you believe it? Did you know that that is the #1 cause of most household fires in America? No bullspit. Completely and utterly true! She just about burned nearly *half* the laundry room! Smoke and everything. I'm not kidding. I was eight. Can still smell it, even till this day. Luckily my dad came home and used the fire extinguisher. My mom was tanning in the backyard when it happened. She had no friggin' *clue*. He yelled and screamed about it. She cried. But it was mostly because she left an eight-year-old girl unattended whilst a dang fire is happening. So crazy. But the funny thing is, I think Dora and I, when we were in one of our "meetings," the ones where I discuss "feelings" and whatever, I told her about my mom. Dora thinks it's possible that my mom had Autism. Makes complete sense. Dora said people can go their whole life not knowing they have it. Imagine. So wicked.

~~Wicked-er than a horse's butt!~~ *Ha!* ~~Made a funny. But anywho,~~ to get back on, Beth and I ended up back at the front office after the tour. It was hella quiet, or something. Ain't spit going on. We started talking. Well, *she* started talking; I just put in two cents, naturally.

"Ever seen that one TV show with the guys that repo stuff?" she said, as her and I sat across from each other at her big, fat oak desk. "You know, the way they go into the, um—Wait. I mean the way they . . ." She trailed off.

"What?" I said. I was confused.

"Brain fart," she said. "Sorry, Sal."

I laughed. "It's coo' . . ."

"But yeah, that show: it's bomb. They have a bunch of guys—big guys, really nice—and they have these crazies that come in and break s■■t."

She cursed, then. Really! She did. I sort of *knew* she wasn't as professional as she seemed to be, but whatever, I'm always right! "What channel is it on?" I asked her.

"I think MTV. Not too sure. Look it up." She put her feet on her desk, and she had her hands behind her head, lounging. She had black heels on, too. The Target kind. Which made me think that she knew what I was talking about earlier with her, the little beezy. "Oh man, I'm beat," she said. "I just got done working out, earlier. You like Coke, Sal?"

"What?"

"Do you like Coke?"

I wasn't really paying too much attention. I was thinking about . . . eggs. Isn't that weird? "Um, yeah. Sure," I told her.

"Go in that mini fridge over there." She pointed. "Just under that desk. Millie's. That's your partner, by the way—but yeah, get us Cokes."

So I sat up and said, "Sure," and I walked over and bent down to where she pointed. Then I sort of pulled on the handle. It was weird. "It's stuck," I told Beth, sort of out loud, so she could hear. Then I turned around and looked at her. "Beth, it's stuck."

"You got to really yank the son of a b■■ch. Just pull!"

So I did. Then finally, *wham!* it budged. I sort of fell back on the carpet, or something. I can be a klutz every now and again.

"Atta girl!" Beth said to me. "Get the Cokes."

I got up and sort of brushed myself off. I looked on in the fridge. Hella Cokes galore! I grabbed two, then shut the dang door. "Finally," I said. Then, I walked back to the desk and put Beth's can in front of her.

"In the old days," she said, snapping open her can, it sizzling after, "these things were a nickel. Now? Forget it! Cost too much like a fortune."

"I hear ya," I said. Then I snapped my can open, too, but really slow and, I guess, "girly-ish"—I don't know. I was sort of afraid it would be all shaken up or something. Don't judge! I'm human. "Ever hear of them putting cocaine in it [referring to the Coke]?" I asked Beth.

"Oh, that's a myth. You really don't believe that, do you?"

"Maybe. Seems legit. Makes them more money if people get some kind of kick from it."

"People already *do* get a kick!" Beth laughed. "I buy these things like crazy!" which, by her saying that, made no sense, considering she (a) Just told me it's expensive, and (b) She works-out? "I hear Pepsi's stock is actually about two times more than Coke's," she said.

"Really?" I said. I didn't believe it. I assumed Coke's stock would be higher. They have a wicked doper image than Pepsi—but then again, Brittany Spears did some crazy commercial for them, and probably more. I don't know.

"Yeah, no s##t," Beth said. Then she dropped her feet down from her desk. "Say, Sal. Do you have a boyfriend?"

"Nope. Don't plan on it, neither."

"That's odd. You're really pretty."

"Thanks. You too."

"Oh hush," Beth said. We chicks always compliment each other, but then we don't accept the compliments we ourselves get. It's really strange. I never get people much, or most, of the time. I seem to say that a lot. "I had my time when I was your age," Beth told me, "and that time is *well* done and over with," and then she sipped her Coke.

There was a weird silence between us. I think it was because we were pretty bored, or pretty out of ideas or things to say.

So I asked Beth, "What do we do around here anyway [because, well, this question fills in the blanks]?"

"We wait. Wait for the people to come in, do this or that, and we tour them." I realize now that my writings are not the real way people speak in my life, but oh well, what's a girl to do? A psycho girl, at that.

"Do you know when they do?" I asked Beth.

"Ah, usually around lunch time. It's when people can. Work and all.

That sort of thing."

"What do you do about insurance?"

"What d'you mean?"

"You know. Like a fire or something."

"A fire or something? Oh. We require the tenants to purchase insurance."

"Oh okay," I said. Frankly she wasn't understanding what I was gawkin' at. People never seem to do. "But I more mean, say, if someone burned down this place, what would you do, Beth?" I said.

"The insurance would cover it."

"Did you know that if you burned down a house, it's a misdemeanor if it's not near another house with living inhabitants inside of it, or inside the actual burning house in question?"

Beth blew out. "*Pfft*. Bulls■t," she said.

"It's true," I said.

"No way. First of all, people who do that are crazy and deserved to be locked up. Secondly, if they labeled it as a misdemeanor and, say, according to your theory" (which she, this b■ch, was assuming was a 'theory,' and not truth. I grinned at this second in time) "they burned something here, it *is* in fact surround by pretty much constant inhabitants. This complex is always inhabited!" Beth was shouting in weirdo disbelief.

I don't know why I even bothered with this entry. It pretty much means nothing. I think I'm wasting my time here.

April, 28th, 10:25 a.m.

Dees entry I li' tu speak een a fransh askscent. Today why doe'cha! Sally-wally Fairfax. Een the golden age o' twen-tee-tu, I's a beat of a charmer. Oh ri'! Nuff said. Now I speak in a aussie askscent. Welcome tu dee *grey* barrior rayff!

Totally messin' with ya! I feel pretty decent today. In fact, I'm almost half of what my potential is. That doesn't seem like much but it is what it is. I go into work soon. I sort of hate Beth. She's a real trooper. She likes to F with me sometimes. She'll say one thing, then mean another thing. I hate it. So confusing.

Anyway, I'd like to tell you about this one time with Tessa and I and how we met our good friend Molly. Molly is the size of a penny, or smaller, and she *loves* to make us happy. She makes lights sway and music boom. She makes us horny, and she makes us feel warm. She's made of MDMA. Ha, *ha!* Don't get it? Well, tough noogies. Deal with it!

Okay, okay. So it starts off with Tess and I. I was at my house, Tessa was at her house. Tessa called me, just right before nine o'clock.

"Sal!"

"Yeah? What?"

"Where the hell are you?!"

"My house . . . Why?"

"Let's go to a rave."

"You know I'm in! Get your butt over here."

"Ditto."

"Can't get here fast enough, sista."

"My car is a piece of sh*t."

"Excuses, excuses," I said. Then I hung up.

I already knew that it would take her ages before she would actually come through. We girls—wow, never ceases to amaze me. Nonetheless, I spent the next hour—no, scratch that—the next *two* hours getting ready, and by getting ready, I mean, like, dressing like a total sleaze-bag. With the red fuzzy boots, colorful bras, and other various, miscellaneous sh*t we chicks wear.

Then finally, *ring ring ringy,* the beezy sista sista named Tessa comes through, dressed exactly like Yours Truly—go figure.

"Hey b*tch," she said once I opened the front door for her, in a way that wasn't insulting, if you catch my drift. "What's cracka-lackin'?"

"Just chillin'," I said. Girl, did we sound like a bunch of goofs. I'm seriously serious.

But Tess just steps on in, like nothing. "This new place is homey, homie," she said.

"It's okay. The fans don't work."

"Oh *God.* I could never!"

"Yep."

"How do you do it?"

"Don't know," I said. But Tessa is like a goodie-two-shoes, without the goodie part. She's like a princess. I should say she and her parents are, like, spoiling her. She's my age and still lives with them. They still pay her dang car note. I'm jealous of it. Wish I had a deal like that. Maybe life would be cooler or something.

"Say, you got somethin' to eat? I'm starved," Tess said. What's funny is I haven't even got my first paycheck yet, not even *today*, even, so really I pretty much have to make due with the groceries I have around the house. Thing is, you can't say that to people, for fear of being judged or something. But back then, it wasn't such a huge biggie. I still get weird about things like that, though, sometimes.

So anyway, I said to her, "Yeah. I got some Hot Pockets in the freezer you can borrow."

"Hot Pockets? Borrow?"

"Just take it."

Gah-*lee!* What a beezy.

"Where's the race at?" I said while I was watching Tess sort of run to the dang kitchen. She and I were in there, and she popped open the fridge door and leaned on in.

"Where are they?" she said {meaning the Pockets}.

"Up. You'll see them," and she did, and then she went on in the box and blah blah. "So, where is the rave, for the second time?" I said to her.

"This microwave is broke, Sal."

"You gotta really press the button. Here, I'll show you." And then I walked over and did it for her. She opened up her Pocket's plastic package and just threw it on in there, the bloody microwave, bare. "So," I said, "for the *third time* now, where is the bloody rave?"

"Sal, why in the world are you talking like a damn Scottish?"

"Don't know." I say "Don't know" a s▮▮t-ton. It's great to say because it leaves room for failure. Ya dig?

"It's at the hash bar," Tessa said to me.

"What?"

"I mean near me. They have this club."

"So it's a *club*, not a rave."

"Yeah," she said. I hate when people mix the two. If you're going to say "Club," don't include "Rave" in the picture. Jesus.

She was eating her Hot Pocket like a beast! Really! She was! Like, honestly, she was making some breathing sound, because it was hot and all, and then she was chumping down on it after. "It's hot," she said. Well, no s██t, Sherlock! It's called a dang "Hot Pocket," for crying out loud!

"Wanna go?" Tess said to me, when she was finally, finally done and over with, with her dang Hot Pocket, it going down into her f██ked prissy, little tummy, the w██re.

"Yeah. Sure, w██re."

She just laughed, I think.

After going through her car's console, this really old Buick her dad gave her because it was minty and vintage (hence the car note), Tessa got out a bag of pills, two sizes too fat for it. It looked like a water balloon pillow. Tess grinned and turned on the car's inside light and said, "Mmmmmmmm. Molly."

"Who's Molly?" I asked.

And basically she told me what I said toward the beginning of this entry: penny-sized, makes you horny, things like that.

"Cool." Then she told me to take one, eat it, and enjoy the ride. "Cool," I said again as I took it. "Take long to work?"

Tess said no. She said it takes a couple of minutes. Just enough time for us to drive over and on to the "club," or something. So yeah, I ate it.

That ride was pretty boring. Tessa had the couth to just sit back, shut up, and calm the F down for once. Not saying she's all excited-type and whatnot—she's not by any means—I just mean to actually enjoy silence. In *Pulp Fiction*, when Uma Thurman says at Jack Rabbit Slims that you know you've found someone special when you can sit back and shut the F up and share silence, I nearly cried, it was so damn magical. I *love* the guy who makes those gosh-darn movies. I always forget his name, for some reason. I think his last name is Tarantino, but I don't know his first name. I always forget first names.

We got to the club, and it was packed full of jig██boos. *Ha!* Jig██boo.

Funny word. Say, I'm not a racist but it *is* pretty funny. You have to admit. But yeah, some white people, too, and dates and dudes and women and ▇▇▇. The ▇▇▇ are ▇▇ to tell just because they do things very ▇▇▇—Let's not talk about *that*, though!

We parked and whatever, whatever, and then I thought of something.

"Tess. When the hell does this Molly friggin' work?"

"You'll feel it—trust me. You'll feel it," she said, grinning her little prissy griny grin grin. Then she got out of the car . . . Well, we both did.

The club life, to some clear, righteous existent, that I can't quite put my *wittle* finger on, is whack; but the righteous part, God help us, comes in, instantaneously, once the lightbulb-like endorphins flush here and there in the ole noggin', from the oddly pulsating strobes, from the bouncing, gyrating hips and grab-a▇ing, from the bass booming thunderously and vibrating the ground beneath your feet, causing you to lose, though you're vibing out and enjoying it, control, amongst the liquor-pouring, the bartending, the hit-on-me or -you, indeed, that blatantly goes on. This is opinionated, you must understand, so take this with a grain of salt. That said, me and Tess (or "Tess and I," if I choose to be grammatically correct), walked passed the line, passed the scalawags that wear threads made of superficial-style mumbo-jumbo or -yumbo, and simply skated on by, like casual queens gracing presence upon peasants. Upon stepping up to the big, big bouncer, the chest out, the tummy sort of tucked in, the smiles presenting, white and bright, Tess says to him, "Hey, let us come in, sweetheart?" and he, too, upon hearing the "sweetheart" part, puffed up his chest and tucked in stomach, making, oppositely to us, himself look bolder and manlier, and he told us, "No problem, ladies," and raised up his red crowd-control rope, and Tess and I skated on in, still like queens, without saying thank-yous or your-welcomes, things unpleasant here in these people's club-ish eyes.

Shoulders moving back and forth, legs clown-ish-ly parading about, Tess was pushing and penguin-walking through the crowd, see, whilst I held those moving shoulders, irritated and bewildered, because I had to keep an eye on Tessa and keep my balance to keep from falling, or being trampled on, or being joked at; and the primates, and their guns (guns being metaphorical, obviously), doing all of this were dancing the night away to the popular Drake songs, loud and auto-tuned, playing in the background.

Tess and I were so dang hot-looking. I know this because grouped men stared at us as if they were savage animals staring at a piece of barbecued, smoked beef, dressed with the dressing of Chanel perfume. We laughed with our heads back when we sat at the bar. "Simps," Tess said. Then she paused. "Say, you want a———" I forgot what she said—it's too far back in the ole noggin'—but as I recall, I believe she asked something along the lines of consuming a particular drink—Patrone, Caption Morgan, Jack 'n' Coke (which you know is my favorite), Spider Bites, Buttery Nipples, et cetera, et cetera—coming from massive varieties on the above neon-lit menu hanging over the bar. "You want *that* one?" she asked me. "Looks de*vine* [even though, God rest her lovely lying soul, she had extensive experience in this particular food industry, the industry of getting mother-F'ers wasted, and she has to try every single thing "alcoholic" on God's green earth in order to properly do her job for the A-holes who ask what is what and all that jazzy jazz]." I shook my head no, and then picked the Jack 'n' Coke (obviously). "You're so plain, Sal," Tessa said. "Gosh.... Bartender!" She waved him over. "Tender! *Yo!* Tender! Get your a■ over here!"

From a distance, he spun around, smiling. He was a burly hunk. You know the kind—tan-skinned, five o'clock shadow. That kind. He came up in front of her.

"What would you like?"

"I'm Tessa; and this is Sally, my friend. She wants a Jack 'n' Coke and I want a shot of Yager-mister, stat!"

The bartender laughed and said, "Coming right up." He didn't I.D. us like most places usually do. Then he walked away, probably doing as he was ordered.

"Tonight is our bowl of fruit. Let's kick it!" Tess said to me.

"Aren't you, um, not supposed to drink alcohol with pills?" The minute I said it, the lights in my peripherals started to gleam in a flower-like way.... Hard to imagine, huh?

"No. Just f**k it." Tessa was such a trooper (and still is), I swear my life on it.

Just then, everything pretty much was a blur. I can only say so much. The ground spun in figure-eight circles, if that's even possible, and I felt like my body was a sponge—and I could suck in all the good vibes everyone was broadcasting. ~~I felt like I couldn't care to do anything~~. My arms were like jelly or jello, and I had to touch Tessa all over, in a very sexual way. She giggled and probably made some off-the-wall comment on how ****g zooted I was, back there, me, inside a room, or box, filled with humans undoubtably equivalent to the euphoria I felt. My senses jolted. Like literally. Jolted to bullspit. Everyone was like a bunny to me, in that moment. I thought everyone was so cute and so free. I felt like I was a god, graciously floating overhead, over everyone, wanting to grace presences humbly rather than like a total b**chy b**ch, like usual. I was dancing like *wow!* I was going *nuts* on that dance floor. The cup of alcohol I had, at some point in time (like I said, I can't remember), had spilled on my wrist, sleeve, knees, the floor, everything, and it was, you can bet your a**, the wildest, craziest, most beautiful thing I had ever, ever seen, girlie. I love Molly. I really, really *love* Molly!

But don't get spit twisted, now. Tess threw up her Hot Pocket—well, *my* Hot Pocket, technically—and made herself look like a dang fool with the guy she was with; him being, no bullspit, the F'ing bartender burly boy. Myself included into this extravaganza of vomiting, I, too, had a go with our fine tender. He had the eyes that could only say "let's f**k" so many times, on Molly, to the point where you had to vomit, too, all over his shoes, and in front of him. Needless to say, when he saw the two of us, Tess and I, the lovely of the lovelies and "hottie" (as in a "verb" kind of way) of the hotties, vomit in front of him, you could bet the last thought he had wasn't "let's f**k" but more along the lines of "I should've never let these b**ches drink." After that, I might as well've been raped, because I can't remember anything. All I remember is screaming and yelling and being pulled out of the club with my arms over two big guys' shoulders, and then being thrown the F out, into the cold, dirty, F'ed Clematis street.

Then, in some miraculously way, I and Tess woke up in my bed, fine and dandy; a little drool out of our mouths, but nothing to write to Santa about. (Get it? *No?* It's okay. Nobody ever does.) "What the hell happened last night," was the first words I heard Tessa say. After this, this entry thingamabob, I probably won't even remember us having ever done that, ever. I like to try and forget embarrassing things. Sometimes I actually cringe and wince when I think of something embarrassing. I'm doing it right now while I'm writing this free-hand.

I'm late as hell for work. I'm probably going to call-in now. *Frick!* I'm about three *hours* late. This writing stuff in my journal is absolutely great. I'm addicted to narcissism, in a way. But don't hate me if you ain't me. *Ha, ha!* My momma used to say that expression all the time. [Sigh.]

May, 5th, 11:26 a.m.

Dora and I spoke a lot the session that passed.

"How was your trip?" I asked her when I came in.

"Good. Me and my husband had a blast."

"Yeah?"

"Oh yeah. First, in Hawaii—"

"Wait," I interrupted, "Hawaii?"

"Mhm"—her nodding, whatever.

"Oh wow. I have friends there . . ."—my hand all out—"Continue. . . ."

"Yeah. So . . . anyway, me and my husband went with some friends and vacationed in Kawaho . . ." and blah blah blah, she was talking about it, and yeah, I could care less.

Anyway, I did the ole pleasantries. It's nice, but I felt sort of fake. I could go on and on about what was said, but it would take forever. Basically we have an hour-long session and we used up ten minutes of that. Which is 5 bucks wasted of my 30 dollar co-pay. Let me get started and stick to the point before I lose my temper.

I was talking to Dora about my frustration with doctors.

"They always try to disprove," I said.

"Why's that?"

"Like, for a quick example, I'd go in, do research and *know* that this and *this* is wrong with me, but then they'd say, 'No. Not true. It's *this*, Sal.' I hate that bullspit."

"You in general hate authority, don't you?" she laughed.

I laughed, too, and then explained, "Oh yeah, most def. Like, it's ridiculous how much adults will try to uncover truths about us kids. Well, I still think I'm a kid, or some bull.

"This one time—you really wouldn't believe it—some kid, his name was Jack [I want to keep his name private; it wasn't really 'Jack'] and my mom, she was a nurse.

"Jack saw my mom in her doctor's office. He said he was having pain in his stomach that hurt him like crazy. Jack was really scared and whatever, and his mom was there.

"My mom told me this story, even though, yeah, she wasn't exactly supposed to—what with confidentiality laws and everything of the sort for nurses.

"Anyway, to make a long story short, Jack had a spray can up his butt, a big one, the fat ones."

Dora's eyes got big. "*What?*"

I laughed about it. "Yeah! Ain't it *wild?* Then my mom sort of suggested that he tell his parents he's gay and all, so that way he could use a regular dildo, which is a lot safer than an F'ing spray can! Then, get this: the kid lied to my mom and told her—Ohhh *man!* Too funny."

Dora was all like, "What? What? *Tell* me!"

"He told her that he slipped and fell and the spray can went up his a██!"

If I ever saw a person laugh, Dora's was undoubtedly the most crazy, once I, you know, said this story to her. You'd think a counselor would keep to themselves on the ole laughing at a broken gay kid, but whatever, it is what it is.

Then I was talking with her about a quite swanky debate.

"Dora, I think it's very safe to say I'm wasting my time here."

"No, Sal. Why in the world do you feel that way?"

"Because."

"Don't just say 'because,' you know what I mean. Tell me. Explain."

Then I reiterated.

"You doctors and counselors and jokesters are doing a job. This job, I might add, is very expensive, quite especially in America. I don't like it, but yeah. We patients know we have problems. We know it. You know it. Everyone knows it. But, what you don't get, Dora, is that we all have problems.

"Take this: we both can agree that humans aren't by any means the brightest lame-Os in the cupboard. We all wonder sh*t and always try to do this and that to make ourselves happy.

"It's a dog-eat-dog world.

"But I'm wondering, Dora, is that if we could, say, help each other more, and not in some beneficial way for ourselves, it would cause a plethora of people that are straight dummies. I think we sort of want to be selfish and dog-eat-dog-ish, so to hellishly speak.

"Take this example: the food industry—I've been around the block a few times in this—I can say to myself that I *know* what I'm friggin' sayin'. Basically it's all a scam.

"If you, this waitress, a college student trying to make a living for themselves, trying to be happy, trying to not have stress, and you go into this job, this place full of people trying to have 'a good time,' well then by God give it to them if they deserve it.

"If a person comes in, has a thirty dollar tab—which is quite normal, if you've ever done that—and he, or her, tip fifteen dollars, fifty percent, you're going to say, 'Wow. They tip well,' and then, if they come in, this high-tipper, and order from you *again*, well, by God, then give 'em a little more rum, for Pete's sake!

"They will tip, tip, tip. My point is this: if you tip well, it's in your best interest. You only gain by doing this. Nobody likes a selfish cat. If you go in there and never tip, they may not remember you, but you sure as sh*t don't deserve a lick of services handed to you. If you got two guys at a table, one tips, one doesn't, then I'm sorry but the guy that tips, I'm putting him at the top of my list for people to serve.

"See, by you not tipping, I already know that no matter what I do, no matter what I say, I'm getting nothing out of it. I'd be broke and not have money for college. I'd lose out tenfold. You're a jackass for not tipping and making everyone's life easier, and for what? Money? *F* that!

"So you see, by serving the awesome guy, the one that tips, I achieve so much. I feel like I have a purpose in this person's life. He's giving me a chance to make his service savvy. S■t, I'll flirt with him, and probably like it. If he's a cool dude and I start up a convo and he's a damn winner, kind, courteous, speaks well, does all that, then by God the dog-eat-dog world is so full of happy s■t!

"You got everyone being happy. I think if there's God, He'd approve of this. Take the time when He decided to make this world. If everyone is hunky-dory, well, F that, too, He probably thinks. He wants to test you. He wants you to tip, and if that waitress or waiter doesn't give you services—in other words, if you put in and not receive back what you put in—you tried, and you can be happy to know you did.

"You knew you weren't the S-head in this transaction. But life isn't a transaction. It's not about trying to do business, because if it was, business is business is business and guess what, you're going to be the one with the shorter stick to pull. Bes' be*lieve*.

"So Dora, this said: take you, this counselor, sitting here in your high-price chair, your fancy job, your college you already graduated from, your success you've already done, the 'waitressing' or whatever the f■k s■t you've done, or did, the husband you've got, Dora, you're beating my ass.

"You win, Dora. You win. Good job. That said—"

She interrupted me. "I get it. 'That said . . . that said.' Go."

"*That* said, you sit there with a person who knows they have a problem and you grin at yourself because you think, 'I'm going to make me some *money* from this pu■y,' because you've already got half the work done for you. The '*patient*,' or whatever, is already needing your help.

"Doctors don't want to find a cure for anything. Why would they? Your business consists of telling people you have a problem. That's why the medical field is all a dang scam. You guys win when us patients say we have an issue. You tell us we have this issue or that and then you make us think we have it. So then we ask you what we can do. Then you mask the help or services you suggest and we have insurance and co-pays to pay not only you but the help and services you endorse. You think we're all winners, but what if, just maybe, I *don't* have an issue?

"If I came in here and said, 'This is my problem, Dora,' and you told me, 'Oh, *that's* normal. That happened to me F'in' this morning!' then I'd probably NOT come back to you because, one, I'd probably think you were a sh▇ty doctor, and two, I already am convinced I have a problem and have a hunch of it, so you tell me what you *think* it may be and I nod my F'ing head off.

"Maybe I need to be told that I have nothing wrong with me, Dora. Maybe I need to be told that."

Then Dora said, "Sal . . . ?"

"Yeah?" I said.

"Do as you want. If that's it, by all means. I'm not going to sit here and take this from somebody. If you don't want my help, then fine, beat it."

Then (to my future self reading this entry, I tell you, though now, by golly, I feel ashamed to say, despite the very angelic moment that I thoroughly told her, the lovely Dora, off)—then *I* was the one that overly laughed and chuckled the F off to myself at her blasted little, wrinkled, olden, F'ed professional face, looking so stern and so proud to have won our little debate, *the* golden debate of retaining my future bi-person gatherings amongst two very philosophical individuals, tinkering with a fresh, disgusting, wronged, and tainted mind lost in self-destructive oblivion.

I said, "Thanks," and left Dora in the dust, never, ever to schedule another blasted appointment ever again. I don't know if it was wrong or, frankly so, if it was yet again another wrongful doing on my part; but it felt satisfactory and ever-external in my anxiety-filled perception to tell a person, one full of helplessly irrelevant medical facts, that *they* were the ones that were, in fact, wrong, and that, no, I would no longer give them my money—for their secured-like future monetary gain, for the next patient to be added to that next dozen or so little mice in their cages.

Oh yeah, before closing the door, "I slept with John," was said. Then she said to me, "No," and I knew it didn't really happen, either. Jerkin' her chain, I guess.

May, 7th, 10:08 a.m.

Goodbye yellow-belly or -button job! Good F'ing riddance! Girl, today Beth gave me the ole stiffy in the A-hole. Canned. Kaput. Fired. Oh well, it seems normal. Wasn't quite catching on. I was getting late and going crazy, even though, yes, I'm about a football-pass away from the job, whatever. Beth was always trying me. She, or anyone, would do it. The chick that worked there (I mentioned her name before, somewhere in this journal, back when, and I should, right now, look for it, but I'm too lazy, and frankly, too bored and too tired to even care to look for the b■ch's name)—she was trying me the most. She would overachieve at her desk and try to beat me at everything; scheduling, saying right spit, doing this or that. Bullspit. I don't have the time or patience for it. But I guess jobs sort of *need* competition. Henry Ford, the guy who pretty much invented the affordable car (in case you've been living under a rock and don't know) —Henry Ford quoted—now I'm paraphrasing—"If I asked customers what they wanted, they would have undoubtably told me, 'Henry, we want faster horses.' " *Imagine*. Can you imagine? I want to laugh at that quote. People do competition to keep along with the demands of others, but the innovators, the ones that I, Sally F'ing Fairfax, want to be, they are the ones that truly make a mark on "modern" (whatever time, I have to put in quotations, mind you, because of the possible "obsolete"-like factor written-word has in our culture) great America, that way that thing we all know and love can prosper.

I must place another newer paragraph, aside from the fact I don't want to, because, well, the confusion factor exceeds the philosophical qualities this piece of literature has on the mind. Why, if I discuss a firing, then Henry Ford (genius of our time, obviously), whilst sitting in a Chinese restaurant at three a.m., you'd probably think this is some crazy, crazy spit. I mention the Chinese food place thingy because, myself needing, I wanted some, and I'm here eating it, now, journal in front, Chicken Chow-*main* and pook fry-*rye* (is that racist?) stuffed in my mouth, cheeks fat, chumping away toward—

Sorry. It's now 10:43 a.m., on May 7th, and I say this because I just got a call from my sister. I'm home now, or whatever. Closed the book up and all that jazz. I *walked*. My sister, her name is, well, unneeded. I won't ever forget it, ever. I call her by her personally unfit choice of name that I picked: Sissy Dukes. She hates it. She's the cutest. One time, back when we were about in elementary school, her and I were at the pool, and I remember it was summer and Mom was at work. We go to this pool and, being she was the older, wiser, bigger Sissy Dukes that she was, Mom gave her the "pool key" (hexagon-shaped, in red, with the number 206, for, *duh*, the symbolization of our trailer's number) to tamper with, handle, all that jazz. We get there, right? We get there in our little teeny-tiny bathing suits, alone, and we played Marko Polo by ourselves. So cute. Then, this really big bearded dude comes in alone, too, and sort of stares at us playing around in the crystal-like Florida water. He was grunting every now and then, so Sissy Dukes, being her sassy self, turns around, at the golden age of ten, beaming at this guy, and says to him, "Can I f▆▆ing help you?" and *he* says, "Maybe . . . ?" and then she says, "Not now, not never [or did she say 'ever'?]"—her hands on her hips, blond pig-tails dripping wet and slump, her eyebrows tilted inward, her eyes dead on him. She was adorable, and that's what I mean. He walked away, never got into the pool, and we never saw him around our small neighborhood ever, ever again, oddly. . . . Well, anyway, Sissy Dukes just called me, just now. I'll put the convo here—or at least try to mimic it. I'm very excited! She was so excited when I answered the phone.

" 'Ello, puppet!"

"Sally! How's it hangin'?"

"A little to the left."

She laughed. "Anyway, *Sal*. Guess who is coming down from Augusta, Georgia, just to see her baby sister!"

"No way!" I said. I was so dang ec*static,* aside from munching on day-old Chicken. "Really, _____?" [Block her actual name out, *duh!]*

"Oh heck yeah! Absolutely," she said to me. "I'm going to drive my happy butt down there and see you and Dad!" and then I noticed her voice getting all falsetto-y

"I don't really talk to Dad much, _____."

"What? *Why not?*"

"Well, he——"

"You know he asks about you all the time, right?"

"I didn't," I said, and I really meant it. Basically, my dad and I, well, we're not the bee's knees anymore. We used to be—don't get your panties in a bunch—but I, like, don't know. I guess he just sort of, you know, fell off the map. It's crazy how things change when you get older, but at the same time, they stand still-ish.

"Oh yeah, he asks about you 'n' stuff when he calls me here," my sissy said to me.

"*Yeah,* Sissy Dukes. Sure you guys are—"

". . . No."

I laughed. "No what?"

"You know what I meant, Sal."

I started to laugh harder! I love my sister! "Enlighten me," I said to her, laughing.

"I hate when you call me 'Sissy Dukes'. It drives me absolutely bonkers."

"I'm excited you're coming. When?"

"You change the subject a lot," Sissy Dukes said, and I do. I have to agree—whatever it takes.

"I know, I know. I'm a really *lovely* person."

"You're such a smarty pants," Sissy Dukes said, but really her voice on the phone sounded as if she was a corny soccer mom. Whatever, I just went with the flow. I had the phone up to my ear and took a bite of my whatever, whatever foody food. Then, after that, Sissy Dukes goes, "What are you eating?"

And I go, "Salad." Ha, *ha!* Such a liar that I am.

"Don't sound like it," Sissy Dukes went on. "I hear rattling. Some foreign languages. Are you at Panera?"

"Oh yeah." I started to laugh. "Totes Mc*Goats!*"

"I haven't heard that expression since we were in high school!" Sissy Dukes said, starting to laugh. "*Ha,* ha! You really crack me up, Sal."

"I'd like for you to get to the point," I said. But I didn't say it rude to my sister. I said it kind of like I was busy at the moment.

"Oh gosh," Sissy Dukes said, huffing and puffing, on a dang roll, on her end of the line. "You're so damn vain. Do you have a boyfriend? Last I talked to you, you were dating some guy."

Oh God. Blimey knew *that* was coming. So I answered Sissy Dukes, all going on and on, like, "You mean Russell? Yeah . . . He was a sleez-bag. Total sleez-bag, I tell you."

Then, no lie, Sissy Dukes laughed. What a—excuse my French—what a total b■ch. I hate that! When you say something and people just laugh at it, like it's, you know, F'ing *noth*ing. People are always laughing. I hate it.

So then I told my sister, "I'm totally over him. *What?*"

"Sal, you and him were the bee's knees."

Bee's F'ing knees. You know what they say: like sister like sister. Ha, *ha*.

"What to you mean?" I said. "He would always be all, you know . . ."

"What? Pretentious?"

"Heck yeah!"

"Sal, you gotta understand, nobody's perfect."

"Oh hush with that. You sound like my therapist."

Sissy Dukes' voice changed. "*Ther*apist?"

"Well, actually, Little Miss Sunshine, she's a counselor."

"You're a strange girl, Sal."

"Why, thank you! I'm proud to be different."

"Why are you seein' one?" Sissy Dukes said to me. ["One" is, well, the therapist/counselor I had told her.] Just making sure I understand when my whatever, whatever future self reads this later. Greetings from the past, Older Sally!

"I'm not seein' one anymore, if you think I am. I'm not. I just feel crappy all the damn time. I just go through—Oh spit."

"What?" Sissy Dukes said. "What happened?"

"F'ing fly is all around me." That wasn't a lie. I really told the truthy truth on that one.

And my sister just laughed. "I *know* where you're at!"

"Oh God," I said, eyes rolling. "Let's hear it."

"You're at the mall, eating Chinese food, the place where you and . . . uh, forgot his name."

"Josh?"

"Yeah. The gay one. How is he?"

"He's good," I told my sis. Then I was thinking, Now, look, you beezy, why are *you* the one changin' the dang subject now? "But no, that's not the place I'm at. I'm at someplace by Dad's."

"Why don't you go say hi?"

"No," I said, then shook my head. "He's probably at work."

"Are *you?*" Sissy asked me.

"Am I what?"

"You know, 'at work.' "

"Okay, nosey. Gah-*lee!*"

"*What?* I can't see how my sister's doing?"

"No. You can't."

"Typical Sally," Sissy Dukes said, and I was really starting to get irritated.

"_____, for about the *hund*redth time, when—are—you—*coming?* I sort of *need* to know, you know."

"In about three weeks. 26th through the 2nd." Then she sighed. "—Is that *cool?* You gonna stop havin' your panties in a bunch and not freak out on me?"

"I hate that we fight. Promise me that we don't when you eventually come, b■ch."

She laughed. "I love you."

I laughed, too. "More!"

"No, Sally-baby, I love *you* more!" Sissy Dukes little-girl'd.

Then I sort of did this, well, little thing where I, um, ask a bunch of questions.

"When you visit, what did you want to do?"

"I think I just want to sit back, relax, kick it with my sis, maybe see a flick, see dad, all that. I miss you guys sooo much."

Then I got up, picked up my tray, walked over to the trash-can, dumped my spit, looked up, accidentally caught eyes with a Chinese man,

71

and told him, "Take a picture, it'll last longer," and then put my phone back up to my ear.

"What happened, Sal?"

"Nothing. Some A-hole staring at me."

"Why don't you appreciate, like, you know, when a guy, like, looks at you?"

"I hate it! Guys always just want me because of my body or something. They never have feelings for me. You know?"

"Oh yeah. I know. Trust me. I know," and I'll bet she does! My sister is so gorgeous. I love her. As much as I'm a total (excuse my French, like all the other times)—a total b■ch, I'm actually totally down for my big sis. She's like, wow. Her hair is all silky and smooth. She's super, super great-looking for her age. I think she uses some salon-quality shampoo; none of that Walmart s■t poor people like me use.

"Hey, how is Alex?" I said to her. "Is he doin' okay?"

"Yeah. He's okay. He's getting better."

"That's good. How's the teachers?"

"It's frustrating sometimes. He's eight now, so it's sort of hard to get him to play with others and everything. His teachers are great, though. His teacher works with him. He's been having less tantrums and . . ." and then, she went on and on and on. . . . Alex is not an Aspie, he's a regular kid on the Autism spectrum. That's why I like him. He's really funny. This one time, he sort of put all his toys out, sorted them on the carpet, and then, you wouldn't frickin' believe it: me and him (God rest his soul)—me and him lined up all the soldiers, the goofy-looking Disney cartoons, the weird barbie dolls, everything. The kid *loves* those spits. Loves them. Absolutely. But then, get this: my sister came in, curlers in hair, toothbrush a-sizzling in her maw, and she stops, dead stops, and looks down at me and Al playing, and then says, "Al! Don't do that!" and she stops everything and picks him up. I thought it was weird. My sister then looks at me, knowing that I, Sally F'ing Fairfax the Thirty-third, has Aspergers, and says, "Alex is NOT suppose to do that. He's suppose to learn how to play with the toys." I explained to her that it's not the toys he sees, it's something else. She didn't get it. She asked me if I would tell her more about that. It was weird. She was irritated, then not. I don't understand it.

But anyway, I told her that he, being a child with Autism, sees the toys more beautifully than the other children. I told her that he sees them as sort of, like, you know, GADGETS, if that makes sense. I told her that the gadgets are more like places that have a specific point in the world, where they can be happy, free, and able to concur. By them being in a single-file line, they have a place in this world. It's not about toys, at that point, even; it's more about, you know, comfort or whatever. My sister was nodding like crazy when I was explaining this, back then. But anyway, that's what Alex is like. I like Alex. He's such a sweetheart.

I'm home now and frankly tired of writing. I want to just sleep now and get the day started. I have a few jobs to apply at. But basically, my Sissy Dukes is visiting, and she's bringing Alex, and I'm so happy about that. I can't wait. My sister is a bad b■ch. Forealzies. I just want to dance right now! I can't wait!

May, 11th, 5:34 p.m.

Looking around, I found a few snags. My job is now FINDING jobs, if that makes sense. I hate it, but whatever, life is life, as they say. I just don't get it. Time for another rant: but first and foremost I'd like to tell you about a guy I knew—one I straight up'll say now, I repeat *now,* that I have NOT slept with, regardless of the want for it—who I met at a party. He told me some crazy stuff. I forgot his name, to be quite honest with you. I knew his friend, though. I dated his friend for, like, five minutes, back when. His name was Edgar. He was a drug-dealer. He sold to Josh a couple of times. Josh was always overly zooted on some weird drugs for the longest time. I always just tagged along at the parties. But anyway, where was I? Oh yeah. This kid chilled with Edgar at this party. This kid was really sad or something. He told me he had just broken up with some girl named Ashley. Ashley was a chick that Josh also knew. She really is the definition of a b■ch. This guy, whatever his name was, dated her, and I thought it was a shame because he was so cute! He was kind of shy but also kind of confident, if that makes any sort of sense. I went up to him at this party, and just sort of struck up a conversation with him.

I asked this guy what he was doing or whatever, with him being all sad with his head down, a beer in his hand. I felt bad for him. I asked if he wanted to dance. He got up to me, and "Cool," he said. "Awesome, yo." He was always saying "Yo" all the dang time; and it was really awkward and weird. I said my name and he pretty much forgot it.

Anyway, we talked and danced and really drank quite a lot. It was like buckets. Just swimming pools of that stuff. We were trashed and I thought he was cute. I don't know what got into me. He was really attractive and mysterious. I just, you know, wanted him to get out of his little bubble of "Comfort Zone"—even HE put it that way. You know? I just wanted him to be happy. It was wild, you know, how I thought like that. But yeah, anyway, I danced and talked with him, and then, get this: we went to some room at the party. Some really lone room off somewhere in the house. This house on Flagler. It was sort of near a restaurant by Cheeburger Cheeburger. (The restaurant is closed down now, though.) So me and this kid go into this room. I was really diggin' him, and I think—well, I'd like to hope I think that he was diggin' me, too. We were having such a great time!

Then he sort of went up to me and said, "I just realized, you're, um, really hot," and then sort of got me against the wall.

I was super horny. There's something about a rebound that really makes me crazy. I love it. So I said that he wasn't so bad himself.

"Thanks . . . girl," he said, and that's when I knew he forgot my name.

Then, we started making out, like pretty hard. It was scary, but you know how it goes. Horniness is crazy. It makes you go bonkers. But then he sort of picked me up. He was making out with me and then, even more, he put me on top of a dresser. My butt was right there on the dang edge. We kissed a lot, and then, he grabbed me off the dresser and we got on top of the bed. He was over me, still making out with me. I started to take his shirt off, real quick. He stopped me—or tried to. But then I slide the shirt over him, but not took it fully off. Get this: scars. *Huge* ones! I got scared. Can you imagine? So I asked him,

"Oh wow. How did you get those?"

He didn't say anything, really. All he said was, "Long story."

So I said, "Oh okay."

And then he put his shirt back down and said, "Listen. I don't want to have sex with you."

I was actually kind of sad when he said that. So I asked him why.

He said, "I just got over a relationship."

"Yeah. Ashley?" I asked.

Then he sort of peered at me. "How did you know?"

"You told me, silly."

"Oh. My bad. I just, I don't know, am not up for this."

"Do you think I'm ugly?" I said. Really I wanted to know why I was being rejected. "Is it something I did?"

"No. Not at all. It's not like that. It's more to do with me being cautious. I feel like I'm not at my best. Like, it's weird. I want to have sex with a girl I like. I want one that is, you know, like a friend. But I wanna be at my best self, yo."

So then I said to him, "I get it. I'm not that way, though. You're a cutie pie."

"Don't call me that. . . . Ashley called me that."

Then I got silent. He was really scaring me.

"Anyway," he went on . . . "I just wanted to make out with you to feel better. I wanted to be, um, kinda sorta nice or whatevs."

"I understand." But really I didn't. You got to say those sorts of things to weird guys. The ones with the weird outlooks, yeah, stand clear of them. He was still sweet, though.

"I just want to be left alone, I guess," the kid said. "I had a lot going on ~~this~~ these passed weeks and I just wanted to feel like I could escape. I want out, if that makes sense."

"All the more reason to have sex," I informed him.

"I want to f██k, but I don't know." (He really said the F-word, as in the *actual* word. Drives me nuts. It's so vulgar.) When he said that, I just *knew* it all was a goner. I refused to take away this guy's, I'm assuming, virginity.

So then he says, "Let's go back. My friend Edgar is somewhere out there."

And then, we both got up and he lead me out the bedroom door. We went into the living room, where Hella people were at, and we went to some random couch. We talked and talked and then, get this: he did something F'ing *nuts!*

He turn to me, randomly, and said, in this deep, croupy, F'ed-up, scary voice and all, "Everything just, ssss, ssss, cave inside, just, ssss, ssss, *sssss,* cave *inside,* just cave inside . . ." and I knew he was F'ing *psycho* from hearing it! Twitchin' and tweakin'. But whatever. I got up and left.

He turned to me, like he didn't say any crazy things, and asked me, "Where you goin'?"

I just left him in the dust. It was too dang weird for me to deal with a psycho like that. Just randomly sprouts out stuff and doesn't remember saying it. Too wild. No wonder why that Ashley chick dumped him.

Now, time for the rant part: I feel as though the male species is lost. They will never know us women. Maybe I'm just young, though. Maybe I'm just a lame-O. I wish I could do more for them. But what they don't get is that, when I get all dolled up, it's never for *them,* it's for the *girls.* Let me explain. Girls are even more judging than men. We like to look at what other girls are wearing. I don't know what I'm trying to say. I guess I just want to say that we truthfully are all messed up. I think it's possible that we're all doomed in some way. It's inevitable, you could say. The guy who told me to beat it has so much going on, it seemed like, that he could care less about me. I'm just wondering that right now. I guess you could say that . . . well, I'm just over everything, and I wish things like make up, flowers, money, cars, clothes, and houses didn't, couldn't, exist. I truly hate this world. It's depressing. I just hate the humans in it. We all are suffering.

May, 12th, 9:04 a.m. (A Dream Log)

I had this dream that I was pissed at a waitress and she gave me my beer and then I held it up to sip it and some guy totally snatched it from me and I got mad and he told me he would pay for another drink with a totally different, totally cheaper flavor and then I told the waitress b■ch that she was horrible and she thought I wasn't going to tip her and then I said, "Here's three reasons why I *am* goin' to tip you . . ." and she stopped listening to me and walked away and I got mad and my mom was in front of me and she was scared because I was yelling and screaming and telling everyone that I hate them and that I want to die and that everyone sucks and then my mom took me out of the bar, at morning time, mind you, and we went into her car to drive off and then I told her I wanted to die and then, outside the car, I saw mammoths walking and I thought it was strange but then we saw meteors hitting us and I knew in that moment that the world was ending so I laughed and walked outside the car and was hearing my mom crying because of how scared she was and, as I was outside, the fire-y wind was crashing all around me, and I embraced it, with open arms, and chanted, "Yes, yes, *yes!* Do it!" and then this shadow in the sky, this big black (or square-like) ball, came and I knew it was a huge meteor and it was coming my way and then everything went black and I woke up and now I'm writing this bullspit and it worries me but I feel happy for this dream I had.

May, 14th, 10:44 a.m. (A Dream Log)[7]

There was a lot that went into this dream, prior to what I'm revealing. Here goes nothing. Basically I was traveling around a roommate's neighborhood. We were just driving and I was in a car and basically my roommate saw a dog. The dog was standing up and had beer and everything. We went inside the house and the dog came into the kitchen, dressed like, well, a dog. Then he shook my hand. I found out that they were just F'in' with me. The roommate and the fake dog, they were men. But anyways, the roommate wanted to stay at the fake dog's house, because his house he said was too far. Even though I knew it was only

---

[7] — Don't be alarmed if everything in the dream log doesn't make sense. I suppose that's the point of it all.

down the street, but I agreed; I always seem to do that in real life, too. So then my roommate's girlfriend came in the picture and then the fake dog's mom and dad and sisters came into the picture. The house was super big. But the fake dog's mom gave my roommate and I and my roommate's girlfriend a video tape, VHS. We left the house and then the roommate broke the tape by sitting on it. Then, for no reason at all, we went back to the house. The mom was there, and, guess what: she asked us if in fifteen minutes we could get her the tape. My roommate said prior that he's scared to break the news to her that he broke it because apparently they rented that movie and had to return it. It was a big deal, even though in actual real life this wouldn't've been a big deal. So then, get this: the mom was saying to get it to her in fifteen minutes because she has cancer and is going to die. So then, my world flashed around me, but others couldn't see it. I told the lady that I broke it and that I would buy her a new one, but I was over-explaining, apparently, and talking too fast for her, because she started to cry. I asked her why she was crying. She said they were tears of joy! "I saw how fast you talked and I was mesmerized," she said. Then things skipped and I basically went back to some kind of living room, then, in the house, there's a register and I see glimpses of me buying her three hardback books—so the dream changes from a VHS tape to books, and it's okay. I didn't really want to buy this lady something, for the sake of saving my roommate's A-hole. So then, basically, I go to the living room, where there was only the fake god's brother, his sister, and that's it —or so I thought. But I had an idea that they were dating. I thought the brother was super cute. So I, Sally the Curious, was flirting, all that, and everyone started to laugh. Then, a third person came into the picture. He was wearing the same color clothes as the couch. He was laughing because I could see him. So I laughed. Then he went back to camo-ing me. I don't know what this dream means. I am kind of scared to know what my dreams mean. I'm just doing this dream thing before my sister gets here, I guess. My future self doesn't wanna hear about these lame job hunts and fails. . . .

May, 15th, 8:14 a.m. (A Dream Log)

Behind eyes, inside my brain, even though they look at me, it feels as though (not beside the point) that they aren't, even though they are and this makes me feel sad. I try to look away but they keep looking back and I feel like I'm choking. It's everyone staring, and I hate it. Then they tell me, "You're so beautiful," with a God-dang smiley face. I hate it. It's not cute.

May, 17th, 6:05 p.m.

I just wanted to write this down because I went to the park to walk, over there on Dixie, near Howley's, and I saw kids playing. One of them I thought was Sam. I remember her name without looking back in this. I was kind of fantasizing about going to Disney World and picking her up some Minnie Mouse ears. The plush ones, not the plastic ones, and then, after coming back home from a monstrous vacation, I would go her house, courtesy of her parents (I can remember their names like Sam's), and then, pretty disappointingly, they would bring a kitten at that same exact moment and then I'd turn Sam around and she would see the ears and I'd say, "Ever heard of a little place called Disney?" and she would smile and nod her head yes. "Well," I'd say, "your auntie Sally" (because that's how she would perceive me; not just as Sally Fairfax, a friend) "went to Disney and she brought you something back." "Really?!" she'd say to me. "Show me! Now, now, now!" "Okay!" and I would take it out behind my back and show her it. She would light up like fireworks and then reach inside the gift bag and pull out the ears. But then she would not wear them right away. I would try to put them on her but she would say no. She would go to her mommy, and have *her* put it on. Because she trusts her mom and not me. Then Sam would have me dance with her to a CD of the newest Disney move called *Frozen,* and I would laugh, and she would laugh, too. And we would take pictures and post them on Instagram, and everyone would be happy because of that or—F■k, I don't know anymore. I would leave and Sam would tell me not to. Then hug me. Then kiss my arm. Then she'd say, "Thank you auntie, Sally." I would be sad because she misses me and I would know it was pure. Then I'd get inside my car and drive all the way back home, crying, in pain, because I miss Sam, too, in this teeny tiny daydream.

May, 25th, 3:02 p.m.

I haven't been writing in this for awhile. Been busy. Super busy finding a job. Just real quick, I wanted to say in this entry that tomorrow my sister comes in. She's taking a taxi because my car took a huge dump on me. If you ever heard of a lemon, well, my car is the biggest of *all* lemons. But I shouldn't veer off into *that* tangent. I wanna try and be happy. I'll do my best to write while she and Alex are here. But I think, Mrs. Future-dooper Sally-Walley, I may be having too much fun and not enough time to, you know, be grabbing this ole journal and writing in it, away from the action and not participating. Nevertheless, tomorrow, tomorrow, TOMORROW!

May, 28th, 11:22 p.m.

Okay, everyone is asleep right now. I'm under my covers and writing this with a flashlight and I'm in my jammies. Gosh, I *love* my sister. We're way too much alike. I love Alex, too. He's really smart now! I'll get to that reasoning in a minute. But gosh, I was thinking about writing in you, Journal, since forever ago. My sister and I have been doing stuff constantly. I don't want to write too much things where you do quotation marks or whatever. I think the word I'm looking for is "dialogue"? But yeah. I'll try to keep that down so I can get this entry done and quick.

So to start this off: May 26th, at around early in the morning sometime (I'm usually good with memorizing the time, but as you could probably guess, I was too busy being excited to look down at my wristwatch or phone), my Sissy Dukes gets off the plane, and I was in that gosh-darn waiting thingy place at the airport, super dang early, and my sister and Al we're were holding hands whilst coming out of the plane's hallway thing.

(And yes, I do have a wristwatch.)

I was waving and waving and waving, but they were still sort of looking around. By "they" I mean Sissy. Alex was just sort of being all scared because you could probably imagine it was a scary place for him.

(Just a fun fact: Me and him, having or being on the spectrum, we have this weird anxiety thing. Basically if I can describe it, it's like this: you are walking around, minding your own business, and then basically you hear people talking, and then more, and then more, and then suddenly you realize you can hear everyone talking all at once and at the same time, even though they aren't talking to you, and it really makes you scared, and then you get confused and your heart races as if you are being chased by a lion. Then a (quote-unquote)—a "Lion" is in your Number. It's a ~~neusense~~ nuisance in this world. Nothing has order and is not in a single file line. You may not get what I'm saying, but that's okay. Just know that that is what it's like.)

Back to scene (love that expression!): I'm waving my a■ off. I'm running toward them, then (Oh my Lordy!)—then Sissy Dukes sees me but doesn't run, probably because, I was assuming, Al couldn't keep up. Lots of strides and running. Sissy Dukes was yelling "Yeah!" and stuff and was saying how happy she was to see me, even before I got up to her and gave her the biggest hug ever! Then I went down and gave little Alex a high-five! He's a little stinker. He was cheesin' like you wouldn't be*lieve*.

After eating, getting their bags, driving in that taxi (that I told to wait because it was my ride *there,* too), we went to my place. They unpacked. My sister commented that my place was a pigsty, even though I cleaned it before she got there. I said she was the B-word and she cupped Al's ears and said no cursing around him. I said sorry, whatever.

We ordered some Papa John's because apparently in her area they don't have it, they only have Domino's, and Sissy Dukes hates Domino's. It came in an hour and fifteen minutes, because of ordering ~~it~~ online. Still good, though. Al ate so good! His belly was all round and full when he was done with those big, cheesy pizza slices. He was a happy camper! (I'm smiling right now while I write this. The thought is too adorable!)

Then we chilled out for quite awhile and just talked. Sissy told me that I looked good and I told her she looked good, too. She was telling me that I should do this or that with my life, because she's kind of got her life together and has the ability to tell me otherwise.

I want to basically put here what she said, but not in "dialogue." I'm going to write it like a monologue. This isn't close to what she actually said, but I'll try to make it all sound gravy:

"Sally, it's the greatest feeling in the world being a girl. You can agree with that. I just *love* dressing up in high-heels 'n' stuff. It's lovely. But sometimes, whilst people being on that stuff, even, and being all cute, you gotta think about it not lasting very long.

"Beauty is short. You have to see the future. Like how I see the future. I mean, like me, and how I see the future. It makes sense when you think about it.

"I worry about you, Sally. I see your apartment and how lame it is. You're not doing okay" (even though Sissy Dukes is not married anymore, being all "temporarily separated," but that's of course not everything) "in this world, if that makes sense. You gotta think about your future, baby. You have to learn responsibilities." [Then I explained about being simple and not worrying about those things and all that, and how I like to have less of things because it makes me not have the burden of owning them.] And Sissy Dukes continued:

"I think you treat relationships like a business proposition, Sal. Your friendships are superficial. You never actually get down to the real person. I'm different because I'm your sister, but that's no excuse. You got to really dig deep into people. You'd be surprised.

"People are crazy. Sometimes they surprise the un-surprise-able, like me. And sometimes (passed what our modern culture is, with regards to popular belief—whatever that may, or may not, be), success in the human aspect is not determined by how much you lie, but how much you can convince. <u>Make people believe in your worth, not just on the surface.</u> People switch up the two and make ~~then~~ them one. This isn't what's so. . . ."

I guess my sister was pretty much saying that I was on, or off, or near, the surface, but never really with it, per se. This conversation went on and on. I went nuts! You could bet that I defended myself, but who wouldn't? I mean, really. If a person is saying something negative about you, regardless if, deep down, you know it is in fact true, you will—I repeat, *will*—defend yourself at *all* costs. This is probably because humans are hardwired—but I rest my case.

I guess right there I just prove my sister's silly little point: I'm untrusting of others and their little lives. It's hard to, though, if you could ever imagine. Sometimes people are always defending their Numbers, their money, their gold, their freedom, their pride, for the sake of feeling good about themselves and feeling "safe." Humans are really a species of animal that thrives on sin, or really, thrives on Life itself.

We use everything around us and mend it to our advantage. <u>I guess you could say success haunts us in a way that we cannot understand.</u> There's the liars, and then there's the convincers. We all say we want to be on the convincer's side, but really, we never can if you're not the type. I personally think I'm losing at life, but never mind that depressing spit. I need to finish this entry real quick.

I can barely keep my eyes open to write. . . .

Okay, so, after all that jazzy jazz, with Sissy Dukes and I sort of, you know, talking, a couple friends of mine—namely Tessa, Josh, and some other newer friend, who I didn't recognize or know of (which Josh probably met at the bar and hit on)—went and drove straight smack dab into the curb in front of my apartment. The wheels were smoking and totally F'ed. I was fed up from the start, that very F'ing instance. Look, if I just got fired, and the place I work at—that is, mind you, at a place where I both lived *and* worked—and I get a noise complaint, *OoooOooo girl!* you're talkin' some serry, serry trouble. Forget cops—they will straight gut a b■ch, if you're not too careful, which these lames totally weren't. (Excuse the name-calling. I was just being all pissed right now writing this.)

Anyway, the three [f■■■eteers] came out of their car, drunk as all skunks care. The first thing I see, Josh with a bottle of Jack, drinking straight from it, not giving a flying f■k. "Sally, baby!" he drunk'd out. "*Ehhhhhh*, wassiz upz?"

"What?" I said, as my arms were crossed, as my sister, from dang Augusta, Georgia, was standing next to me, as her son, an Autistic child, sleeps on the couch in my room, and me thinking, What the flying F, guys?

Tessa had the guy who I didn't know slung over her shoulders and looking like a zombie. She was dragging him by the feet, giving the ole zombie shuffle. Then:

"*Ha! ha! ha! haaa! Ay, Sally!*" I heard Tessa say. "I'm so F'ing drunk, gurrrrl!"

I was laughing, and "Shhh!" I said. "You mothers are going to wake the neighbors up. Come on."

Sissy was *all* about it, I'm tellin' you.

No more "dialogue." Sorry. I'm getting way too tired for this bullshit.

Anyways, Tessa and Josh, as they came in, started fighting with each other. They took shirts off. Tessa's tits, I'm so dang jealous of them. But anyway, they fought. Their friend sat on the couch and all, and totally just watched and laughed. They all were like *children,* for Pete's sake. I was laughing, too, but still, they were like dang children! They were scratching and carrying on.

Then, all of a sudden, we see Alex come in, wearing his Jammies, like how I wear them right now: poka-dots—main color yellow. He came in, thumb in his mouth, and he was rubbing his eyes. Sissy said, "Aw, poor baby," and picked him up and gave him a kiss. She didn't seem mad that my "un-welcomed" friends showed, but you still can't assume things of the sort. You just keep truckin' on, lady.

What's the crazy part . . . Get this: Alex said, sort of out loud, "Now, listen." Tess and Josh did. They just stared; their friend was too. "Listen, listen," Alex said. "We's are tryin' ta *sleep,* see! Go away, José. *Go!* Outta my sight, outta my sight!" He kept sucking his thumb. His voice was really all sounding muffled. "Beat it. Scram!" That's how ole Alex is so *smart!* He took charge! and you know what, Tessa and Josh and their friend did leave. And me and Sissy and Al totally went to bed. And we slept like F'ing kings (or *queens!*).

Next day, May 27th, in the good ole mornin' t*i*me, we made a helluva killer breakfast! None of the crummy Starbucks spit. No. *Heck* no. We ate some eggs and bacon and pork and sausage. I felt like I was Arnold! *"Heee-alllll! Mariaaaaaa! Look a' mi maaa-sales! Arrrrhhhggggg! Heee-allllll!"* [(a crazy 'Arnold' sound) Ah, Maria. Look at my muscles. (Another 'Arnold' sound . . . and another 'Arnold' sound), in case you didn't understand.] That was my crap expression of a once-upon-a-time governater. But yeah, I more mean the crazy amount of protein that that B-fast was. It was delicious, though.

That morning we ate, didn't talk much, whatever. I put on my shoes and everything, dressed in whatever, and then, basically in a heartbeat of a second, my Sissy comes in and tells me, "Let's go see Dad." I was petrified, but I did anyway. So we went. We drove down Foresthill Boulevard, in a taxi, and Sissy was making comments about all the new buildings and architecture and everything. I said it was no biggie, but I was trying to keep my mind off Dad.

I love my dad. But again, we lost touch. I call him every now and then —don't get me wrong—but he's overly optimistic. He's *lame* optimistic. The kind of dang optimism that makes you want to hurl. I shouldn't really dislike him, per se, because of it, but it does get on my nerves. I just hate it when he compliments this or that about me and he's all smiley and genuine. It's like he's mocking me. Like he's an actor, acting, and I don't believe it at all. We have issues about it. I don't know.

We got to the front of Dad's house. It hadn't changed. Let me describe it: the fence, it's slidable; the drive way, it's made from asphalt cracking everywhere; there's a carport, too; dogs running around (four of them, one new); rectangle garden planter in the front, with a wheel-barrel tire in the exact middle (and this garden hasn't been used in years); grass perfectly cut; fence wrapped around the entire place; the backyard is huge, and behind it, passed the fence, a gigantic Palm Tree nursery; a square thing of dead grass from a cage being dismantled; the house color, it's blue, but if it peels, you'll see white underneath; a swinging, squeaking door with a hangy sign that reads, in red-painted font, REDNECK IN RESIDENCE; and a front door, just before the carport, that is very new, normal, and nice. The place is a place I've always called "home." I love it.

So I pull up, park, yada-yada . . . The dogs are all going bananas, barking and all. But it was probably because they hadn't seen my sister, and though she hadn't got out of the car yet, she said "Puppies!" as loud as any ears could hear. F'ed me up, big time.

So we open the gate, mind whatever, and go in and the dogs are just licking us absolutely everywhere. You wouldn't believe it. Then we just went on by the car port and my sister was like, "Wow! Still looks the same." It really did. You bet. But they did clean it. I think it was because the new puppy was probably playing in the grass, getting his paws dirty, and then wiping and scraping his paws all on the clean ground. There was streaks everywhere or whatever, at one point in time.

I didn't even knock. *We* didn't even knock. I just went on in like it was nothing. I can do things like that at my old house. My step mother (we'll get to that in a second), she was in her room, probably sleeping or reading, but my dad, he was in the living room, watching Law-and-Order. . . . Yeah. He's one of *those* guys.

So anyway, I snuck up on him and Sissy was giggling like crazy. At first, I was tip-toeing and everything, then I sat down next to Dad on the sofa. He didn't move an inch. His eyes were all heavy and everything. It looked like he was about to fall asleep. So I snapped my fingers.

"Dad. . . . *Dad*"—*snap snap*—"y'awake? Huh?"

He really, I s██t you not, didn't answer. And I was, like, snapping loud! Like, wow! So I did the whole thing again, except my sister tip-toed into the room, too.

"Dad. DAD!"

He heard *that* one.

"*Ah!* Who's there?" He spun around like a madman, then he held his heart. "Oh gosh, Jesus Christ, *Sal!* How the heck are ya? and _____! You look *great!*" He stood wayyy the heck up and gave us those crazy bear hugs guys give. They hurt sometimes.

"Oh my God, it's great to see you, Dad!" Sissy said.

I was more silent than I should have been.

"Sal? Why the long face? Why haven't you called? I think about you a lot, you know."

I just told him that I've been busy.

The conversation went on and on and on. But don't get me wrong, I was totally enjoying myself. I just hate events like these. You know. Family things. *Those* kind of things. It sucks because everyone is so happy and grateful to be alive and well around the people they "love" that it makes me all sick inside. I don't know. It seems fake to me. I generally hate adults and their ways.

We did this and that, whatever. Dad talked about work, the car he was building, the new mortgage he took on the house, the other *blah blah blah* stuff you always hear out of parents. Sissy just talked about kids and getting a home and also the usual *blah blah blah* spit. . . .

Then they came to me, while we were all sitting at the table, drinking wine.

"What's been going on with you, Sal?"

It's hard to say what I said. It's fuzzy now. But I started talking about politics. I told them I was sick of a lot of things. Like minimum wage, for example. I told them that are economy could not possibly have a minimum wage increase because, if you look at it this way—because most people don't look at it this way—"Desperation" equals every-man-for-himself ideals that sink you deeper and deeper into more "Desperation." We all want money. The company, like most people don't seem to see, is also a customer. They buy labor, they buy humans. When you work for a job, you are pretty much selling your labor to the place. If the labor is forced to be pricier, then I'm sorry, you're out of the job, my little Miss. Fancy-Pants. That big raise you got, imagine doing double the work in *less* hours. Yeah. It'll all be the same, and then the prices—don't get me started on that. The prices will then go *way* the heck up to the sky! Because since people got the money, the places know this and meet to the demand of people buying more, almost immediately. Gosh, I hate people. They are like little F'ing maggots. There's a zebra everyone wants, but the zebra is almost gone. So a frenzy happens. I hate America in some ways. Capitalism is for chumps. Lions in Numbers, girl.

Then, Dad stopped everything and stared. He thought I was nuts or something. You know the look: the eyes low, the hands on faces, the leaning against elbows, the listening intently. . . . Then, after I noticed this, he asked me something else: "Well, Sal—what about the people that work hard for nothing?" and dude, after he said this, I was so happy. So I explained.

"Daddy, basically it's like this: the world is full of people looking for a type of 'fair' in their little dull lives. They want this happiness and all. What I mean is, they basically will do all they can to reach their little fix of joy. <u>They will buy things, do things wrong, kill things, do good things and bad things, and do everything they can, regardless of right and wrong.</u>

"People know this, especially people in the business field. Sometimes they actually use your 'want' for their 'profit.' They force you. They will create little ideas in your head that are meant to attract you in some way. I hate it, but it's part of making a living. Every man is really for themselves.

"As they say, 'Maximize Profits.' That's all it ever is, and all it ever is going to be. Profits. Who is coming on top? It's always a winner and a loser. The losers are in a surplus. They may seem dumb, but if your life never had something of value given to it, that leads you to your desired goal—you may have to find that value that sparks you out of neutral and into drive or over-drive. This isn't a joke, Daddy—I'm serious. Stop laughing. Stop!"

"Sal, you really are a hoot!" My dad was laughing and everything at me. "Baby, you have to not think so much. It's a bit much. Here. Let me get you a beer," and this bastard really got the mother-F up and went to the fridge and got me a beer. I was pretending to be happy by giving some kind of smile and he bought it. He thought it was real. I drank the beer without effort. I hate when somebody doesn't listen or think things are truly valid or possible in life. *Darn it!*

But anyways, back to plot: after all the beer drinking, the grilling, the endless conversations of work, life, logic, politics, money, loves, dogs, cats, the sun, over-driving, super-driving, flavoring, dying, winning, losing, your face, my face, the world, meteor showers, money (again!), being the best, being the worst, what guys were dated before, what guys were let down, possible scenarios [I almost wrote "scenery" but then stopped] for synergy our world can do (and that was Yours Truly saying that), any kind of shampoos we can buy ~~the~~ to enhance or make hair fuller (that was Dad asking me and Sissy), possible entrapments that cops do when they pull you over (that was Sissy Dukes!), we finally ate, all four of us (the fourth being Daddy's wife), and talked. I hate my dad's wife. She's a b■ch and a half, to the second power! which means she's three times a b■ch!

She once made me go to the doctor's and I was pissed the whole time and pouting—I was thirteen—and I got home and she made me do one-hundred pushups, me being all cold and heated at the same damn time. I called her a w■re and got grounded. Then she made me do endless sorts of chores and stuff.... LAME!!

But now that I'm older, I apologized for my actions to her. She's not so bad. She likes when my dad plays with the dogs and hunts them. My dad is a hunter, like a Wall Street boy! Takes them dogs out and has them winning ~~is~~ in stocks! #WINNING. So lovely.

We basically didn't say really anything important, except that I need to visit Dad and my [step]mom more. They said it was actually really important that I did. I told them I will when I actually become a somebody in this world. They told me that I already am, but I beg to differ.

We went home, slept, and oh, I forgot to mention Alex had a great time playing with my stepmom and Sissy in the living room the whole time or whatever.

After that, May 28th, which is today (duh!), we woke up and my sister decided that, Hey, Sally, we need to go to Disney and get our tickets! So I said yes, naturally. We went online and bought our tickets. (My sister had to pay more because, well, she is a resident of Georgia, and technically, as Disney would probably say, we have to make more money from her because she couldn't *possibly* get the non-out-of-state charge to go to "Happiest Place on Earth" or whatever-spit.) Then my sister told me my computer was slow. I have an 2010 Apple MacBook Pro and it's pretty okay but nothing to write home about. She told me to go to the computer place and get me a SSH (Solid State Hard-drive). Says it would make my s■t go faster, faster, FASTER! So I bought one. Suckers are *expensive,* girl! A little bit under four-hundred bucks! That was the best one, though. We installed it and everything. I played with Alex. He likes Angry Birds like crazy. I'll have him draw me an Angry Bird in the morning when he wakes up. I'll put it after this entry or something. I'll have Alex draw while we're there at Disney World. I'm so excited to see it! I can't wait. I'll probably write live while I walk or something. I want to make sure I get everything down. Just notes probably. I'll have Al draw or something. With crayon. Two days. Two days we're there for. My sister is paying for my ticket and everything. She's two-hundo and I'm about one-fifty. Not bad, I guess. Not bad because it's free! *Ha! ha! ha!* I'm tired as F, and it's now over one o'clock in the F'ing morning. I hope I didn't wake Sissy or Al up. They are snoring so peacefully right now. I love it.

May, 29th, 8:12 a.m.

So I told Al to draw this, like I said, and he had no issues at all. He loves drawing. I think I'm going to have him do a puzzle piece tattoo on my arm or chest or stomach or something. Like he draws the puzzle piece and I basically have it be a childish-like look and have it all symbolize mine and his Autism or whatever. I think that would be cool. So anyway, I'm leaning over the table writing this on a notepad or whatever. I'm going to copy the notepad stuff verbatim into my actual journal. Sissy is cooking some breakfast or something. She wants to leave but I have to write this. She keeps telling me to hurry up, but the longer she does this, the longer I'm explaining it here. So yeah, she's going to have to slow her roll! I'm going to keep this notepad and have Alex draw in this. I want to show the time I wrote it. I'll keep my wristwatch on and I'll just write the time like this

"[time]:"

and just keep it like that. Then I'll just write whatever I see and have Alex draw it. I'll probably bring a small sketchbook or something and rip it out and put it in the final journal entry I make. This is so exciting! Wish me luck!

8:47 A.M.: What I'm thinking right now . . . you won't friggin' believe . . . I'm thinking that everyone at Disney is going to have their cameras and stuff and I'll be having this notepad and everything, all getting the memories in order by not pictures but words. I can't write too many commas because it's way too hard to do it quick. I'm seeing the roads whip on by so I'll tell Alex to draw me a road.

10:03 A.M.: We're here! Gosh! So many cars parked. It's insane! I saw the Disney World sign and it was epic! The toll lady smiles the whole time and was very very helpful. Gosh almighty. *Yuk Yuk!* That's a Goofy laugh!

10:23 A.M.: So we parked and what's crazy is the parking is about $15.00! Mickey likes to steal money!

10:33 A.M.: We're just waiting right now for the bus thingy that they take for mass amounts of people. Everyone seems sort of uptight and fussy but they look like they are anticipating something. Alex is definitely fussy like wow but we are trying to calm him down with soothing hand-holding and such. I'm going to tell him to draw a butterfly!

10:38 A.M.: Okay he totally felt better after that. Gotta get on the bus now! It's here!

10:41-ish A.M. (I'm not looking at my watch): ←frown-y face! Ha, *ha!* So yeah, anyways, I'm hearing the tour guide guy and he's really hot and hunky and saying corny jokes: "Don't play cards with the lions, people! They are a bunch of Cheetahs!" Everyone laughs anyway. I'm telling Al to draw me something but he's saying no. I think he's not as excited as I am about this notepad.

10:54 A.M.: We're here and I'm trying to look down at this thing so I don't get anxiety from everyone running and screaming and jumping and swarming and laughing and having a good time. It's 68°, though. Like an AC unit. Or a ▮▮▮▮. ▮▮▮▮ We're walking up to the ticket stand▮s and everything. My ticket we found out didn't work online so I have to buy it straight from the horse's mouth, which doesn't make any sense because the lady at the ticket booth is not a horse; although she has a Donald Duck thing on her T shirt. Like a metal pin.

10:58 A.M.: Wow! The lady was so nice! She told me that my last name was really interesting because "Fairfax" is from a street in California, where she said she was from, and that brought her back to her childhood. She gave me a map of where we were so I and Al don't ever get lost if Sissy goes away or something. I wanted to shake her hand but she was behind glass sadly.

11:24 A.M.: My sister keeps saying to not write. She says I need to enjoy myself.

11:24 A.M.: We were totally walking. I'm trying to write this quick or ▮▮▮▮▮ at least. Alex and Sissy are asking the lady for directions and she's trying to type something. This place is so bright/vivid! I think it's truly bringing me back to my childhood memories of when I used to come here. If there's a Heaven, it most certainly is at Disney World! Oh yes, and that top drawing is what Alex drew right before we got to the biggest Disney shop in the world! Looks great, huh? It's the Epcot ball!

11:45 A.M.: Taking a minute ▇ ▇ to write. Oh my gosh! Okay, so, it's this weird thing going on where Disney's artists sculpt the Disney characters out of bushes and flowers and stuff. They look so real! You go passed the gift shop and take a left ▇ and see this huge dome-like greenhouse. You walk in and there's about a dozen tour guides. Butterflies everywhere! Alex was so damn happy! He was clapping his hands and everything. It was too, *too* adorable. Sissy was cheesin' the whole time. They had the Mickey Mouse sculpture there and everything. Tons of people were taking photos of the stuff. The tour guide that was there showed me a chrysalis that was hanging above the bush in the entrance and I was like wow! It was really amazing to see that. I honestly feel so happy right now. I love Disney World! So kick▇s!

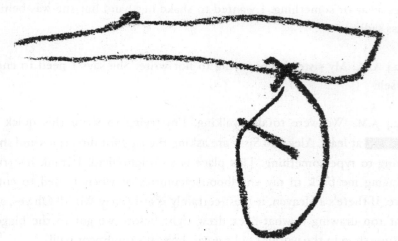

12:02 P.M.: It's very hard to write fast. I hope I can read my stuff later! We're walking along the pathways and it's so sunny and perfect. I'm worried about getting a sunburn, though. Alex is trying to hold my hand. Bye!

12:09 P.M.: There's fountains everywhere! Water and whatever. The people around here really give this place character. Imagine kids ▇▇▇ playing and laughing everywhere and the adults can just sit back and enjoy the sweetness of their children. This is Disney World! I'm at frickin' Epcot!

12:23 P.M.: My sister is taking a smoke break for a minute so I have some time to write a long one here. There's this duck literally standing next to me while I write this. Not kidding. He is about 3 inches from my arm while I'm in the grass here. He is chillin' like a villain. It's really cute. I love how life is totally different here. I wish it didn't have to cost so much. I wish life was always a vacation. But if I start a rant I may not stop and then I'll probably have a bad time so let's not and say we did on all the negativity I spew out on the regular. Disney is playing this really crazy music here. Like from *The Rescuers: Down Under*. I love it. I remember that movie being really speedy at the beginning when the camera slides passed the crops and reaches the farm house. Okay Alex wants to draw something. BRB . . .

Aww! Al! So dang *cute*. He drew a picture of me I think. I swear I just now saw it. But anyway I'd like to say that we are all connected in the "circle of life." Seems appropriate when a sculpture of Simba is next to me. . . . Very well!

12:33 P.M.: I asked Sissy what I've been wondering: "Why can't you smoke while walking around Disney World? We're in open air." My sister said because. I asked why, and she told me it's "tacky" and also inappropriate and disrespectful of the children running around. I guess I don't think it is such a big deal. I also should mention that we're passed the Epcot entrance. Wicked!

12:43 P.M.: This place is magical. Okay, so, you're walking around and everyone is laughing and honestly, I like their laughs and smiles[8]. I do! I'm just with my family, us three, and we walk passed "England" and the first thing I see is a huge thing of Mickey with brooms dancing ▓▓ from *Fantasia*. It was so dang great. I'll take a picture with my sister's phone.

1:01 P.M.: Oh my God! Won't believe this! Seeing Alice. Hold the phone!

To Sal,
Alice was here!

Okay, back now. Okay, so, Alice freakin' comes up dressed in skimpy blue and white, looking *exactly* like her! This girl was so stickin' adorable! She had to've been nine*teen*. She was, like, just under five feet tall or something. I was jealous! She came up to me, while me and Al and Sissy

---

[8] — I'm looking at this right now, and I totally, um, feel like this contradicts my previous entries. I know that I said before I hate smiles, but yeah, listen. At Disney, the smiles made sense!

Dukes were just about to leave "England," and Alice comes up to me and says, "Excuse me! Pardon me! but have you seen the white rabbit?!" Oh my God I flipped out! So yeah, I basically asked her for her autograph. (Had to trace it from the notepad, but still, it's Alice's!)

1:20 P.M.: We're walking and taking looks at the different actors. My Sissy says her Disney friends who come all the time tell her that she needs to really check out the "Frozen Beer" in "Japan." Or was it "China"?

1:26 P.M.: Super quick: The cray-cray *Peter Pan* bushes are phenomenal! Captain Hook looks so realistic.

Note: Listening to Daft Punk's "Make Love" while I look back at my notes, writing this all down. Continue:

1:29 P.M.: Oh my good Jesus, a train! They have them whirling around tracks like private jets! whatever that could mean! Sissy is taking pictures of them. Lil' Allie is giggling like you wouldn't be*lieve*. . . . Little Allie. *Ha!* I'm an A-hole!

1:39 P.M.: We're in "France" and I see the Eiffel Tower but it's in the background where we can't reach it and this sort of makes me go bonkers.

2:13 P.M.: Been awhile. Okay, let me make this quick: We got the Frozen Beers and they were absolutely awesome. I love, love, *loved* it! Took pictures with a Kodak even though they went out of business forever ago. No skin off my sister's bone, though.

2:28 P.M.: I don't want you to think Disney is all peachy. It's sort of like a place you go to to forget you're at somewhere normally. Like somewhere special where all the people don't care to laugh or smile, that's Disney. I mean, look, you pay all this money, you better have the time of your life by golly. The employees make sure of it, and they frickin' better. They had some Minnie Mouse lip gloss at the gift shop. I totally wanted to snag a piece but I thought I would have been a hypocrite or some bullspit thing. It's b■chy to be or to think that way, but whatever, we'll all live to be a thousand someday (whenever the heck *that'll* be). I just think little girls shouldn't get the wrong idea about being a beautiful girl. It's not at all what it's cracked up to be. I sometimes regret watching those Disney movies and wanting to be exactly like those dang damsel-in-distress types. They have combs now where they are foldable. Crazy, huh? Like Swiss army knife combs. Makes kids get the wrong idea about being an adult. I think kids have it easier because nobody has tainted them yet. I sort of envy little kids who play and laugh and have fun and never have to really ever see all the madness and the bills and the car notes and the dang crying that happens every day. I just feel jealous, is all.

2:34 P.M.: I'm so f■king cynical. F■k!

2:56 P.M.: We're just eating some pretzels before we go on Fast Track, this ride that's at Epcot where you ride on a car that does twists and turns and goes hella fast. I think it's great because I road it once when I was a small kid. Around ten. I vaguely remember it but my dad was dating some girl and her family were real jerks because they were rich and even though they knew I had mental issues, they still looked at me funny and told my dad he needs to watch me and be a better father. What I'm thinking now, I'm thinking about when I was younger than ten and how I use to think, regardless if true or not, that black moms produced chocolate milk and white moms produced regular milk. I remember I thought this in kindergarten. I even told a black kid that I was jealous of him because he had chocolate milk when he was a baby and I had regular milk. He cried and told the teacher and there was a parent-teacher discussion on Yours Truly. There always was. My dad always kept cool about it and talked slow to me, but very clearly, and I got to say, I loved it, and I loved him, too. My dad is very special to me. I'm glad he found somebody to marry, even though she's a total b■ch.

3:23 P.M.: My stomach really friggin' hurts, girlie. It isn't helping that we

are waiting in line and the estimated time is about, like, a million days. I hope it comes soon. I wanna bust this bad boy out! Hot damn!

4:12 P.M.: Oh my God! So much to say! We were waiting for about an hour or so, then got on this big line, then this other big line. What they did—get this: they have the screens there while you wait and you build you're own car. You basically shape it and put different parts and everything and it's really, really cool! Alex got a real kick out of it. He told me that it was the most fun he had in forever. I said good! Grand! It was very special. Until we got on the ride. . . . Okay, I was having a real ball, but Alex, oh Jesus in God's green Earth, Alex was screaming his whole head off. I was too, but his was fear. I guess he was having sensory overload. I get like that, so I feel for him. But then after the ride, he was perfectly, perfectly fine and dandy. He was actually asking if we could do it again! Sissy was over it so she of course said no. I would've waited again for the little tike. He was too adorable! But yeah, we had a huge blast. We didn't get the picture that they take of you when you scream at the grand finale, which was sort of lame, if I do say so myself.

5:02 P.M.: Trying to hang in there. We went to this space simulation of rockets and I got pretty sick. At the last minute, Alex got too scared and my sister had to take him away from all the excitement. I don't know why we picked the orange side, the side with all the G-forces. Poor guy. I would be scared, too, if I'd been on that ride at his age. But yeah, I went on it alone and everything was very bright. I may have to correct some things on this bright paper. Oh well. What can a girl do? Not throw up, that's what!

5:32 P.M.: ███████. ███████, th████ ██ wasn't cool to be doing that. F███ that guy!

(Note: Don't want to be reminded of what happened in that second. Not ever.)

6:09 P.M.: So much running around trying to find tables and food and all that nonsense. It sucks. My feet hurt and I can totally feel a sunburn coming along that's totally going to be the death of me. I'm cranky. So is Alex, too. Sissy is a mad hatter and a half. Tee-*hee!*

6:32 P.M.: We are deciding to walk around all of Epcot, again, for the *third time* today, and I'm really starting to get pissed off. We went into this a Chinese gift shop and the sales rep showed me this crazy drawing pad thingy. I can't remember what it's called, but whatever. It was basically like writing calligraphy but the ink is just water, and you draw with the brush on the pad with water, and basically the water dries up and you never, ever have to worry about a mess or anything. Basically you just let it dry and you can reuse it. What the rep said, anyway.

7:22 P.M.: Three's my limit. Three. That's it. That's what I told my sister, and then I graciously sit down on the curb here. Give no Fs. Simple.

7:32 P.M.: Disney announced some firework show happening at 9. So you know it's epic!

9:21 P.M.: My anxiety is through the roof right now. I'm trying to write in this notebook to look away from all the fireworks. Alex is pretty uncomfortable, too. We're both holding our ears; Alex has is eyes shut, ears tightly held by both palms; I have the tight-whatever ears, too, but I'm squinting down at this notepad, and I have one hand writing all this junk down. It's hard to hold a pen down and keep a notepad put. It sucks. But yeah, anyway, Sissy and I talked for a very, very, *very* long, long time. I mean it. We spoke a lot about the future, to be honest. She was telling me about how she wants to go to FSU when Fall comes. She always says "when Fall comes" a lot. Why not now? I tell her. But I was being a hypocrite when I told her I had no plans and no "nows" for the future. I told her that I was happy for her (even though, yes, I was more jealous and envious than anything else), and that she was the one that should have all the glory. I'll just be the cheerleader. She said phooey! I told her the only thing I have going for me is my looks. She told me that that won't last forever. Beauty is only for a very short time. The real thing that lasts is how much you know, Sissy Dukes the Great told me. To be quite frank, I didn't really listen. All that's alive and here is beauty. The fireworks explode and make pretty pictures of flowers and butterflies. People say their wows and I'm here missing all of it. Head is in the stars.

Sissy has her arms crossed and we were standing on the stone planters. I keep balancing my feet and all, and I'm basically writing on my boobs. People are staring, but oh well, it is what it is. Maybe I am cynical in some ways. I just don't believe in the American Dream anymore. I believe that people just want things and that's it. That's all that life is about. Wanting things, wanting this or that. Even me, Sally F'ing Fairfax, I wanted Disney World with my sissy and Alex. They are having a blast and I'm stuck here missing out on everything. I'm always missing out on everything. Story of my life. My legs hurt. What I'm trying to say is that maybe my life is hopeless and that nothing really ever lasts. Happiness doesn't last. The only thing that lasts is the past, the memories in it, the infernal, or blasted, narcotics of life's results of success. Or the "feeling" of success. Pursuit is all we want. I hate everyone and everything. And now, finally, the fireworks have stopped, and I feel better that they did. . . . My sister just asked if I enjoyed it. I said no and I'm ready for either home, a hotel, or her departure. She said that that wasn't very nice, and I said it's not nice to talk about the possible success that hopeless people can't, won't, ever, ever have. Whatever.

2:29 A.M.: I just had a disturbing dream. Or should I say, a nightmare. Here, I'll tell you; see what you think. I'm writing this on barely any notepad. Gotta buy some in the morning down at the hotel's gift shop. If I have no more room left at the end of this, I apologize. Sissy and Alex are asleep. I'm trying not to wake them. Okay, here's the dream: I had a dream I was in a room, a bedroom, and perpetually it's as if I just got off work, but constant. Anyway, there's frogs and beetles coming from nowhere in the room—I have no idea, and I'm scared. I'm terrified. So I told this female roommate next door about it and she always gives the run around. I also try to call my dad, but again, the runaround. Then something scary happens. Everyone is gone. So I'm alone in this room dealing with frogs and beetles. They are coming from what looks like poop-ey shirts on my bedside. My room has two lights. My room's door has the two switches. One switch is a light to my room. The other is the hallway outside of my room. If I think someone is coming down the hall to knock, I get scared and turn both lights off because I don't want to see them and I don't what them to see me. But then, I turned on the hallway light. There was a little girl with pigtails at the end of the hall. She doesn't notice me. So I turn the light back off. I'm in complete darkness and I hide so maybe she'll knock and go away. But I forget the door is unlocked. She peeks in and says, "Mommy, I'm scared," but I know I'm not a mother. So I walk closer to her and she walks closer to me. Then this part scared me. She always looked like she was hiding something. I was paranoid a demon of some kind sent her in from the living room out from the hall. The girl keeps telling me to come to the living room and pulling me but she looks very scary and has a grin. I keep saying no. Then I pull back and close the door and lock it and shut the lights off. Then I hear giggling outside the door. More frogs and beetles swarm around at my feet while I hold my head in the darkness, feeling helpless and as if I'll never, ever leave the

May, 30th

9:18 A.M.: My sleep was awful. I just bought a new notepad though. Its paper is a lot easier to write on. Sissy and some beezy at the front counter were arguing because she double charged her and didn't look for the payment Sissy made in advance. Manager and all happened. I'm just waiting for her to pull the car up she rented. She rented one for the whole trip, except the Dad visit. My sister probably spent a fortune. I hate money. But anyways, she is now pulling up. Round Two of Disney World. Next stop: Animal Kingdom!

9:32 A.M.: Back to the ole grind. Line waiting, bus catching, tour guides saying crappy jokes. Yeah.

9:48 A.M.: Animal Kingdom smells really funky. It smells like wood chips, in a way. The lines were bad. I didn't choose this place. What I choose was Universal. Wanted to go to Universal but Sissy said that right now all the Star Wars geeks are going to be everywhere around there. I think "geek" is a strong word, because I sort of like Star Wars, but what I don't like, I don't like long lines and a small park with tons of people making noises and making me go bonkers in the ole noggin'. No matter, we're here! and I'm trying to stay as positive as possible!

10:23 A.M.: We had breakfast or whatever. The food was honestly wild. *Ha!* Wild. What a word, what a word. We ate some burgers and fries, oddly. Weird thing for breakfast. It was good, though. Then we started walking and I saw a pathway that lead down some stairs. "Look!" I said to Sissy and Alex. "Let's go *there!*"—and we, of course, did. Some lady heard me and said: "By God, Jim! Look at the *size* of those *fishies!*" Sissy and I laugh our A-holes off. We're just walking now, trying to find something fun to do. Odd. You'd never think to say that at Disney World.

10:40 A.M.: We are walking around and I see some chick on stilts with some green leaves all over her. Many, many tourist are talking and taking pictures of her. How degrading, I'm thinking.

10:52 A.M.: Now, look. I'm not some girl that is a debbie-downer to the extreme, but what I'd very much *like* to say is, well, walking around here, with Sissy and Alex, them holding hands, being all great to one another, gives me a sense of hope and happiness.

11:04 A.M.: Oh my God! We're just walking along and some tour guide lures us into this wild ride! She takes us, and quite a few others, into this tour "of the jungle," as she puts.

11:11 A.M.: Already on it. Did you know that there's this type of bat that has a wingspan of 6 whole feet? I thought that was crazy. This chick that wasn't our guide asked Sissy the question. She told her 3 feet. Wrong! Then see asked me and I told her 3 feet, too. She looked at me funny, but then said, "This bat has the wingspan of 6 whole feet," and I yippie'd, jumping up and down. Not only just the tour guide, but Sissy and Alex looked at me weird, too! The whole group of people looked at me weird. . . . Weird.

11:20 A.M.: There's these bunches of cages around. They aren't cages, per se, but they are binding. The tigers are behind them, and the lions, too, and I feel pretty dang sad about it. Those lions have no chance to live a lion's life, not ever. They are going to be hand-feed for the rest of their lives and never see the outside of glass. They will always see children, day after day, month after month, year after year, in front of them, smiling, throwing chips or something at them, laughing while they do it, and the lions'll just have to take it. The lions and tigers and bears become an attraction, not an animal; which, in turn, makes the viewers, meaning *us*, the ones that are the predators and monstrous animals.

11:26 A.M.: I asked the tour guide if it would be okay to let the lions and tigers and bears sort of "roam free," with the supervision of a person, of course, and a leash. The tour guide laughed and thought I was joking, but clearly I'm not, "and everyone here deserves for the 'lion to eat[9] them,' " I thought; "good riddance and good-bye!"

11:41 A.M.: Okay so we're in the bird part of the tour. Let's see how it goes. I have to pay attention to this new guide.

12:00 P.M.[10]: On the dot. Okay. Sissy, me, and Alex are sitting somewhere to eat. We just got out of the bird tour. Oh my God. That tour guide was the sweetest. I can't describe the feeling of her talking to us. The only way I can describe it is when you were little and it was quiet and the librarian at your school came up and tickled your ear with a teddy bear because you were being so good today and you get this really funny tickle-y feeling inside your head. It feels all warm and nice and it makes you feel right as

---

[9] — I totally, totally am feeling like I'm foreshadowing something extraordinary, here. I don't know what it is but I think it's great that I started this journal knowing nothing about how to really give a crap about things like that. I'm glad I started making this journal thingamajigger. I think it's making me a better person.

[10] — This note was a lot shorter, but I remember it better, now, as I'm copying it into a my journal. So I'm just going to go ahead and make it more detailed.

rain[11]. You get all warm and you can't help but smile. That's what the tour guide was like. She started off talking to us in the entrance and telling us stories of the birds. There was one in the water. You could tell she really did love birds. I mean it. She had a soft voice and was super sweet. Then we turn around and she goes, "Oh! my favorite!" and she started to explain this pigeon and how it was gigantic; the biggest pigeon in the whole planet! she said. My sister shook her hand and told her it was truly pleasant to have her be our guide. She told us, "Well, not good-bye, yet. I have a route. I can follow you three around this bird 'area' [she may have said another word for 'area' but I'm not too sure. She probably did, though]." Then we said okay and it was weird, at first, because it was stalker-status, but then she really gave us such great advice on things and such great facts. I mean you could ask her anything and she knew it. If it involves birds, well, by God she knew it! She was talking about these Dodo birds and how they got extinct because people were coming onto this island, an island the Dodos were at, and basically it was a disease-free place. She said the Dodos' island was the only island they were at in the whole world. So when these people came in on these boats, they actually hurt the Dodos bad because all the parasites they brought onto the island from their ships killed all the Dodos, indefinitely. I thought is was sad but then this sweet, old tour guide lady said, "—but it's okay that the Dodos are extinct. Since this happened, everyone is always very careful not to let it happen again. The Dodo had an unfortunate death but we learned from that death and have saved quite a few species of bird because of this," and that really made me feel warm. Then she explained another bird that was up high, way up in this cliff, about 20 feet up, and the guide was saying how this bird actually will spend I think all winter, if I remember correctly, trying to put the sticks up there, away from danger. They will spend their whole time going back and forth, back and forth, back and forth, up and down, on this cliff. They carry sticks in their beaks and do this all day long. That's dedication! The guide was saying how the people that work on this bird portion of the park have to take down the nest

---

11 — Got this from *The Matrix*.

after the eggs hatch because they can actually fall on peoples' heads. Alex laughed when she said that! The guide just laugh, too, and went on to explain how birds are wonderful creatures and it's a shame things like extinction happen to them. "But it's part of Life," she said; "and frankly, there's not much that a researcher, like I, can do, you know?" I and Sissy nodded. "You guys are sweet," the guide told us. She gave out her hand for a shake and I think it was the first time in my life (and I'm 22 years old, mind you) where I've never been so eager to shake a person's hand. She walked us out of the bird tour and told us how she studied at the lower north part of Florida and studied herself silly on birds and how when she got out of college she applied for Disney ("even though it was a second choice," she said (and I asked her this)), and how Disney really helped her out and gave her everything she wanted to do, which was ultimately tell people about birds and how these people are truly the reason for the birds' survivals in a lot of ways. Things like recycling, not polluting, walking instead of driving, et cetera, can make or break a bird from living amongst the very beings that are doing these "bad things"; "and wow!" I thought, "I hope *I'm* not selfish! Thanks, Cindy!" The guide's name was Cindy; she told us, and she never tells customers her name, even though she has a name-tag nobody reads. So since she told me, Sissy, and Alex, it meant that we were her favorite customers of the day! Gosh, I can't *tell* you how great it was to hear that. We all smiled and waved at each other when we left the bird tour. Gosh, and how sweet it was.

12:32 P.M.: Sissy was waiting long and hard for me to finish that last one at the table. She got mad at me. But now we're off to some ride that has dinosaurs or something.

12:50 P.M.: Just waiting in line, is all.

1:12 P.M.: WHAT A RUSH! We just got done with the dinosaur ride. Oh man, Disney gets it! You had to go into this chamber and get a "briefing" from your "captain," and he's saying that they are going to go back in time to get a dinosaur or something. The time is during the moment when the meteors killed all the dinosaurs. So you go through this ride and it's flashing all these lights and dinosaurs come at you, in your face. I loved it! Alex was such a big-boy. He wasn't too afraid. He was screaming, and yeah —don't get me wrong—but he was a big-boy, because after it he said he wanted to ride again. It was really entertaining. The gift shop was really great, too. WHAT A RUSH!

1:34 P.M.: We're trying to find a water fountain because these water bottle stands charge 5 bucks a pop!

1:43 P.M.: So it's hot as heck and I'm complaining and my sister is getting mad. We're going passed this carnival and I thought it was rather curious because, well, "what is a carnival," I thought, "doing at Disney World? Isn't the whole *park* a carnival?" I was asking too many questions to Sissy, so I didn't say anything. I kept silent and guessed why the carnival was there: "because of money?" was my answer.

~~1:58 P.M.: I'm seeing an ice cream cone stand and I think it looks absolutely delicious, so yeah, HELLO! YUM YUM!~~

2:08 P.M.: There's an F'ing bird show! I flippin', F'ing *bird* show! We're going in now[12]!

2:32 P.M.: I'll have to recollect from memory from this note because I think I was too excited and most of it is extremely hard to read. It looks like basically I was there at the show and there was this really prissy chick that was smiling a lot, and then there was this older guy, Tim, that was with her on stage. They were all positively giddy and whatever, and they were showing off these different birds. The lady was saying, in this one portion of the show, "Does anyone have a dollar?" and some guy, some stupid motherf█k, stands up and says yeah. It was a twenty, we all found out, because the lady had the guy hold the twenty out and the bird took it from his hands and then flew back to the lady. Pretty wicked, I must say. Then she made a joke about how she'll keep the money or whatever. The crowd laughed because we knew she was full of s█t. Then the bird flew back and gave him the money. Then, get this: the older guy on stage comes in and says, "A theme park that gives your money *back?!*" Then everyone *really* laughed. Jesus Christ. There were so much more birds after that. Bald Eagle was the best. They said it was no longer extinct anymore (or on the "list" of extinction, I should say). After the whole thing this lady, oh my God, this lady was saying that we all need to help the environment because we are the ones that decide. It honestly pissed me off. It left me thinking that humans are like a virus, and any biologist would classify an animal as such if it kills that mercilessly.

2:57 P.M.: We're trying really hard to go see the yeti ride. Wish us luck.

---

[12] — Just a small note that before writing this section on the notepad, I was complaining about how hot it was and how I want to leave and go home. Sissy said no. Even Al said no. I asked him to draw me something and he stuck his tongue out at me. Can you believe it?! So yeah, we were walking, running, walking, and basically we stopped at this crazy fan thingy. It was a fan that was blowing while streaking mist was oozing out of it in balls of clear clouds. It felt nice and safe. I spread my arms out wide and embraced the cool hug from God. Then, ironically, I saw the bird show, next to me, roaring and full, in my peripherals.

3:23 P.M.: This line is murder. We actually ran from one side of the park, the side with the birds, to the other side, passed the dino-carnival. Epic!

3:39 P.M.: Just keep swimming just keep swimming just swimming, swimming, *swim*ming . . .

3:48 P.M.: Just about to get on. Wish me luck! This looks F'ing scary!

3:58 P.M.: That was great! Oh my God! It was too short though. Like really short. I screamed the loudest and my sister was laughing her A off the whole time. The guy next to me was laughing, too. He was some Mexican guy. I think he touched my leg at one point. I didn't care though. It's Disney. I'd give him a taste. But anyway, it was awesome! The ride went backwards and forwards and the Yeti was so crazy! They had a projector show him pulling the track from its "stilts" thingamajigger. Hella saucy! We actually had a blast.

4:12 P.M.: It's getting to be that time of day. The sun is murder at this point. Sissy is starting to feel it, too. She has Raybans on and I'm totally jealous of her. I was going to buy some yesterday at the car ride, inside its gift shop, but it was about $150 and money is tight so I decided not to. We're waiting in line at some restaurant called the "Yakking Yeti," or something like that. That's what I thought my sister said, but really, it was actually the "Yak and Yeti," not "Yakking." The food is coming soon . . .

4:20 P.M.: WEED! Just kidding. So anyway, the food is to die for. But there's no seats anywhere to be found. We have to go around and look.

4:24 P.M.: Some A-hole really is saying that the 4 seats around him are taken. What . . . a . . . F'ing . . . *tool!* So now we all three have to seat down on the ground and eat our bullspit. Let me take a bite. . . . *Wow!* It's lovely!

4:44 P.M.: My sister wants to check out the Safari before we head out. I'm actually really excited for this. . . . Also, I want to point out that I haven't been looking up much while I've been here. All these guys keep staring at me. Even the guys with wives or girlfriends. I actually even notice the girlfriends saying that they shouldn't look at me. I think it's because I have my blue-jean daisy dukes on and my booty looks really big and nice in them. I'm a ▮▮▮ girl but I have a perfect ▮▮▮ girl's booty! Also I'm wearing this tiny shirt on and my boobs are pushing the shirt up so much so that you can see my tummy. That's how small the shirt is. Guys are so funny[13]! I loathe them. . . .

4:52 P.M.: Running for some reason. Yeah. Hold on.

5:09 P.M.: I'm out of breath, now. Thanks, Sissy Dukes, you beezy. I feel all sick, but that's nothing unusual. I feel sort of sad because we passed the *A Bug's Life* showing and I really want to see it. I remember it, back when. It was really great because they had liquid that shoots out. And air. And lights. I wanted to see that. Sensory-overload is great sometimes.

5:19 P.M.: This line sucks.

5:22 P.M.: Some fat b▮ch just fell just now. *Ha!* Dumba▮ Alert! I'd hate for that to happen to me.

5:29 P.M.: Karma. Some kid dropped his ice cream on my foot. This sucks.

5:39 P.M.: Sissy wants to talk but she's getting mad because I'm writing so much. We have a long time before the safari starts for our line. I'll let Alex draw something while I talk to Sissy. She's genuinely sort of pissed at me because I'm obsessing over this notepad.

---

[13] — Not "funny"—PIGS! All pigs!

5:55 P.M.: It's lovely that I can see the line ending soon, and wow! Alex's drawing is hella saucy! What's more, I'm not even going to take photos of what I see—I'm going to write down everything as quick as humanly possible[14]:

The tour guide is saying that we're going to be on this trip for 2 weeks and I'm laughing about that. I love how Disney says things for added effect.

The first thing I see is a fat rhino. Wicked!

There's a hippo just chillin' in the water. It's mommy or something is swimming around beside it. Crap! Even then you can see a black ball where another one is underwater. Double wicked!

A dang Falcon!

I look over and my Sissy is totally checking out the Gators.

---

[14] — I realize I'm not going to be able to put the exact time of things, so if you could, big, big beautiful Future Sally, please be patient with me. Thanks a bunch. XOXO.

A waterfall!

The tour guide is so funny! He was talking about this upside-down tree and then he said some joke. I can't remember what it is because I'm laughing so hard, right now, but trust me, it's halar' 'lar'!

F'ing dingos. . . .

There's a tall ant hill thingy. A bunch of them actually. Apparently they can be as tall as *me*. Now *that's* some heavy ants-in-pants, girl.

This antelope with horns is chillin' like you wouldn't know.

God. I have to write quick. Driving fast.

Okay so we're stopped at this "Dead-end Road," right? The tour guide is saying how the Elephants ahead have stomped the road over and he has to go around. I feel like this is totally staged! *Ha!*[15]

Another upside-down tree!

There's palms on an island in a small pond and these white tall birds are chillin' there, fighting over something.

There's these rocks that are stacked and it reminds me of *The Lion King*.

ZEBRAS!

There's a dang Zebra next to me!

A "herd"[16] of Rhinos! *Ha!*

---

[15] — I came to find out that it totally was. . . .

[16] — Totally not sure if that's the correct terminology.

Okay, now I'm seeing this "Pride Rock"-looking thingy. It literally looks like it. And there's Cheetahs everywhere around it! Gah-*lee!*

The tour guide talks too much, I'm thinking. We are running over these chain-linked roads and I'm thinking it's markers for the people lining others up.

There's these rocks that are F'ed up and it's because Elephants or something like to eat the clay or something and they rub their horns on the clay and F it up. Wicked!

That was fun! I'm talking a pano on my sister's iPhone.

6:29 P.M.: I'm beat. We're all beat. Time to go home.

7:34 P.M.: This drive back blows. . . .

May, 30th, around 9:00 p.m.

Sissy and I just came back not too long ago, and honestly, I am pretty darn good. I wasn't happy, none whatsoever, about little Alex leaving. He's really such a doll. He says he wants to start writing something. Like a journal or something. He says I inspired him! I love it! Warms my heart to hear things like that. Sissy smiled, too.

    Alex—this little rascal—before everything, we go into my room and basically, yeah, I showed him this journal thing. His eyes scanned it back and forth and grew *big!* "Woah, cool!" He was so excited! Him and I drew on it with colored pencils and watercolor. You see, my journal is all-white, see. So basically it was easy as pie to draw on. I just told him to draw a star on the spine while I draw, get this: "A Lion In Your Number." So crazy, huh? It was lookin' like a *real* book! He drew a lion on the cover!

I'm so proud of Alex. I truly am. But sadly, Sissy and him had to leave just about a couple minutes ago. Sissy has to get back home and everything—do work, things like that. The normal adult stuff. I envy my sister and what she does. She really is such a sweetie pie.

Not much details to say, right now, but when they left I started bawling. I know I put up a front but I really do cry a lot. Really. It's lame of me, and I always feel like a retard, but it makes me feel better. Look. If you sit there and never say you've never cried, Future Sally, well by God you're a liar. So much crying goes on. But anyway, Sissy just now left, pretty much, and so I'm crying, sobbing, all that, as I write this.

May, 30th, around 10:00 p.m.

I'm calling up Tessa. . . .[17]

"Hey, b■ch."

"Hey, turd-muffin. What's up? Been awhile."

"Yup, yup . . ." and then I didn't say anything.

"Can I, uh, help you, Sal?" Tessa finally said. "You always do this to me. Never say a word. *What?*"

"Well, um, Tess, I'm pretty sad."

"Why, hun?" Tessa can actually be sympathetic when I need it, even though she's a total beasty[18].

I hesitated, at first.

"It's all an illusion. I feel very sleepy right now. I think my anxiety spikes when I don't get any sleep," I said, which makes sense, considering

---

[17] — and whatever I put after this is the conversation I got . . . live.

[18] — I got this saying from a movie. Again, totally not a word I, like, use on a daily basis. Tee-*hee!*

I have my sleep disorder, "and it is so dang *lame!*" I thought. "Jesus."

"Sal, you gotta relax. Whatcha doin' today? Anything?"

"I wanted to hang with you."

"I'm, ah, going to a bar soon, with Josh. You can come."

"Which one?"

"Wong's."

"Wrong's? What's that?"

"No, Sal. *Wong.*"

I was F'in' with her at that point!

"I gotta go, hoe," Tess said. "Meet me at Wong's. I'll text the address."

"*Wait*. I actually need to talk to you."

"Sal, I'm busy. What is it?"

"I'm sorry. You're busy. Okay. I'll leave you alone, in peace."

"No. Just say it."

"I just . . . I don't know. I feel trapped. Like people tell me to be positive and I can't he positive. People never listen to me—"

"Sal, I can't talk about this right now, no."

"—and, like, my anxiety is turning into anger; my anger into hatred; my hatred into rude-ness. F k," due excuse the French, Future Sally.

And Tess goes, "Anything else?"

"Yeah. Shoot me."

"Okay, Sal. Just come to Wong's . . ." and she hung up.

Such bull, and yeah, she said this an hour ago. I feel like I should go. I'll write and sulk later.

May, 30th, 11:02 p.m.

"When someone says to make a change for yourself," (for happiness, *duh!*), "I go bonkers," I said at Tess and Josh's table, when I sat down, them actually still, well, being there. "But what if I am actually in fact a failure?"

"Shut the heck up and have a beer," Josh said.

"Or when I'm unsuccessful with romance. What if I'm actually a terrible person and people genuinely don't see me romantically because of it? Or I'm too good-looking or something?" I was scared to ask this, because immediately my anxiety shot through the roof. "Ugh, my head hurts . . ." and I crossed my arms and buried my head into them, sort of on the table and yeah, "whatever," I thought.

Sally this, Sally that. Sally, Sally, Sally. That's all they did was say my name. I wasn't really listening, kind of.

"Sally, baby, you gotta enjoy the festivities of life," Josh said while drinking his beer.

"Yeah, yeah," Tessa agreed, sipping on hers, too; "you can't just be miserable all the time."

"Well I *am* miserable. I am." I was starting to feel sick when I said it. "You guys don't get it," and I sort of lifted up my head slightly. "Tessa. Josh. Listen to me. I—am—going—in*sane*. In-f⬛king-sane! I hate it. People don't like me. I hate everyone! I do."

"Sal. Keep your voice down," Tessa said, worried a little bit. "You're causing a scene."

I looked around and you know what, nobody was looking at me. Nobody. They just kept eating, all silent or whatever. Nobody was talking with "friends." I swear. It made me feel so lame and inferior. Then I *really* started raising my voice.

"I'm tired of this! I'm just darn tired of it. All of you, you simps, you all can go to Hell! I hate you all. I hope a f⬛king meteor hits this gay a⬛ planet" (and remember, Josh is gay, so the word "Gay," like every other swear, is insulting, especially to him) "and leaves you all dead! F⬛k you! F⬛k!" Then I got up, after saying this, and held my face to keep everyone from looking at me while I cried. I hate things too much. I literally went there for maybe ten minutes. I friggin' walked home. No buses. No rides.

And you know what else? Nor Josh or Tessa even followed me or comforted me. But I guess that's what happens when you condemn everyone to death, or whatever.

Royally speaking, though, I did it all the correct way: hate should be done whilst shouting at tops of lungs, at tops of windpipes, because, frankly, hating is the absolute best coping mechanism, I think. You don't have to agree, Future Sally. But just know that you—yes, *you*—were once a little spit, back there over yonder, a time of complete desperation you couldn't possibly recollect.

I have no clue where the heck my brain went, after all this mess. I was walking home and I started to see things. Nothing made much sense. Okay, so I sort of saw this guy that was all walking off behind houses. Like zig-zagging back and forth, right as I was walking. The guy looked like a weirdo. I mean, like, he was going door to door, in kind of daylight, and going between houses, probably for no apparent reason. I was rubbing my eyes because I just knew it wasn't real. Things like that are never real. The guy saw me and started running after me, so I sort of ran, too, but away from the guy. I lost him, thank God. Don't ever let guys like that catch you, ladies, because you may come up on the backs of milk cartons, or be on one of those crazy rape brochures. I know it's whack of me to say, but as a girl, I just *know* guys can't control themselves. Why, even *I* can't control myself, and *I'm* a friggin' girl! Sometimes I purposely try to look like a hot mess. I can't ever not wear a bra, even though I'd like to, but the ole ta-tas are very, very perky, now, and they don't sag the way I'd like. Sometimes I want guys to just leave me alone. It's weird, I know, because if I was ugly I'd want guys to look at me. But I'm not ugly, and I know this, so I guess I want to be ugly. It's funny. <u>You never want the things you got. You always got the thing you don't want</u>. It's funny.

But yeah, and then, while walking, I saw this couple kissing behind a tree. They could have not been there—I was out of it—but anyways, they were kissing and having sex under a tree, off behind someone's house. I saw it for a split second.

Then I saw some trees dancing. I'm not kidding. Live trees! They had faces and they were sort of swinging and twisting back and forth. It could of been wind, in reality, but *I* don't know. I never know these things.

Then I thought of Russell and I decided I missed him. What's crazy—you're going to think I'm crazy—what's crazy is that I sort of, you know, *miss* him being a d■k to me. I liked it, even though it was a death of me. At one point, I hated his guts. But I always thought he was the sexiest man alive. Like I would honestly go out of my way just to pick an argument with him. I liked to make him mad because it showed me that I had an affect on him. Gosh, if I ever tried him, even, and he just sat still, not getting mad, I'd've dumped him *months* ago. I swear my life on it.

Just An Undated Thought . . .

What I keep thinking about is how life has a series of things that happen as you get older. Like when you're born you see a doctor, although you don't remember, or can't remember, him. Then they teach you to walk. You cry, complain, do whatever. Then it's time for school. You go there, cry, complain, do whatever. As you keep going there, though, teachers keep saying to, like, be more serious, but you don't want to, so you cry, complain, do whatever, yet again. Then you see others around you doing better than you and it makes you sad. You keep pushing and seeing everyone making the type of friends they want but you're just stuck in time. You're perpetually stuck in time; all the time, you're guessing. Then you keep going to school and then, before you know it, you're in middle school, where depression first starts. This time is most awkward because you realize you're not all there. Or everyone is more normal than you. And you, in turn, get more depressed and try to "fit in" as best you can. Then you do s■tty in school because everything seems like a blur with all the kids talking about sex and girls and drugs and partying. Things you didn't know existed. You still thought there was a Santa Claus, back then. You get laughed at because everyone is ahead of you, always. But you keep going and, before you know it, high school starts. You have to switch schools so much that you can't function. No teacher works with you because you are too stupid to teach, but here, there, everywhere. So they coast you on by and by the time you are about to graduate, at the almost-fifth year, the principal finally brings you to her office and says that you probably should drop out because you're grades are too bad and she makes up a bulls■t lie that "people passed 18 can't go to high school here legally." They bring your Dad in and basically he calls bullsh■. He tells them that my daughter is going to be here whether they like it or not, regardless of them losing points toward school funding by my staying there, as a five-year student, and not graduating with the others. Then, get this: you go and have the crappiest time because no teacher cares. So you take virtual school and pass, and then, after all this, you get kicked out of your house because you posted some unfair, unacceptable status update on your stepmother, who you hated at the time, that says: "This lady has no job, no anything, and she's raising my dang rent. Phooey!" and your stepmom, who is signed into your dad's account, says for you to get out, you have thirty days to pack your spit and leave. So you find a nice, easy apartment down the street, near Wellington, because that was where you're current job was at the time, and you left. Then you see others going to college, having a ball, having parents that care about them and can afford to pay for their stuff like college, books, cars, clothes, a roof over their head, and you're stuck messing with your $1100/month job that barely makes you pay for anything, and you have no other opportunities because Florida's economy is so, so terrible. Then you get so depressed at your full-time job that you go to a hospital because of thoughts of suicide and then you owe a bill. You get health insurance and spend all this money you have, just so these doctors can stand there and give bullsh*t, un-helpable answers of the "help" they can give, but oh, we still want you to go here because we, um, need to make sure you're "okay"; when in reality they just want your insurance to pay them so they can spend the money on their cars, their kids for college, and live a happy, happy life full of goodies you won't ever get, not in a million friggin' years. Then you, in turn, get more depressed and think "bad thoughts" and everyone—and I mean everyone—thinks you're some kind of psycho for even thinking the thoughts. So you pretty much ease on by in life, never to find love or happiness. You don't gain weight, you don't buy cars, you don't buy houses, you don't do anything but sleep to try and get to the finish line of Life as fast as possible without you being conscious. That's the thing. Depression is not the word for this, no. What it is, it's hatred of the feeling of Life. The eyes that see and look at colors, why? There isn't a singular reasoning for it. The feeling of handshakes. The feeling of anything at all. All your senses collide into one another and make you cave inside with terror and everything else negative. You find that everything doesn't make any crap of sense, ever. Not ever. But whatever, you keep going, get better jobs, and still coast on by life, writing in your stupid journal that even *you* don't read, not even the hopeful "future self." The reason a future self is even in the equation is because of Hope. Hope is a sonuvab■ch. It is. Then, you keeping going on, lonely and lost, into this aimless adulthood and watch everyone you've ever known become happy with kids, cars, money, clothes, expensive spit, yards, pure-bred dogs, and so, so much friggin' more. Then you gain some sort of disease and have no assets to give to your nonexistent family, and nobody remembers your name . . . at all. You don't want to see this, Sally. You don't. But you keep living for the sake of Ha-ha's *ha-ha*. It's all a scam. Forget cry-for-helps. They do nothing for anyone. Nobody can actually help because it's all gone and lost. I guess I'm being rather negative right now, and I'm sorry for that.

June, 22nd, 8:23 p.m.

I've been slacking a bit. Not writing. Been busy. I've kind of been looking over the game plan of my life. I barely have any money to do anything. My friends don't really talk to me, so I had to asked Tessa for help. She totally forgot about my outburst. I asked her if she knew anyone that could get me a job. She told me about a girl named so-and-so, who I don't want to say the name of, that works for Kelly Bluebook, a staffing agency, and how she could help me. Tessa also gave me a number.

So yeah, I called it, whatever. This chick was nice. I felt like the line was recorded, though, because she didn't talk to me like a friend or anything, especially since Tessa, who I said was the chick that referred me, wasn't really a difference in the so-called "spice" of the conversation. I asked her what I could get.

"Cigna is hiring, ma'am."

Now, I know this is crazy, crazy. But hear me out, because I was skeptical, at first, too. This chick told me they start you at $12/hr. Holy spit! Wow! My ears actually stood up! I swear! She told me that basically all I get are inbound calls from customers asking questions regarding why their hospital bill wasn't paid, or if they are covered, or this or that. It seems easy enough.

But yeah, that's not even the half of it. Turns out, they give you a pay increase every. Three. Months! Wow! and not only that, but yeah, it's paid weekly, not bi-weekly, because it's through Kelly, not Cigna. Cigna I guess pays out Kelly and they disperse. I could be wrong but that sounds about likely.

This was about a week ago, mind you. This chick sent me an email to fill out. It's a Kelly Bluebook email, to signup. It's just crazy because of how scary it is. It's a lot of money, yeah, but is it what I really want? I mean really, *really* want? I don't know. Seems like a good move, though. I think I should take it. I should. It's time to not be unhappy anymore. It's time to be a big girl and stop being so gosh-darn afraid of everything already.

I'm inspired to do the signup. Wish me luck. Bye!

June, 28th, 1:05 p.m.

Wheelin' and dealin'... wheelin' and dealin'. All I'm doing. I just got off the phone with the hiring chick at Cigna, I think it's called. She was very nice and professional. Good thing, too, because my rent is due, and I don't think Beth will put up with anything late, especially from me, God bless her heart. But anyway, this girl was nice. She is going to start me off at $10/hr because I'm not experienced. The training, she said, is extensive. I thought she said "Expensive," and she kind of raised her voice a bit and spoke up like I was an old person. I hate that, you know? You ask a question and people freak out. If it was expensive, then yeah—NOT taking the job because my money is slim to nothing! I am glad she told me, though.

Besides that, um, I do want to say that she did get me the interview-y, quite fancily, I must say! It's ASAP. She said tomorrow—"Crap," I said to myself! I may even start darn near in three days! If, of course, I play my cards right. But yeah, again, besides that, I have this new obsession with Jim Carrey. He's hot. I saw this YouTube video of him at a college: he was saying some pretty inspirational stuff: he said that life is between fear and love, awesome and not-awesome. Most people choose fear and mask it as an intellectual decision toward their future—and most people are stuck doing the things they hate. Like, he said people should make mistakes doing what they love because if you make mistakes doing what you hate, well, then you're just going to be miserable, is what I picked up on it. Pretty wild, huh? Jim makes me wet. I'm actually touching myself while writing this! *Ha!* Is that weird? I know it sounds rather slutty, but come on! It's Jim Carrey. But nothing—and I mean *nothing*—beats my obsession over Joseph Gordon Levitt. Oh my *God!* Holy. I would literally ride him raw!

June, 28th, 8:01 p.m.

■[19].

June, 3rd, 7:00 p.m.

I started my new job, but I've been too busy to write about it. The training is wild. I'm still in T1 (Training #1). The people are nice, and it feels like the first day of school. We do ice-breakers and everything, just like high school. What's crazy is the booklets are pre-used, so I get to see notes taken from the previous people. What's funny is only some of the answers are correct so you have to be careful if you decide to use their stuff. Even the big fat training lady said this.

Get this: on one page, this page passed "H.I.P.P.A. Laws," there was this really odd poem from some person. It looked like the type of poem

---

[19] — Let's just not look at this. It was a bad day, let's just say that. Let's also say that I hate myself sometimes, and it's a problem. It's hard to be positive.

you'd see if you were really bored and suddenly got inspired. I mean, I'm in insurance, now, so you have to think about the people that work here and the monotonous stuff you hear in training.

I'll bet whomever wrote this was bored to death. Or maybe they were thinking of a person they really liked and couldn't have sex with. I'm a pig in the head, as a chick, but nonetheless, what I did was, I wrote down this poem from the booklet just so I could put it here. Let me put it:

"Silhouettes" by Thomaz Nadeau:

>*She wore clichés in her hair,*
>*Silhouettes etched beneath—*
>*A jeweler's moon.*
>
>*I sat there*
>*Refrigerated with fear.*
>*Three words:*
>
>*Cushion the unknown.*
>*Stained, paned*
>*Glass heart—*
>*Stone-cold reasons*
>*Break me down.*
>
>*I am leaving—*
>*Eyes melt*
>*Upon the stars*
>
>*Heart break*
>*With every step*
>*That I take.*

I honestly thought it was beautiful, to say the least. It made my day feel better. I felt like I could deal. I actually sort of felt like this guy. What

I took from it, I took that basically the person you see from afar can appear like something else, something mysterious or un-take-able, if that makes sense. It's like having fear in the thing you want most and then walking away from it, never to ever feel the satisfaction in the very thing you desire. I hate that sometimes.

It's a good thing I started this new job.

July, 4th, 5:20 p.m.

Apparently I was wrong about this place. It's not insurance at all! but it's close! I'm working at a collection agency. Yeah. I know. Lame. I'm the person who asks for you to pay your bill, I know, I know. But apparently the bonus checks are good. I guess it's weird. You collect around $42,000 in a month, they give you $300 and 20% overage, in the agency's fee, of whatever else you collect. It seems really crazy. I feel important.

Today, this beat-down, hair-split-ended lady named Victoria was teaching. She's new, apparently, which makes no sense to me. But yeah, she was talking about tone and the way we say things. She was saying that a person on the phone only hears, like, conversation or voice. Part of conversation, the thing of it is is that about 60% of it is body language, 30% is face, 10% is what you actually say. I think that's pretty standard and makes sense but also I hate it.

I hate it so much so that I raised my hand and asked Vic (that's what she wants us to call her), "Why is it that way, if I may ask?"

And she said, "Because this is what the customers are feeling."

"What's In It For *Me?*" I asked with a falsetto on the "me" part.

"Correct, Sally!"

This sort of made me feel weird. I don't know why. I guess it's because I sort of felt like all companies are the same and looking to seek money. I think money rules the nation. I hate it so much, I could just blow everything up around me.

Besides, I just hate money and how it makes you not get the things you want in the time you need them. But I'm starting to wonder if material goods are even that cool or great.

Sure—I'd like an iPhone, like every dang American does, like how my sister has one and I want to be like her, but I can't. Know why? Money, that's why.

Money, money, money! That's all I ever hear. Money. Moola. The big cheese. The big cheddar. The big green-y spit. And the funny thing is that I'm employed at the one place that literally *runs* on money.

People owing is our business. Without debt, we'd be broke.

There's only a few jobs that make money from mistakes. Police Officers. In some cases, Doctors. Debt Collectors, *duh!* Maybe Fire Fighters. There's pretty much people everywhere in fields where people are "in need" that make their dough from mistakes. Take Politicians, for example—*Act*ually, never mind. Let's not and say we did.

But yeah, this all said, this is all I'm learning. I guess you could say I'm growing up. Which also means I have to cut my entries shorter because I have to sleep and stuff. I may not have time like always and before....

July, 10th, 5:56 p.m.

Today at work was too wild for words.

But let me go back. This whole training week has been a nightmare. Basically I'm all nervous on the phone but yeah, customers seem to like me. Especially since my voice is so high and peachy-sounding. I guess I'm using my timid mannerisms to get money. I collected the most in T_2 (Training #2).

You won't believe it if I told you. Okay, so basically everyone, except the guys, has been totally jelly of me. These girls are always giving me "The Stare," or "The Stink Eye." They snap their tongues whenever I do something great and all the boys keep staring at me. I know it must be hard to stop looking at me when I'm in a polka-dot knee-short skirt that practically is see-through. I have a business shirt with these cute flower prints on the front pocket. I really like it. I have every color. It makes my tits look big, *huge*.

The boys have been staring me down like crazy. They always look at my butt. Okay, ladies, you know how when you get up, get out of bed, spend an hour or more dressing up, and you go to work, struttin' your stuff? You know days when you look F'ing killer? That's what it was like for me. But what's crazy is while I walk I can feel a sort of presence behind me. Do you ever get that feeling? Like a shadow or a guy or something is behind you checking your booty out?

Anyway, that's how I've been feeling. It actually makes me smile to myself when I feel it. I know that sounds lame or something, but I can't help it. It's true! But yeah, the girls definitely are noticing it.

What I do want to tell you, I want to tell you about how I've been on the phone getting payment after payment after payment. They have this thing called a "Hot." Basically if you think someone is going to pay, you "Hot" it. Then you call them back or something and if they pay, you get the credit for it toward your budget. Seems simple enough.

What I'm getting at is that I hotted this account in Texas or something —about a seven-thousand dollar account—and then I had lunch. You won't believe what happened!

So firstly I went to lunch and came back. Everyone was staring—I mean everyone and their mother. It was eerie. Me, myself, and I, we just strutted on in, in T2, minding business, and this lady comes barging in the moment I sat down.

"Who's 438?!"

That's my collector number, by the way. We all have different collector numbers to differentiate ourselves from the other collectors. To keep moola safe, you know?

"Me," I told this lady that barged in. But what's crazy is I hadn't looked up, not at all. I was doodling on some paper.

"Where? Who said that?" said this chick in a rather alert tone. "Was it you? *You?*"

Then, I looked up. "It was me! How can I—" I stopped right away. I had to. The lady that was right there, right smack dab in the very front of T2, it was Sherry!

And so I was all, "Sherry!" and she was like, "Sally, honey! Oh, what a lovely surprise to see you! You work here, now?" and she said the "work here, now" like it wasn't the most obvious thing in the whole, wide world.

"Yeah," I was all. "How are you!" Okay, okay, I know I'm being a total hypocrite with the "how are you"s to her, but honestly, I wanted to say it.

"I'm doing real good," answered the lovely Sherry. "Okay, basically—Guys!" she said aloud. "Sally just got a payment of seven-thousand five-hundred dollars!"

And, oh Lordy, everyone clapped.

I held my ears because it was too loud and I said, "Oh . . . Really?"

"Yeah, really!" Sherry all congrats'd. "By the way, you're in my group. I'm your supervisor!"

What was a supervisor of a fortune 500 company, I thought, doing riding on the PalmTran? "All righty," I told her.

"So yeah, Sal. I just came to congratulate you on your payment. You're now at budget."

"Yeah?"

"You're bonus is going to be low—about one-hundred bucks—but don't fret, you still can collect more and get your overage. I'm so proud of you!" cheered Sherry.

"Oh," I said.

She said good-byes to everyone and walked out.

Apparently money here can happen at the blink of an eye, no problemo.

A Letter to a F███ead

Dear Bob Dylan[20],

F█k me, please. Now. Your music makes me insane and just a *lit*tle bit █.

July, 14th, 5:26 p.m.

First day on the floor. No biggie. . . . No biggie?! Of *course* it's an F'ing

---

[20] — Younger Bob, not Older Bob. I should have reiterated that.

biggie, Sally! Jeez! Ha, *ha!* Whatever. So I'm actually pretty excited to write about this day, even though I'm not exactly thrilled. Is that weird? To be excited but not thrilled? I don't know anymore. Maybe I'm retarded.

What was the highlight was rather embarrassing. I'll talk about it in a second. First I want to say that I was dressed insanely scrumptious. I wasn't doing all this just sweater and underwear stuff while watching TV. Uh-*uh!* No way. I was in this cute red and white-striped top that I got at Macy's, totally on sale. And I got this really cute skirt—but nothing short—and I got these long socks to match it. Striped socks rule the nation!

The girls around here are really weird. Some of them actually want to get pregnant. Like, I'm foreal. I overheard some girls talking, all being next to each other, and the girls kept saying things like that they want this guy to have kids with them and this other guy is their baby-daddy and all this *other* bull.

The girls here are not get-along-able. No. Heck to the mother-F *no*. I feel like I can't relate. But all of them have this crazy A stare toward me, and it's really, really freaking me out slash pissing me off, and I mean it. I want to straight gut the next b▮▮▮ who ▮▮▮s with Sally. You got another thing coming.

But anyway! like yeah! Where was I? Oh yeah. Getting onto the floor for the first time. . . . Well, technically not the first, first time, but very close. I did side-by-sides[21] with another collector on the floor, as part of training, but that doesn't count.

When I got out there, holy crap, you won't friggin' believe who I saw. It was Russell! *and* he's the friggin' lead! Like, this is just my luck: an old psycho boyfriend working with me at a job I finally am okay with, and he's my boss. Now, I'm thinking if I should ever bring it up to Sherry's attention.

"All right, guys," Sherry said aloud during pre-shift. "We're starting off today with compliance, as always, but first I'd like you all to welcome Sally. She's new."

---

[21] — A "side-by-side" pretty much means that our phones are connected, or wait—our *headsets* are connected to each other, and the person on the phone can speak but I can't. It's to train you to hear what a conversation on the phones here sound like.

Everyone—and I mean *every*one—was staring at me. The guys there were whispering sh!t like they would hit it or they got dibs or something; as if I wasn't hearing, and as if I actually would even bother with them. Russell was all looking like I wasn't a big deal. Even though I am.

Pre-shift starts. Blah, blah, blah.

"Okay, guys," Sherry goes, "Today I want you all to stay on the phone. You know this is important. I don't want anyone off the call. Stay on." (She looks down at her sheet.)

"And also," she said, "congrats to Russell. He ended the day off with four-thousand three-hundred and fifty-six dollars!"

And everyone starts clapping.

"I want everyone to know that there's no dress code."

"What? No dress code?" someone asked Sherry.

"Yes. The director said that it's too hot outside so you all can where jeans."

"Can I wear flip-flops?" a chick who had really cute high socks on said.

"No. That's not approved."

"So just jeans. That's it? *Jeans?*"

"Yes."

"That's stupid!"

Sherry sighed, then said, "Yeah, well, tough. I'll see if we can get extra stuff. But for now, jeans are available till the end of summer. Let's get on the phone and have a productive day."

And then everyone all scatters. I went up to Sherry's desk and asked, "Where do I sit?"

"Over there by our lead, Russell. But you can call him 'Russ.' He'll teach you the ropes."

Ropes. *Ha*. The only ropes that joker'll teach me, all dang *summer*, is how to lose your temper.

So I bit my tongue, sucked in the horse spit I was about to face, and turned around and walked on over to Russell.

"Hey, Russ."

He turned to me, grinning. "Who told you to call me that?"

"Sherr-bear."

"Typical. Miss you."

"Missed you, too."

"*Missed?* Wait, wait—hold on. That's it?"

"Yeah, duh. What else?"

He all looked at me like a joke and then, get this: he told me how he "feels."

"Sally. Missed as in past-tense? The *sssssta* sound. You know? E-D. Missed."

"Stop trippin'," I told him; "you're freakin' out over nothing. Where do I sit?"

"Sit here, to my left. So yeah, why didn't you call me after that night?"

"Is that a serious question?" I said, sitting in the chair, at the cubical next to him.

"You know, you're a b▇ch. You know that? I swear. Every time we run into each other it's nothing good."

Russell and I have some issues, yeah, but it wasn't always like that, like he was saying. We had good times—I'll admit that—but we also had not-so-good times. Actually, skip good times and go straight to bad. The guy went psycho.

"Russell, you need to cool it," I said; "and have you been taking your meds?"

"F▇k you."

" 'Kay, José," I said, matter-of-factly.

I sort of don't get it, really. The guy and I had problems, but this one night—oh my good *God*—it was horrible. I'll tell you it. But yeah, nothing much happened after that. Russ wasn't helping and I was hanging up on everybody and not staying on calls, whatever. . . . More bull:

Russell and I dated, yeah, but our breakup was really dumb. I was already fed up with him anyway, but no, he just *has* to go around talking smack. He's a control freak. Really. He is. I swear.

We basically decided to go to some club, even though I really didn't want to go. Russ was like, "Let's go to Dr. FeelGoods," and I was like,

"No," and he was like, "No, b■ch, we're going." I got mad. I truly hate when guys call me a b■ch. It irks me!

Anyway, so I went. The guy goes and picks me up and basically we fight all the way up till the door. I was messin' with his pea-brain a lot, so you could bet he was frustrated. I was a happy camper because I was at a club.

We go in, yeah, and the first thing we do—or the first thing *I* do—is start dancing. Russ didn't like that. Not the dancing type, as he said. But whatever.

Long story short, we fought *about* some bullspit—I don't know *what*—and basically, yeah, I left him at the booth and started dancing. Basically while I was dancing, though, I turned around and guess what: him and two scalawags—or should I say "Hoes"—were *all* up on him. All up on. It made me furious, girl.

So I said, "F this," and danced with some cute guy. He was in a nice suit and nice fedora. I'm a sucker for fedoras. It's super hipster. The guy's name was Clyde—and he looked really super familiar. Ultra familiar. That sucker could dance like you wouldn't know! I had a real good time.

So anyway, we danced and the A-hole comes up, after getting all slobbered on by two beezies, and he literally slams his fist into the guy's face.

(Mind you, this guy, Clyde, he bought everyone in the entire bar a round of shots. So you know he had moola. I was all about it. I'm not a gold digger, but yeah, money is definitely an additive to my attraction. Which Russell really doesn't have, even though he *says* he has.)

I'll just end it here. Russ pretty much got his butt beat by Clyde's friends and I was saying "Stop, baby!" at Russell when I did see him hit Clyde. Russ got it pretty good. Friends slung him over their shoulders and walked him out. I just walked home, all the way from Clematis to City Place, which isn't *too* bad. But if you're a ■■■■ ■■■■ ■■■, ■■■■ ■ ■■■, you'd *know* ■■■ ■■ ■■ ■■ ■■■.

As I passed Muvico, what was weird, I saw Clyde behind some bushes and his friend sort of speeding and parking near the sidewalk. Clyde looked like he was running. His suit was all messed up. But yeah, from that moment, looking at them driving off, I decided not to mess with egotistical thugs anymore. So that meant Russell. And that's the story of our breakup.

July, 17th, 5:54 p.m.

The antics around this place are silly. I don't want to say the company I work for, because it's probably unneeded, but it's not Cigna—*that's* for sure. The drama is silly, like I said. These people are ~~19 to 25~~ 17 to 45 years old, and all of them act like this is high school. They treat this place like it's their life, and even I just noticed this and I've not even been here a month. I hope I don't turn into these mother-F'ers.

Russell is continuing not to speak to me, so I'm just like whatever, minding my own. Sherry keeps asking if I need help and it's getting really hard to say no because I do. I'm already at budget so it's not a big deal, I guess. If I mess up on a call, oh well, no skin off my bone.

Sometimes I wish I was a movie star so that way I could be a lovely princess inside a big castle and have butlers and servants, but yeah, I shouldn't go on dreaming about it because dreams never come true.

At lunchtime, I was in the break room, pretty much alone, and I got out my Campbell's Split-Pea Soup™ and got it all heated up. When I turned around, though, hot bowl of soup in hand, I saw these groups of guys sitting and they were all peeking over at me with really messed up grins and were whispering. I'll bet they were talking about sex.

But anyways, I sat down and started to eat my soup. It was good but nothing too great. But then, get this: Sherry comes up being all happy and she sits down next me. She started talking with me.

"Sal! What's up, my golden goose!"

"Just eating soup. Can I help you?"

"Want company?"

I hesitated. "Uh . . . Sure, I guess."

She sat down and wouldn't keep her eyes off me. This would be a good time to have an actual smartphone to browse on the internet, but I'm working at a crap job so no, not happening.

"So how are you likin' the place?" Sherry asked me. "I mean, the group seems to like you. Everyone is saying nice things."

"Yeah. Only to your face."

"Beg your pardon?"

"Oh nothing. Don't worry about it. It's nothing."

Sherry squinted. "Something buggin' you, Sal? You seem upset."

"Just worried about money, is all." I really was trippin', too—no lie on that one. I just wanted her to scram. I hate this lady.

So yeah, she goes, "The money will come. I promise. It's easy to do this job—you just havta focus hard."

"It's also other things."

"Well tell me. I can try and help."

"What do you think of Russell?" I asked.

She answers like, "Russ? He's, well, sort of pretentious in a way." Then she started to laugh. "Woo! I mean, he's just controlling."

I grinned. "Oh! trust me! I know," I told her. "Me and him used to date."

"No kidding? Holy smokes. We only have one lead and he's carrying you. I have to make sure there's no conflict of interest."

"Well, I mean, we *used* to date," I emphasized, looking down at my bowl that was then empty.

"You sure you don't want me to get you out of his hands, Sal? I could."

"I know you could. I know. But he's just, I don't know, a total jerk," I said. "He and I butt heads."

"Well for sure I'm moving your seats—Hey wait! Is *that* why you were not asking so many questions?"

I shrugged.

"Because if it is—as your manager—I'll make sure he doesn't make you uncomfortable. I'll sit you next to another girl that's in the group. She's not a lead but she can help you."

I said thanks and the next thing I knew, lunch was over. Bam! Done. Blink of an eye.

So Sherry kept to her word and moved me. It's not such a big deal but the girl I'm sitting next to, Shelby, she's hilarious. She's also really hot. I think me and her will click. I can only hope.

July, 17th, 5:54 p.m.

The days are swinging on by . . . I can't help myself. The weekends are probably the worst part because I can't do jack *spit*. I went on Facebook, though, like I never do, and basically I had endless amounts of friend requests and messages from weird men. They always say dumb compliments like the next guy down from their message. Pretty much it's sad. It's pathetic actually. Some guys actually message me dozens of times. I never respond back to any, any, *any* of them. Never. I'm a beezy but I'm also not F'ed. For example, if a guy hits on me, I'll literally reject him—I don't give an F. I'll tell him, also, what he's doing wrong. Some guys have no clue what we want, ladies—you really got to pay attention to those little details. I read them so dang much. If you actually research body language you can really find out about your romantic interest a lot quicker. There's too many signs to say ~~which~~ what, but I can assure you, it works wonders. You can sift through the fakes from the gold stars.

July, 18th, 7:30 p.m.

I love Shelby. She's the bomb-diggity. She told me so much. Basically she said that she wants to chill with me at lunch and I totally said yes. The thing about Shelby, she quit her previous job at a hookah bar down on Clematis. I've never been inside but I heard about it. Well, anyway, I'll just put the conversation here:

"What it do, Sally-baby!" Shelby said with her highest voice possible, staring at me when she got to our table we chose in the break room.

"I'm doing okay, I guess." I shrugged. "Nothing too bad."

"Whatcha eattin'?"

"Hot Pocket."

"*Ew!* Gross!"

I laughed, then said, "*Whelp!* you're not the beezy who hasta eat it, now do ya?"

"Don't push me, Smalls!" Shelby said.

We just laughed like you wouldn't believe. I'm telling you, girlie, she's my twin, or at least it feels like it.

"So, Sal, how you likin' it here all right? Pretty wild, huh?"

I said, "Getting the hang of a things, or the swing of things, but I don't know, it's weird. How long have you been here?"

Small-talk commenced!

She said, "I used to work at a hookah bar," and this is where the story comes into play, "but not until me and my now boyfriend found each other," she continued.

I told her, "Wow. What crazy spit."

"Crazy *spit?*"

"Yeah! Nobody ever gets it. Just roll with it," and I really meant it, too.

She was all, "But yeah, anyways, me and my boyfriend [who I can't remember the name of because I never remember names] met from him randomly coming over my house 'n' stuff."

"Really?" I wanted to know.

"Yeah. He came over and sort of confessed his love toward me. We spent the day together or whatever."

"I wish I had that!" I said. "That's too adorable!"

Shelby smiled. "I know. I love him. He's really special to me. But what's crazy is the whole day he was acting funny. I knew something was up."

Okay. Stop. At this point in the conversation, I just thought she was being the everyday-average broad that worries all day long, but she wasn't. "So what was up?" I asked.

"He wanted to kill himself at the end of the day. That's why he was confessing his love. He was going to end himself and he just wanted to say goodbye to a girl he really liked."

I said, "Christ. Wowie. Really?"

"Mhm," she nodded. "I thought it was sweet after all of it, but you could imagine the shock when he was on top of a building and stuff."

"He was a jumper?"

"Mhm. Yes. He was gonna jump. Cops and lots of people were there. They had a megaphone and I finally convinced him to not jump. He didn't —thank God—and we've just been inseparable ever since."

"That's nice," I said. "You b■ch," I thought about saying.

"Oh yeah, Sal. It is! But yeah, he goes to college and works a lot. I got the job here to make more cash. So yeah, this is me. Lame, huh?"

"You're not lame," I told her; "you're the bee's knees."

She smiled. "Thanks."

After a bit of a pause, I said, "So he wanted to kill himself, why?"

She goes, "Life, I guess."

"I can understand that. We should all three chill one of these days."

"I'd love that," Shelly said.

Then I said, ". . . Shelly."

And she goes, "Oh hush! My *grand*ma calls me that!"

I love Shelby.

July, 21st, 5:49 p.m.

The group is full of alkies. I'm dead-A serious. The good news, they all have invited me out to the bar. I don't know if I'll go because Mr. A-face is going. I hate Russ with a burning passion. He honestly thinks he knows everything, but he dang sure doesn't! Aside from that, I'm eating alone at lunch, now, pretty much. But there's this one guy always staring at me. He seems like a creeper but I'm really not too sure. You're never too sure with creepers nowadays.

July, 22nd, 5:34 p.m.

Days are all the same to me, now. Weekends, work-days—all the same. When a person asks me what I'm doing, it really doesn't matter. Everyday is a day to do something, in my book. I just wish people could understand such an idea.

I've been insanely tired, insanely bored, and insanely over-it, and I think people at my job are noticing. Shelby especially. She keeps asking me about myself during break and lunch. Heck, even Sherry joins in. They tend to look at me funny when I give answers. Like they aren't correct.

It's like, yeah, opinions are a test and really, the opinion has to be correct for people. People want other people to agree, but not I! I could give a dang. Aside from all that, tonight I'm going out with the group. I hope they don't influence me too, *too* bad. Know what I mean?

July, 22nd, 11:14 p.m.

I'm drunk as ell riting thiz. I ho you understand it. I hop i remember. F̶ ̶k̶ ̶y̶o̶u̶! SALLY! F̶ ̶K̶!²²

July, 23rd, 9:42 a.m.

Luckily today's my late day—I go in a 12 o'clock. I'm going to try and recall last night. So, pretty much Shelby, Russ, Sherry, the entire group, they all kept buying me drink after drink after drink. I had everything. I feel like they wanted to see little ole Sally-cakes drunk as a skunk on wheels.

On top of Russell's table, yeah, "ay! guys!" shouted Crunk Sally, "him een diss guy, meaning I"—point, point, downward—"used to date!" and Russell cracks up; everyone, too.

A person goes, "Oh yeah?"

"Precisely!" I wise-cracked. "He also has a little wee-wee!"

From there, Russell went, "Sit down, Sally. You're making a ▮▮ing *fool* of yourself. Come on, now. Sit, sit," and he was tugging all up on my pant-leg.

"NO!" I was acting like a little kid. "NEVER! Na-na! You can't catch me!" I lil'-kid'd. Then I hopped down off the table anyway and started dancing toward whomever.

I heard "What a dumb b▮ ch," all behind me, but I didn't care! I was straight-up on a roll. I was clapping my hands around and giving random guys hugs. They didn't care. They were all grinning. Some were really following me. I guess when a cute drunk girl gives you hugs and kisses,

---

²² — I didn't block the cursing out naturally. So I crossed them out. Sorry if it's offensive.

you think she wants you, but no, *not* actual. Really it means she's just excited, is all. Or at least that's what *we* think about.

But never mind that. I was all giggin'[23] around, trying to have a good time, when all of the sudden, some b■ch in a bright-blue skirt comes up behind me and pushes me.

"Slut!"

So I turn around, naturally, and get this: it's Tessa.

"Hey!" is the first thing I say, next to her, near her, trying to not shout as much from all the noises. I guess I thought she was pissed at me when she said the "Slut!" part. When you're drunk, all things seem hateful.

"Sally-baby!" Tess gave me a big, big hug, all tight or whatever. "I didn't know you went here!"

"As if!" I said. "—Say! You want a brewski! I'm buyin'!"

"I saw Russell over there," she all reminds me. "He looks *pissed.*"

"Heck yes! I told everyone he has a small d■k!"

"Serves him right, the f■khead!"

I just love her. Really, I do.

So I go, "You want that beer, or no?"

"No, Sal. Just get home safe. Don't f■k anybody tonight. Keep it in your pants!" and she winks.

"But, Tess! I'mma vir—"

"NO! Like I said, keep. It. In. Your. F'ing. Pants!"

I just laugh. "Cya, b■ch."

"Cya, s■t!" she says back, and then she goes off wherever.

So I turn back around to, you know, dance or whatever, and the moment I do, some guy is all there.

"Wanna dance?" he says, but he was all, like, saying it like demanding.

So I go, "Ew. Gross. Hell to the mother■ no!" and then I turn back around. But this guy sort of stops me.

"You have no choice," and then he spins me and starts grabbing my hands or whatever.

I told him, "F■K OFF!" and everyone started looking at us.

---

[23] — "Gigging." It means, like, dancing a fool.

140

"Hey, hey, hey. Woah. No trouble," he said. "Just thought you wanted to dance."

"Well, I didn't. Now beat it, f▇." I really said f▇. That's so not like me. I *love* gay people.

He huffs, "B▇ch," and then walks off.

I'm a human repellant. You tell somebody I'm coming around, they all run like flies from a buzz zapper. Except, they don't actually come. I don't know what I'm saying. Maybe I'm still drunk.

So yeah, anyways, I stop dancing like a fool after about five seconds, and then go back to my group. Sherry's all there with Jeff or whatever, and Jeff is fired up to see me.

"Sally? That you? Wow!"

You got to understand, this guy, Jeff, never, ever talked to me after he and his wife saw me on the PalmTran. The guy just never did. I swear. Weirdest thing, ever.

So I go, "Yup," and just turn to Sherry, and "Sherr-bear!" is what I go ahead and say!

"Sally! You drunk? Oh wow!" Her eyes got all big. "You look loaded! Here. You want some of my water." She hands her glass over to me. Mind you, they are sitting and I'm at the edge of their table, standing.

I wave my hand. "Nah. I'm good."

"You sure?"

"Positive. Affirmative, commander!"

They both laugh, Sherry and Jeff.

Jeff goes, "Well, hey, Sally. Sherry tells me a lot about you. She says you started working at ▇▇▇▇[24]. That true?"

"Yes! I hate it!"

He laughs. "Why's that?"

So I turn to Sherry, saying, "Do you know this guy?"

She just squints, confusingly, like you wouldn't believe. "Sally. This is my husband. You remember him, don't you?"

I laughed. "See you two. Ciao!" and I walked all away, away, away.

---

[24] — Don't want to say my company I work for's name. *Shhh!*

Two feet away, pretty much, I see Shelby with her boyfriend. Him and her look like the type of couple you see in movies or novels, the type you *dream* about, the type you F'ing wish about, God▮▮ it! When drunk like that, mind you, I get mad. But what's weird, I'm mad now, too.

" 'Ello!" I annoy'd toward Shelby and her boyfriend. "How's *you* two . . . ?"

He goes, "What?" very briefly.

"Sal!" Shelby goes, "this is _____, my boyfriend I told you about!" (I can't remember the guy's name, dang-it!)

I held my hand out, but like a slump a▮hole.

"AY, _____!"

"Hello," he said, then shook. "Sally. Good ole Sally. Shelby keeps bragging about you."

"No! *She* keeps bragging about *you*," I corrected. "She told me the story that you two were on the" (she was waving her hands behind him, as if to tell me "No! Don't go there, Sally-baby," but I ignored it anyway) "—I mean, *she* was on the ground, and you were on a roof, and—"

"You told 'er that, babe?" _____ interrupted, looking directly at Shelby.

She's all, ". . . well . . . um . . ."

And I say, "Yeah! It's sweet!"

"Sal—can I call you 'Sal'?"—he gestures for me to nod, and I did— " 'Kay, cool. Sal, it was a very bad time for me, when I did that, so . . ."

Okay, listen. I'm all drunk right then, so I had no—repeat, *no*—clue what the F he was sayin', right then. Nothing. He just kept talking and talking, but then he goes:

"Did I have a hard time? Yes. Did it suck? Yes. Did cops come and I had to do a bunch of bull▮▮ that I didn't want? Yes, and yes. But I'm telling you, Sally, you're going to feel all right. Tellin' ya."

Apparently I said something that made him say that. Not too sure what. I'm sure I'll find out today.

"Yeah, yeah, sure, sure, amigo. Step aside," I said, sort of pushing on through people.

As I was perfectly centered around the fat crowd of my group, beer down my shirt, high-fashion mini-skirt on, face glistening with sweat and, more than likely, Dos Equis, I shouted, "LET'S GET F▮KED UP! A-L-C-O-H-O-L!" I actually spelled it like an F'ing beezy!

That's when Russell, the fa▮y-est boy I know, came up behind me, grabbed me, and started sort of *pulling* me out wherever the hell . . .

"Sally! You've had enough!" He was dragging me and everything. "Come on!" (One dude almost stepped on in, weirdly, oddly. It was the dude I rejected. You know . . . the dance dude-guy.)

Long story short, Russell took me home, to my apartment (I told him where I live), and I was calling him nasty names. He was pissed, girlie. *Super* pissed. Boy, am I going to hear an earful today when I get to work. But yeah, it's almost 11 o'clock. I have to get ready for it. An hour is not a lot to get ready, especially for us girls. Tee-*hee*! I'm silly. A super silly goose!

July, 23rd, 9:30 p.m.

Didn't realize how hungover I was today. Gah-*lee*. It was murder. REDRUM! Tee-*hee*. I suffered through it, though. When I got there, everyone was all giggling and looking at me and whispering in each other's little areas or groups. I got all embarrassed because, honestly, when you know a person is talking about you, and you *know* it . . . um, yeah, it feels terrible. Russell was just staring at his computer and didn't look at me. That's whatever, but Shelby—oh man, the craziest thing—Shelby told me, at break-time, that I was drunk and telling her boyfriend about my suicidal thoughts I've been having, right there at the club or bar last night. That's why he gave the advice. Totally weird, right? I didn't even remember this. Apparently I said it clear as day, Shelby said, and I meant it, too. Should I be worried, Future Sally? I mean, yeah, I should be because that means—Oh spit, that means *you'll* be gone! That means . . . *Oh dear!* That means I'm alone when I write this. Crap! I don't want to be alone. *Crap!* My anxiety is through the roof right now while I write this bull. I'm going to lie down or something. Sorry.

July, 24th, 4:12 a.m.

It's hard for me to hit the hay. Right now, as I'm writing this, what I'm doing, I pretty much am laying down in my bed, bored out of my mind, and I'm writing this all down with both my legs hanging hella off the bed, literally touching the ground. I'm scared right now because so many things are on my mind. Oh, and also, the light from my night-light is bright enough to make me see my paper—that's how I can do it. But anyways, the two things on my mind. Ready? Okay. This night-light is not typical. Basically it pulses this *wooooo-woooweeeeeee-wooooooo*-ing bulb and I kept staring at it shortly before indulging in this fine piece of bullspit. What I keep thinking is this: When I'm older, an old hag, the old hag Sally, am I going to remember this on my deathbed? It shouldn't freak me out so much, but it does. The idea that I'm immortal sort of scares me ▮less. Like, if I go my entire life, I'm going to keep looking at the past as a sort of series of events, not the actual life itself. Pretty much I'm thinking that right now, the present, is sort of passing me by, second after second after second, and I can't control it. It's like somebody is pushing me constantly in one direction and I'm saying, No, stop, please. Don't. It sucks because once I have all those wrinkles, I'll just remember all these times staring at this light-bulb and saying to myself, you're right, Sally. It was all a game. I'm just afraid that I'm too smart, or either too dumb, to follow everyday life like a normal human-being. I need sleep. Bye.

July, 29th, 7:30 p.m.

Basically everything is bottling up, I told Shelby. Basically it's all one big waste of time, this life. I want this to go away.

Shelby was calm as rain.

"Sally?"

"—and I am sick of it. I hate it. I don't like it."

"But Sally, you—"

"*And* it's all a scam."

"Sally!"

I finally looked up. "What?"

"You going to finish your soup?"

I looked down at it and said, "F the F'ing soup," and I tossed it, and it smashed, and everyone was looking at me in the break room.

"Jesus . . ." said Shelby, shaking her lovely little head. "What's your deal? You pickin' that up?"

"No," I told her. "I'm just over it. Russell is pissing me the heck off."

"What's he saying?"

"He's saying nothing, and that's the problem!"

"Do you still have feelings for him?"

Just then, pretty much Sherry comes up and says, "Hey, hey, hey!" like we're—or, sorry—I'M into being all excited or whatever.

She sits down next to me, close as hell. "Shelby. Sally. You guys eat anything. Oh CRAP! Why's this—Who made this mess on the ground?" As she was stepping around it, I heard cracking of glass.

"It was me," I said.

"Well, are you gonna pick it up?"

"Nope." I said it insanely matter-of-fact.

"Why not? You have to!"

"Keep the janitor guessing . . ."

Sherry looked at Shelby and, with me imagining that they were laughing, they didn't.

Shelby's like, "That's messed up," and Sherry's all, "You better pick this up. I can't let you do that, Sal."

So I got up, walked out the doors of break room, and went back to my desk, pissed and probably embarrassed.

That was my first write-up, and probably not my last.

Coming back from that gosh-darn conference room, the "hell room," I immediately went to the bathroom because of how pissed I was.

I sat in that toilet for about, uh, fifteen, sixteen minutes or so. I was on my phone or whatever.

Anyway, I got up, pulled up my crappy Macy's poka-dot panties with a tiny blood stain in the front that I should throw out, and my pants, too, which are ripped like crazy and totally an HR issue, and I walked out of the stall.

This b⬛ch—*ooooOoooo*, this b⬛ch—she was washing her filthy hands at the sink. This fat b⬛ch. Big ole booty. She turns around as I leave and says, "Aren't you going to wash your hands?! Gross!"

I didn't even *know* the b⬛ch, and yet, still tryin' me.

"I don't have to," I said; "I didn't really have to go. I didn't touch anything. Just my pants—and mind your bizz-nat."

"Still!" she said, sort of like she was better than me, even though I'm oh so much hotter than *her*. "You still got to wash! It's company policy! I don't care *how* close you were. If you're a foot near your privates, wash your hands," she emphasized. "Please."

If I hadn't been in trouble already, with, you know, the pin and all, you could bet I would have done this: I would have had my hand over my crotch, about two inches away, "and oh my!" I would've said; "do I have to wash them *now?*" f%#$ing with her! and then this beezy would've *told* or whatever, and I would be in more deep doo-doo.

So I went ahead and said, in my nicest, most pleasant voice, "I'll get on that, stat," and walked around her, about a mile around her (because of how fat she was), and washed my already-clean-ass hands.

I left, just then.

The b⬛ch is so fat her belt-size is "Equator!" *Ha!* I just *love* Eddie Murphy. Love him.

August, 11th, 5:16 p.m.

I'm sorry. I just want to vent a little bit. It's been awhile since I last wrote. I know I'm always saying I'm busy, just like everyone in the god-dang planet, but I'm serious—I am! Okay. Ready? You know, for the rant? Okay. I want to talk about Russell. I know I've been talking about him a lot and strangely, I probably do still like him. But I don't really have a clue why that is. I mean, the guy is a pretty-boy. He's actually nothing like my type. Remember, I like hipsters. Russell is just so . . . how can I say it? He's a "basic bch." That's the only way. The guy literally will buy Axe from friggin' Walmart, use it, and pretend like it's cool or something; and, on top of *that*, the guy makes the big bucks at the collection agency. I make around 9 bucks an hour. He makes about 11. 11's dope, but 9's like bum-status. He kills it on the phone, but it's probably because he's cheating. I'll probably watch and see what he does once I get used to the system more. We'll see.

August, 16th, 10:10 p.m.

I actually decided to go ahead and cook something tonight. I made some home-made mac-and-cheese. It was bomb as fork. Basically I put the noodles into this pot, boiled them, drained them, and then loaded them with butter. After that, Velveeda cheese galore! I drenched that hoe. Seriously. I ate it like crazy, too.

Today, though, oh man, today was really cool! You see, over my cubical is another directory. It's the healthcare side. I work HCA accounts; they pretty much work clients that, um, rent out rental equipment. Like crutches, things like that. Oh man! So much to say!

So there's this guy named Jeremy. He's smart as heck. Smarter than me (not saying much)! and this guy was telling me all the messed up crap healthcare does. Not within are agency but they themselves doing stuff.

So anyway, Jeremy is smacking his keyboard around, all huffing and puffing, and my desk was shaking, so of course I said something.

"Could you not *do* that? Please? It's messing me up." I said it real stern and probably, *boom!* condescending.

"Oh! I'm sorry, dude. It's just these people piss me off. I fking hate Aa."

I asked what it was; and don't worry, because I didn't know either.

"It's hell is what it is," he said. "If you believe in God, and you believe that there's a Heaven and a Hell, Hell is most certainly in an Aa call center."

I laughed like hell, girl. It was his delivery! Priceless!

"Oh man!" I said to him, "why's all that?"

"They are geniuses. Okay, so. They created this pool—it's genius. What they do, they set their customers up with accounts, all that normal crap, and then the freaking people ask them, "Hey, could you take your equipment back? I can't—"

"Wait. Why?" I asked.

"Why what?"

"Why in the world would they want equipment and then not?"

"You didn't let me finish. They ask the place if they could take it back because they couldn't afford it."

"Oooooh," I said. "Continue."

"So anyway, they immediately send them to collections after, is what I'm told by a majority of these people."

"That's F'ed!"

"I know, man. And the thing of it is is that (a) These people truly can't afford your crap, and are genuinely telling you they can't pay for it, and (b) A███a created this pool that one person works—*one* person works—for three measly hours a day."

"Holy . . ." I was surprised.

"Yeah. So these people call in, pissed, because collection agency after collection agency calls them—new ones, every few months—and these people keep saying, 'I already paid.' So yeah, we tell them, 'Whelp! ma'am or sir, looks like you didn't pay it.' "

"So basically they are paying dozens of times," I guessed.

"Correct," lil' Jeremy said. "Right you are. So it could take up to a *year* for this account to be updated as paid. So that means I guess s██t posted, like, months after someone pays me."

"Jesus . . ."

"I've kept a hot in my route for nine months one time until it finally posted into my number."

"A Lion in your Number," I said.

"What?" he said. "—Hey, what's your name?"

"Sally."

"Cool. My name is Jay. Short for 'Jeremy.' "

"I like 'Jeremy' better," I said.

And he goes, "My mother is the only one that calls me that," and then he flirts by saying, "But you can call me that, if you want, doll."

Doll. Jesus. Wowie zowie. I can't believe . . . But whatever, that was how I met Jay. Only thing interesting today.

August, 22nd, 12:10 p.m.

Miami! The big M.I.A.! Shelby invited me this weekend. I'm so excited! I love Miami. Shelby was saying how there's a band that's down there called Roots Shakedown. I've never heard of them, but hey! life's about experiencing, right?!

August, 23rd, 10:31 p.m.

Just got a call from Shelby. She's telling me that at 4 that's when she'll pick me up. I'm excited, but I don't know, I'm also scared! I haven't ever been to Miami. Over 22 years and haven't been to it. I hear that when you go to Miami, you go through some crazy, crazy spit. I hear that it's like an adventure. I can't wait.

August, 24th, 4:14 p.m.

I woke up this morning with my throat completely sore and the balls of my ankles F'ed. I remember everything but I'm not sure what the hell happened to make me feel so crappy. So you *know* you had a good night!

So at 4:15 I call Shelby, and yeah:

"Hey, Shelby. You comin'?"

"Yeah. We're on our way."

"We're?"

"Yeah. Me and ____, and another chick, Tessa."

"Tess?"

No . . . F'ing . . . way!

So I go, "What Tessa? *Who?*"

"Noodel. Her."

"Oh god. She's my homie!"

"You guys cool?"

"Oh yes, she's just . . . well, you know . . ."

Shelby laughs. "I know. Well, get dressed. We're almost there. I got the address you sent me and my iPhone says ten more minutes until your place."

"Awesome," and then I hung up.

So I was about to put my socks on, but *ew!* my feet were dirty! I was checking the mail because my Sissy sent me some make-up in the mail. So my feet were super dirty but I was too lazy to take a shower. So I wiped off my feet with a friggin' napkin and then put on socks, shoes, pants, and a tank-top. My boobs looked too big, so I put a sweater on over whatever.

They came, blah blah blah. We stopped at a gas station, got some beer, whatever, and drove on. The highway was smooth. I didn't talk much, but Tessa, on the other newer hand, was talkin' up a storm! She was talking about how she takes Adderall and how she smokes weed a lot now and has "anxiety" and she can't *wait* to try the free beer.

I just ignored it. I know how she can get.

So anyway, we get into Miami and Shelby and her boyfriend start jabbering about how she missed the parking at "The Door," which is where this band we're about to see is playing. Shelby turns around and finally parks.

The moment she steps out, some guy tells her that the parking is ten dollars. Only, the guy just says, "Ten dollars." After she pays him, the guy walks off.

Tessa goes, "Did you know that sometimes bums act like the parking guys just to take your money?"

And Shelby goes, "Oh Jesus. Really?"

And Tessa says, "Yeah, but that guy had the venue's shirt on, so I think it was legit."

"Better be," I said.

So then all of us start lollygagging around, with nothing to do really, and Tessa gets out her cigarettes and starts smoking up a storm. I don't smoke, see, so it makes me irritated in some ways.

Shelby asks me, "Hey, you got ten bucks for the entry?"

I go, "No."

"That Seven-Eleven over there has an ATM," Tessa suggests.

"Awesome. Let's go," Shelby says, and we all start running across the street.

"Tag! You're it!" Tessa says, tagging me, cigarette in her mouth, sprinting.

~~I care about a few things that~~ I didn't really care. I was just walking. Some guys honked at me and said, "Woo! Look at that fine piece of a▇!" ~~I wanted to kill them.~~

So we finally get to the Seven-Eleven and Shelby goes, "I look terrible. Everyone at The Door looks so rad and I'm just plain."

I reminded her that basically she isn't plain and she just needs new threads. So we go up to some hat display and I tell her to try on the goofiest-looking hat there.

"No way!" she says, and then she tries it on and her and her boyfriend laugh at it.

I just mind my business and walk passed aisles and go the ATM. At first, it didn't bring up the option for cash and I thought it was fake for a second but then realized I didn't press in my PIN. So I do and get twenty bucks. Then I walk over to Shelby and ask her if she has any change. She takes the twenty and gives me two fives and then gives me a ticket.

Apparently she was one of the people advertising and handling the tickets. Which makes no sense because I could have gotten it for free, in essence.

So we go back to The Door and pretty much Tessa is talking about how her friend is down at some brewery and can get her free beers. This was how she could get the free beers. I thought it was bullspit, but yeah, apparently some things in life *are* in fact free.

After bickering on how Shelby and her boyfriend aren't hungry and how they are lame, and how they suck, and how, woo woo woo, they are "party-fouls," Tessa and I embark on our very own journey.

Tessa is just rambling. She was talking about things that I pretty much had no interest in. She was talking about bands and how they suck or are cool, whatever. So I was listening, but you know, also not? Yeah. That. But anyway, we finally get to some vintage store and I got all giddy.

"Let's go in there!"

So we do and we see a bunch of treasures here and there. We check out the records and basically sift through piles and piles of this stuff. The first thing Tessa sees is an album by T-Rex. She said she has to have it, and calls dibs. I didn't care, like I said. But then we saw Tom Waits, Fleetwood Mac, a first album of Stevie Nicks that was about a dollar and probably worth a fortune, and some other stuff like a Star Wars soundtrack from the '70s.

As we get out, Tessa sees some keyboard and starts freaking out because it's the same keyboard that Radiohead uses. She wants to buy it but then sees that there's a "Rental Only" sign on it, and she says, "Screw them!" and starts playing it. Me, though, I was playing a Sega for a bit because I saw some kid get off of it. Sonic the Hedgehog was on that hoe, so I played it and it was hella fun.

So blah, blah, blah, we get out of there, go into the head shop a door down and the first thing the owner says is "Buy something!" so we left.

A bum that smelled funny and had a guitar around her came up to Tessa and started to talk to us. The bum was a female, though, and she was showing us her guitar and how it makes her money, "a ton of money," she said. And she told us how she has to get to Kansas City and go back home because she's a tattoo artist and lost her portfolio and she needs to go back and re-up on some supplies. Tessa grabs her guitar and plays it smoothly. At first, playing "Loving You," by Minnie Riperton. She was saying how it would be funny to go up to randoms and sing it in their ears to freak them out.

The bum laughs and tells us her stage name is Gordo Pastrami. Tessa and me just laugh at how dumb that crap is and then Gordo tells us that this is her business card and hands us a cardboard rip-out with her stage name on it. She tells us to search it on Google. She tells us that in Austin, Texas, for South-by-Southwest, she made $1,400 in 4 days. We were shocked, needless to say, but then we asked her where the brewery we're heading at is, because Tessa didn't know where the hell *anything* was. Tessa likes to front.

"Go back to Malcolm X Dr.," Gordo said, "then take a left and go down four blocks and you'll see a red building: that's the brewery."

"Cool," Tessa said, and then reaches in her pocket and gives Gordo a dollar. She said thank-yous or whatever, and then Tessa and I just walked back because we passed Malcolm X Dr. already.

So after getting ask by two—count 'em two—bums if we would like to help a veteran out, and after Tessa said yes to them and I said no, and Tessa pays the guys each a quarter and the guys both stare me down, hard, we finally find the brewery ahead of us. We passed the door, though, because it wasn't the type of door that was out in the open. In fact, the brewery was almost in the middle of nowhere. Very many times did I tell Tessa that I think we're in the ghetto. She always laughed, though, for some odd reason. But we really were lost and Tessa decides to call her "Free Beer" friend up and he tells her that he's outside standing. So we turn around and he came out of some planter trees in front of the door, therefore making the place entirely hidden, and Tessa goes bunkers and skips on over to the guy.

After hellos were said to this guy, he shakes my hand and tells me his actual name is "Bunkers," which is odd, obviously, because I was just thinking that Tessa goes "Bunkers." I think Tessa is sleeping with the guy.

Anyway, we go inside and there's 4 people at a table and it's not like a bar or anything. It looks more like a meeting room but with wooden panels and sort of looking like a bar or pub. I don't say hi to everybody because it was too awkward for me. I hate people.

There was this secret door that Bunks took me and Tessa through. The first thing in this place/secret room, it was full of cubicles but under construction. Tessa asks Bunks what it's about and he tells her, "Office renovations," and that really we're not suppose to be in here.

Okay, so. We go in, yeah. Then we see a bunch of Donkey Kong barrels, the size of Texas, and I got all giddy. Never seen such things. So anyways, we go back there and there's these *huge* brewers all the way up to the ceiling, which seemed like two-stores high. I said a bunch of wows and everything because I genuinely was impressed.

So there's this place Bunkers led us to. It was probably the biggest freezer I ever did see. It was an alcoholic's dream. There were cases upon cases of beer of so many different varieties. But this beer wasn't name-brand stuff. This was Miami's finest beer, only sold in Miami. So Bunkers tells me this and asks, "What flavor do you like?"

I told him I like Blue Moon with an orange peel, so anything similar would be fine.

"I got just the thing," he said. "Here." And he pulls out this beer that was wheat-based but was also mixed with Grapefruit. I got super giddy, popped it open, sipped, said "*Ahhhh*," and thanked Bunkers for the lovely beer.

He told me thanks, too. Or no-problems, whichever the two. But yeah, we get out of there because it was too cold. So we go to this big dispenser and he poured another beer out for me and tells me to keep the glass. Heck yeah! I drank beer like crazy!

We go back through the secret door and I see this girl who looked really familiar. I told her she did and she tells me that she and I went to some AdvoCare meeting with Russell, and how he introduced us. She asked if we were still dating, and I totally turned around blatantly and didn't answer her. She said she was a Jesus-freak, too, later on in the night, so F her!

We all five walk, walk, walk back to The Door, drunk or buzzing, depending on how long you stayed at the brewery (which I was there for about 35 minutes), and crossed streets and stuff. I got a text from Shelby asking where I was and that the event starts fairly soon, around 10-ish. It was only 8 o'clock, mind you. So I told her I'd be there soon, and left it at that.

Our group got to The Door basically right about 5 minutes after I sent the text. When we got there, Shelby was all, "The show starts soon," and Tess was like, "Sally. I want to try the pizza down the street. Let's go there," and I go, "Okay," and Shelby goes, "You mean Serious Pizza?" "Yes," Tessa says. "It's awesome." "Be back at 10," Tessa "our mom" 'd. And we all just laughed at her crazy a██.

We walked down the street and, with Shelby deciding to come along, we all three got asked by 4 bums if we had any money. We all said we didn't have anything. And then they all told us that we were the most beautiful things they ever did see. And Tessa told them all, "Wish I could say the same." Wow. What a cunt.

So we finally are coming up close to Serious Pizza when, get this: Gordo Pastrami, in just her underwear and taped nipples. Black tape! That's it. Shelby goes, "Look at this retard," and Tessa and I just say that we know her and that we have to try and pass her without her knowing. Tessa grabbed a cone and put it over her head, and I put my shades on . . . at night, mind you.

And as we were walked up, I was singing Corey Hart's "Sunglasses At Night," and laughing my A off.

"Howdy!" Gordo says. "Why, if it isn't the two most-lovely ladies strolling on through. Tessa, why are you being a cone head! [and Tessa was laughing] and you! *Sally!* Sunglasses at night?" and she sung the song, too! [I laughed like hell.] "Why are you guys here?" Gordo asked. "And who's this?"

"This is Shelby," I answered. "And we are going to Serious Pizza."

"Could you get me a water? Gosh! I'm sweaty as all heck."

"Sure," I told her. "It'll be a sec, though. Is that cool?"

"Take your time. And Tessa?"

"Yeah, Gordie?"

"You got to check this one out." And just when Gordo said that, she turns around and everyone gets all silent. Some guy walks by and Gordo goes, "—Hey! Ever seen a Texas Rattlesnake? [The guy looked confused as hell as he was walking passed us, but he was looking right at Gordo.] — Here!" and she humps the air and you could hear some maraca sound! Too, *too* funny! [The guy laughed as he passed.]

"How?" Tessa said, excited.

Gordo goes, "Look," and she pulls out this plastic ball from her panties and shakes it and it makes the sound. "Works every time," she said to us. "But yeah, get me water, please, if you guys could."

We nodded and walked passed.

The line was terrible. It was all the way to the door. Everyone was eating, and pizza was everywhere: on the ground, on the ceiling, probably even on the roof. I don't know. So we waited in line. The whole time, though, Tessa would not . . . shut . . . the F . . . *up!* I swear! There was one chick at register and she was taking calls and taking orders. The people behind us kept saying that this is ridiculous every minute or so and annoying the F out of me.

Dude, we literally were waiting longer than I ever waited in an F'ing line. Longer than a dang Disney line. I was over-it, and 10 o'clock was looming toward us. Literally it was 9:30 and we *still* didn't even order yet.

Finally, thank Jesus, we got there. This chick that was there was stressed—you could tell—but still was truckin' away.

Tessa ordered a pep with a Corona. Shelby was next and she order and pep and some water. When it was my turn, a call came up and the register chick was all, "One second," picking up the phone. Then she told the guy on the other end, "Placing you on hold," simply, and took my order: a pep, a glass-bottle Coke, and a bottle of water. She gave us all a number.

We went outside and gave Gordo the water and it was taking dang near ages for the food to actually happen. But no matter. We watched Gordo work her magic on these three fatty men. One of them had a birthday. So Gordo sang "Happy Birthday," with her own twist to it—I don't know what—and they were all smiling and laughing and getting a real kick out of her.

One of them told her that she has to do yoga—like a yoga pose—if she wants their money. She shrugged and smiled and nodded and said all right. The three dudes went up to her and did poses and everything. Then one of them stops and takes a picture of Gordo, the birthday boy, and their friend, I guess. Gordo, she is so confident! I swear it. I wish I could look that silly and get away with it. I'll bet she gets into fights all the time, though. I'm jealous.

So anyway, it was seriously 5 minutes till 10 o'clock and Tessa was getting ants in her pants. We were at the line and everything. Tessa says she's leaving and can't wait any longer and she does in fact leave.

Me and Shelby wait for another 4 minutes and our slices come out.

The guy asks where's the other girl and we tell him that she left and he says if she wants her pizza she has to come in with us[25] later.

We walk all the way back to The Door and no bums asks us for money, oddly, as we eat our huge friggin' 'zas.

We get in and Shelby sees her boyfriend and he hands her a drink or whatever. I go up to the bar but realize I spent my ten dollars at Serious pizza, so basically the guy tells me cash only. I didn't drink anything. How lame.

The band takes a while to setup, but yeah, the lead singer guy was a hottie. Shelby told me that he was a serious hunk. But she also told me not to tell her boyfriend that, because he doesn't like the guy. I said that's psycho spit, but whatever.

The band's songs were really great, but what stood out the most for me was their second song. It had a bunch of pauses and fast-pace sounds and they sounded crazily reggae. I loved it. They're my new favorite band.

The lead's mic, though, was lowering or whatever, so Tessa goes up at the front and holds his mic up and he finishes his last two songs with her holding his mic up right from the stages ground[26].

So we leave the place and outside, there were these people making the most bomb briskets ever. These black people. They were saying that the food was for support toward legalizing Marijuana. Pretty wild. ~~It had nothing to do with weed, though.~~

After mingling in the parking lot with everyone, our entire group, plus others, decided to go to Steak'n'shake.

Tessa, Shelby, her boyfriend, and I, we all drove down there, got lost briefly, and then found it.

Everyone was there. All Tessa's friends she met, all Shelby's friends, her boyfriend's friends, everyone was sitting down and everything. But I didn't have any new friends. I got pretty bummed about that. Then again, I never try.

---

[25] — She never did, though. She totally forgot by the end of the concert. So basically she wasted ten bucks. So apparently this type of thing happens quite often.

[26] — I later found out that her and the guy were dating.

I don't even know what to say that happened at Steak'n'Shake. It's all a blur to me. I keep having this crazy anxiety happen to me. The food was terrible there. Sissy Dukes told me it was better, back whenever. I should have listen to her advice and just ordered just a shake and nothing else. Oh well. The anxiety was terrible, though. I was gone. I kept rocking back and forth and I kept thinking really bizarre thoughts and I was unconvinced things were real.

I got up and simply just left the table and didn't listen to anybody speaking to me. I walked out on my tab and just said F it. I didn't even care. All I knew was that I was unhappy. I was unhappy with everything and I dang-near cried.

Tessa came out and said how lame it was that I left the place. Shelby did, too. Her boyfriend was just sort of not speaking. We just go in the car, after, when they all paid faithfully. They were ordered to tell me to never come back to Steak'n'Shake directly from the manager because I got free food when I wasn't suppose to. I didn't care. Good riddance.

After Shelby took everyone home, because my house was so far away, her and I talked the ride back, all alone together. I laid down some pretty philosophical stuff. I was just saying how I feel. My anxiety was through the roof, but all I wanted was to be heard. That's all. That's all I wanted, see. I was talking about how I love to write and how, well, here, let me explain. I'm not going to include her side of the dialogue because it was mostly just agreeing and head-nodding type of stuff. Here:

"Shelby, it's just whack. This life freaks me out too much. I remember in high school I used to read so much fiction that it was unbelievable. I used to read Salinger, Faulkner, Haddon, Ellis, Shakespeare, all that bullcrap. I'm not a dumb-dumb like how everyone sees me. I actually want to be a somebody, but sometimes—*some*times—I'm always feeling like I'm going insane.

"Sometimes, I feel like Easy never is good. I'm addicted to Easy. I hate how things react within each other. It's never a fair game of cat-and-mouse. It's always a winner and a loser. In some ways, Shelby, I don't even know right from wrong.

"It's all an opinion. This right and wrong is purely just a fabrication of something larger. If you have a guy who murdered another guy's entire family, and you hear the victim's side of the story, almost always you'll hate the murderer and never hear *his* side.

"But what if you heard the murder's side and he told you that *his* entire family was killed by this guy, and that's why he killed his whole family, it would make you wonder.

"But then you got legal ideas floating around. You figure all the morals involved. But at the end of the day, it all boils down to proof. The proof's in the ~~pudding~~ puddin', as they say. If there's absolutely no proof of the victim killing the murderer's family, then I'm sorry, the murderer will lose every time.

"Right and wrong don't even make sense to me anymore. There's too many variations. I'm just sort of aimlessly going about this life and just seeing the next thing that comes up in front of me. I hate it, to be honest.

"The Now is never what it seems. Sometimes it's just your imagination playing tricks on you. I can say all day to grab the thing you want most, but at the end of the day it all matters on how you feel after you get it. Most of the time—all of the time—whenever I get the thing I want, I feel disappointed.

"I'm never fulfilled.

"Most of the time I feel like the past ~~disctates~~ dictates all your choices you make.

"There is no Free Will.

"There is only what you have encountered and what you will encounter. Every choice becomes a passing of past in disguise. It all is just an illusion. You don't have a choice because the choice you make is already made even before the choice was presented to you.

"You could say, 'I can choose yes or no if I want. I don't care.' But it's a lie because you already picked one even before you saw it. And it's because of impulses and past encounters with things you have past seen in this life. That's why Free Will is a joke, or not reality.

"If I was Hitler, for example, and I really and truly thought that the killing of Jews would be better for my country, and I convinced the entire nation to such depths that they themselves even agreed, then by all means, Captain, I'm going to think that what I'm doing is for the good.

"People who are evil have no idea what they are doing is evil. Nobody does evil on purpose. It's all two-sided. One person will always favor something over the other, by the choices, or past choices, seen.

"So if I, Hitler, die and go to the pearly gates for judgement, I'm going to say, 'All right! This is in the bag!' and then God tells me finally that what I did was wrong. Then it's all a paradox. I'm going to say, 'F off, God!' because He, to me, makes no sense.

"Imagine if everyone knew each other. . . . Oh gosh, that would be magical! Then you wouldn't be able to judge people. Like, for instance, a person choosing to be gay. Maybe that person picked it because it makes more sense to their feelings. Or maybe they got F'ed in the past by some psycho beezy and she changed the outlook of the guy so much so that he no longer chooses the P over the D.

"We don't know, but we judge anyway if it's not okay with how *we* feel. . . . F how we feel! That's such a one-sided thought.

"So I hope you see my point, Shelby, that people's rights and wrongs are so not black and white. It's the greyest possible thing ever.

"Look. Let's say humans go to Heaven and Hell. Humans'll naturally change those places, in essence, if we still have Free Will. We literally would turn Heaven and Hell both back into Earth. You'd say, 'Gosh, this place is warm,' and then turn on an AC unit in Hell.

"In Heaven you'll see a bunch of naked people who are all beautiful. Holy smokes. The lust around there must be insane! So then you got all these people partying in paradise and turning it back into Hell or Earth.

"God won't be able to control those amounts of lustful humans. We would have sex so much.

"My point is that humans are humans, nothing more. We turn anywhere we go into a place that benefits *us*, not the place itself.

"We come from Earth, which is the *only* place we got, and yet, we created bombs to destroy parts of the country that we hate. Just because of their choices and beliefs. You don't know what they been through.

"It's all a cycle.

"It's a cycle of right and wrong, and pretty much everything a human does is both right and wrong depending on the viewer.

"Shelby, darling, I wish I could make my own religion. But instead of trying to tell someone what is right and wrong, I simply would put the world in front of them, and make sure that they know how the world works before going into the choice.

"If you have *a* and *b*, and someone told you the pros and cons of both, you'd be able to choose which one is better for you. Companies and people tend to shy away from that ideal.

"What Christian wants you to read the Satanic Bible? What company wants you to know their hidden fees? What guy is going to tell you the truth before his lust?

"The idea is simple: if truth was all around us, we would be infinite beings.

"The choices should be throughly examined, without it being timed. But that's silly to think about, isn't it?

"Well, Shelby. I know you must be tired. Thanks for the ride, love. I hope everything is well with you. Be safe."

"Be safe, Sally," Shelby said. "You're the most deepest person I've ever met. And I love you."

I just laughed and shut her door.

And after spending all those hours talking with her in front of my house, well after she got there, my throat hurt me like crazy. I sacrificed my throat to get my message across. You win some, you lost some. Hopefully it goes away soon.

And this, Future Sally, the Reader, was my first time in the lovely, lovely Miami!

I hope nothing is weird tomorrow with me and Shelby. I hope what I said was acceptable. I never know anymore. But I can only hope so.

September, 1st, 12:10 p.m.

It's just my lunch break. I brought Journal along with me. People were looking at it and asking me what it is because it looks like a regular book. I'm hoping it looks like a journal and not a regular book, but oh well! what can I say? Besides, if I walk around pretending to hold a book and not really liking it, why would I continue with it? Very curious. Word of advice: if you hate a book, never read it all the way to the end. You'll just forget about it anyways, and the author will forget you, too. Trust me. The author doesn't care.

I'm talking nonsense. I wanted to say that things are pretty good in the office. I hit budget for the month of August. I forgot to write here that I got my first bonus check. It was pretty fat. It was over a thousand bucks. I'm happy with it. I want to make more. This new month is suppose to be good, they say. I just want to be successful.

Russell is pissing me off, though, as usual. He keeps doing these really shady things on the phone. I'll have to dig a little deeper into it, but I'll put it down here whenever I found out.

Okay. This is weird now. Some guy has been staring at me in the break room this whole time. Every time I look up I see him look down and grin. It's kind of cute but kind of weird, you know? Why won't the guy talk to me if he likes me? I never understood that about these really shy guys. But anywho, I'm going to eat my salad from McAlister's. Success!

September, 3rd, 12:23 p.m.

Dude, people get jelly around here quick. I'm getting payment after payment on the phone and people *stay* talkin' spit. I say whatever to that. It actually makes me mad, but still, nothing I can do about it. The people are sharks and jerks around here. The most ignorant people, ever, aside from Shelby, Jeremy, Sherry, et cetera. But yeah, people hate you when you get an inch of success. I think it's rather cute, see.

September, 10th, 6:30 a.m.

I want to talk about Sherry. She's lovely. What I found, though, was that she was from Africa. She met this guy Jeff online or whatever, in Africa; both of them were from there. They really hit it off and then they decided to move to the States. I have no idea why, though, but they do seem happy about that choice. I'm finding out all this stuff from lunch. Her and I and Shelby eat together all the time. We've been called the Trio of S's! It's pretty cute. I do love them. They are my girls. We always gossip about the craziest things, though.

"Hey, guys," Shelby says coming up to Sherry and I's table. "D'you here about the new dress-code policy?"

"Yeah," Sherry goes, "and don't think that just because I'm a sup [pronounced "Soup"] doesn't mean I agree with the crap that goes on around here."

"Ditto," I said.

Sherry turned to me. "*Ditto?*"

"Yeah. Duh."

"Sal, you act like you're a supervisor," and she laughs.

So, serious-like, almost wearily, though, in essence, I say, "I am, thank you very little."

"You're *far* from it!" and Sherry literally laughs again; and I think lil' miss Shelby joined in, too.

After a pause, I ask Sherry, "Have you ever seen a lion?"

She paused; but then, almost expectantly, she looks at Shelby and says, "So's you are going to college soon, yeah?"

Shelly smiles. "Oh yeah. I can't wait. I'll actually become a somebody."

"That's good, Shelby. That's good. I'm proud of you. What are you going to study?"

"Psychology."

"Oh? Wow! What a card! Congrats!"

"Thanks, Sherr-bear."

And they laugh.

I just felt left out, to be frank.

So I go, "Last night I had a dream that I could fly."

Sherry was about to say . . . something, but then, Shelby stops her. "I got this. Sally. Baby. You really gotta stop monopolizing the conversation. It's scary sometimes. You talk crazy. Talk about normal things."

"But I do. I swear I do."

"I never see you doing that."

"Didn't you say the other day that I'm 'the deepest person you've ever met,' or something?"

"Yes. I did. But you don't have to go around blabbing about nonsense. Why don't you talk about something *normal* for once."

"Guys, guys . . ." Sherry settles us down. "Enough. I don't want to hear you two fight. You're my best employees."

"We're not fighting, Sherr-bear. Right, Sally?"

I nod.

"Okay," Sherry says, "but remember, if you don't have anything nice to say, then *please* don't say it at all! Please. I beg it."

"I can't guarantee that," I admitted.

Sherry just gave me "The Look." "And *why not,* missy?" she asks. "I'm tired of your reluctance or whatever. Just learn to listen."

"What I mean is this: I can't guarantee that the things coming to and from my mouth'll be positive. It's unrealistic."

"Unrealistic to be positive?" Shelby says. "I can understand that but— Hey! Jeremy!"

I turn around and he's there. Right F'ing there, the tall bastard. I love him!

"Hey, three S's!" he goes.

" 'Ello, 'ello," I said, bouncing my eyebrows up and down.

"I'm not staying long, I just wanted to say what's up."

"Stay awhile!" said Sherry. "Over the bend and through the roof!"

"What?" Jeremy didn't get it; and I didn't either.

"Oh you guys are *lame-Os!*"

"No, you are, Sherr-bear," said Shelby, making fun of her old-ness.

"*Oh,* screw you, Shelly!"

And she laughs. "Don't call me that!"

And then I started laughing.

Jeremy goes, "You guys are so stupid," and he laughs. He meant it silly, not mean. "Whelp," he claps once like a total butthead, "on that note, bye!"

"Bye!" we all say, and he leaves, whatever.

"*So,*" I suddenly say, "where you guys living? We should plan a group party."

"Can't," Sherry says. "The company doesn't allow bosses to do that sort of thing."

"Really . . . ?"

"Mhm."

"Oh come on, Sher," Shelby says, laughing; "you and I *both* know that you don't listen to that bull."

"Yeah, and you even said you don't, you lil' butthead-face," I added.

"No. What I said was, I don't *agree*. Not listen, *agree*. And plus, it's probably best if we don't. I'm not a party-er."

"I heard different," I comment, scratching my eye.

"From who? Jeremy?"

"From, um, I Don't Know-land."

"Good. Jay is a son of a b■ch."

"Sherry! Shame on you! You cursed!" I was only kiddin'.

But she laughed, though, "but anyway," she said to me, "I have a newborn, now. I can't throw parties like that at my place."

"Parties are lame anyways."

"But you said—"

I held my hand up. "I know what I said." Then I stood up and did a curtsy. "Like, yeah, totally," I said.

"What are you talking about?" Shelby said. "You're weird. I swear to God you're weird."

I just start laughing. "So, Sherr-bear [mimicking Shelby], where are you from?"

"Why do you wanna know?"

"Because that's what friends are for!"

"Are you okay?" Shelby asked me. "You're acting strange."

"I'm fine! Where are you from, Sherr-bear?"

She goes, "Uh, Africa. That."

"Really?"

"No. I'm just saying that because I feel like it. Of course!"

"Why you got to say it like that?" I said. "I mean, really, why? I was just asking."

"You're being defensive for no reason," Shelby said. "Take a seat. You're scaring us."

"I wanna know more about Africa," I said. "Tell me . . . *now,*" I pretty much demanded. "Please, now. Tell me!"

"All right, Sally. Take it easy," Sherry said; "enough with the crap. Leave if you want, we don't care. We're just having a pleasant time with ourselves. But you're more than happy to join us when you get your act together."

"Ditto!" I said.

"What?" Shelby didn't get it.

"Ditto, *ditto!*" I was feeling euphoric. "Guys, I just want to know what Africa is like! Is that too much to ask?"

"Then *sit,*" said Sherry, tugging my dang arm back, trying to seat me. "Jesus. Everyone is looking. Just cool it, relax, take a seat. Gosh. I'll tell you about Africa.

"I'm from Uganda. It's a really great part of Africa. It's not what you're probably—"

"Is there safaris?" I interrupted.

"Yes. 'Course—it's Africa!"

"Oh okay. Is there nice people?"

"There's nice people everywhere, Sal," goes Shelby. "You just got to look for them."

"—and another thing about Africa," Sherry continued, "is that people there are more into saving, not spending. Like they won't just frivolous spend. I don't really get it, to be real with you" (she was scratching her eye) "but it is what it is. The people in America, for example, get paid but live like they have twice of whatever pay they have. They go out, drive fancy cars, spoil themselves. It's really weird."

"I know exactly what you mean," I said, nodding. I was also leaning more forward, investing. "I hate America. I hate Capitalism. It only favors the rich. Corporations have too much power."

"I agree," said Sherry, "but—"

"I'm out. Goodbye," Shelby said, grabbing her things.

The moment I was about to say a "Cya!" Sherry says, "Wait. Why? Is this boring?"

"Sally talks too much about politics. It makes me roll my eyes."

"Thanks for your support," I said.

"Don't mention it," and she skips away.

"*Any*ways," Sherry went on, "Africa is really great. I met Jeff there. What's crazy is he's white but when he got to America he picked up on some fake southern accent. It makes no sense.

"My accent is almost gone, though—as you can see. Sometimes when I talk to family, it comes back. It's really strange.

"But yeah, Africa. It's an amazing place."

"Isn't there genocide?" I asked. "I mean, I hear there is."

"It's a stereotype," Sherry said. "Not all of Africa is like that. Sort of like not all of America is full of rich fat people. That's the Africa stereotype."

"I want to visit Africa, Sherry."

"You *do?*"

"Yes."

"We should plan a visit!"

"I have no money."

"You will . . . you will. You just really gotta push for budget. I have faith in you."

"I hope so, Sherry. I really hope so," I sighed out. . . .

September, 13th, 8:20 p.m.

Sherry put something into my route[27] at work. It's this crazy insurance account. Pretty much the insurance company didn't pay on the claim because they were needing medical records. It's a half a million dollar account. If I get it, say, then I should get over 10,000 dollars! But that's

---

[27] — At work we have a thing called "Routes." It's pretty much our difference between each other. You have a hot, and it goes into your route. It's how the company knows that *you* collected on that specific account.

kind of far-fetched, because usually insurance pays way lower than the total hospital charge, and then the contractual adjustment[28] is added after that smaller payment. We'll see how it goes. . . . The thing about collections is that most people never answer their phones because they think we automatically are out to get them and just want you to pay. That's if you're just not paying an account that is all correct with billing, that we actually do that. But if there's an error, like this account Sherry gave me, then by God, I'm going to ask that we try to get this squared away without you spending a nickel or dime. Call me crazy, but I think it's fair! This lady's case, though, is that they are needing the medical records of the last 5 years, because they think she was a smoker without telling them; in which case they deny the claim. If you lie, you get F'ed in the butt. Big time. Swear it.

September, 15th, 5:11 p.m.

Need sleep, *bad*. I may crash after writing this. What I'm finding out, regretfully, is that everything in my life is not what I want to be doing, and what's more, Future Sally, you're the only real person I have left to talk to. Everyone else is so far up their A-holes it's sickening. This journal is literally the only thing that . . . well, is keeping me in line. But sometimes life gives you lemons, and when the lemons are too big for words, quite literally, then I'm sorry, I have to break. Or rid of the lemons entirely. I feel like I'm depersonalizing, right now. I pretty much have no control over my arms, legs, anything. I'm just laying down and watching myself slip dully into psychosis. I want to get out of this body. So many people want it, but I don't. I hate my body. I hate this vessel I'm stuck inside. The driver is tired of driving. I keep thinking about leaving everything and sleeping in alleyways. Maybe having nothing is better than having something. I'm starting to think that this is completely true. Bye. Going to sleep, now. A thousand happy lions.

---

[28] — An agreement with the hospital, that's a "Contractual Adjustment." Or what I personally think it is. . . .

September, 23rd, 7:11 p.m.

Today was crazy only because of this phone call I had. Turns out, the account Sherry gave me, the insurance one, the big, *big* insurance one, is a gold mine! Okay, so. This old lady answers the phone. Sherry called it for me because I was too afraid. It's a good thing, too, because this lady was irate from the start. Sherry built rapport with her, for about, like, twenty whole minutes, and then she transfers the call to me.

The lady's voice was super sweet. Sherry said, afterward, that her voice was mean as heck! Who knew! But yeah, she was telling me how unfair the insurance was because the claim was large and they didn't seem to want to pay it. I don't want to say the insurance company's name, but they really did F her over. They are wanting medical records for a condition that she doesn't even have. Smoking. I say "condition" but that's how they're treating it. I just don't get big companies and how they treat people who are unfortunate.

This lady literally is on disability and she *for sure* can't pay jack spit. But whatever, the insurance doesn't care. I told her I agree with her and that it should pay. I'll get to the bottom of this. She told me that I was sweet, and nice, and understanding. And I told her that she was nice and sweet, too.

September, 29th, 12:01 a.m.

Midnight. It seems like all I talk about is work. That's okay, sometimes, but I think the bigger picture is life as a whole. Work is work, yes, but you have to look at the magic in it. I don't ever see magic. But what I do see is life swarming all around me with endless arrays of varieties. That's cool. People are people doing people stuff. I think it's all a balancing act. People want this for this or that. Not in just business but in everything. <u>I don't even really know what happiness is anymore</u>. What I'm seeing is people playing games. The game of life. <u>Life *is* a game</u>. Cat and mouse. I feel like I'm beating a dead horse, though. Just stop. But aside from that, my bills are up-to-date, and I'm cool about that. My checks are steady, and it's nice to have security for once in my life.

October, 8th, 12:08 p.m.

I brought my journal into work today to make some corrections here and there and cross things out and underline, all that, and I'm glad I did—but not because I actually did the corrections but because there was a big meeting amongst our group about Shelby. Apparently Shelby was trying to be a lead this whole time. She was being overly into her work and stuff, and I thought it was great but I thought it was strange.

At pre-shift, Sherry tells us to go to this meeting she just up and decided to make, right off the bat. So we do, blah blah blah, and we all sit there and don't know what's going on. So yeah, Sherry comes in with Russell and Shelby, and Sherry is all excited.

"Okay, guys! Sit, sit. I have an announcement to make with all of you."

With all of you? I thought. Didn't she mean, *to* all of you? Strange. We all were sitting and some of us leaned forward.

"Shelby is going to be our new lead!"

Everyone was all like "WOO!" and stuff, and Shelby was blushing.

"Congrats!" a chick, who I hate, said to Shelby, out loud, in front of everyone. "You're on your way to being successful."

"Thanks, lovey. Between work and school, life is good."

Oh yeah. Shelby started online schooling recently.

I was actually kind of bummed. Everyone got up and sort of hugged Shelby and everything, but I didn't get up.

"Sal, get up and give your friend a hug. Be happy for her," their eyes all seemed to say when they saw me not giving a hoot.

I just got up and said, "Can we get back on the phones now?"

Sherry goes, "We can. I just thought"—she was saying this, out loud, not just to me—"that everyone would like to know about this. Come on. Get back on the phone."

So it's going. I walked along and bumped into a couple of them and they would say excuse me but I didn't pay any attention. I guess you could say I was selfish.

I was the first one to sit back down. Once I did, I got on the phone and called my big insurance lady. Or no—what I really did, I *checked* the account, not called it. Now I remember.

So okay, there were new notes[29] and yada-yada, and I saw that our insurance review department didn't get the medical records, even though, Cecilia, the patient on the account, told me specifically that she called her doctor to have that be faxed over to us.

I told Sherry about it, coming up to her desk. She told me to call the lady, get the doctor to fax or mail *her* the medical records, and then *she* will fax it over to *us*. I thought it was a long-shot and that there's no way somebody will really do that.

Well, turns out, she ended up wanting to do that, but she picked a fight about it. She was saying how the insurance is out to get her and all this. I advised that, look, all you have to do is do this and this. There's multiple entities on this account: me, the collector, the hospital, your creditor, your insurance, the people paying this, my insurance review, the people researching to get your insurance to pay, and then there's you, Cecilia. She understood when I told her in that tone.

She tells me she has a fax machine and will fax it over as soon as possible. I think it's great to have such powerful rapport with a customer like that.

So I get up and go over to Shelby.

"Hey, Shelly," I said, "I'm going to get a *huge* insurance payment, not you. If it pays, I get a ten-thousand dollar bonus, and you don't. So *ha!* Forget your position!"

She frowned. "Sal, you do know that I'm carrying you, right?"

"What does that mean?"

"It means that I have a budget based on the people I carry. I have a group budget, like Sherry. Since I'm carrying you, your money is added into my group budget. I get as much of a bonus as you, even *if* it pays. From just you alone."

---

[29] — There's "Notes" in the account that tells you what's going on, what happened in each conversation you had with the customer, and overall it gives you an idea of the future.

"Oh," I said, feeling stupid.

"So *ha!* Get back on the phone and make me some moo-*la*, silly goose!" She is starting to use my sayings. . . .

I'm glad after all of this because she was staying humble about it and I was being a total A-hole. But anyway, I love Shelby.

October, 17th, 6:57 p.m.

Halloween is coming up, obviously. I got a call from Tessa and Josh, on three-way, and they want to go to the place in Miami for Fright Nights. It's a big deal because the haunted houses are big and gnarly and scary. They invited me out tonight because they need a third person in order for the tickets to be affordable. They are picking me up now. I'm scared but excited! It's Friday!

October, 18th, 2:17 a.m.

I just got home. Wow. What a card [a Sherry saying]. That place was off the chain. I go into the line and the person there swiped my debit card and then Tessa and Josh paid me with cash. Not exactly what I wanted, but oh well. . . .

So we go in. The first thing I see is a strong flashing and statues of gargoyles or whatever. I was first in line with our group; that's always the worst if you ever go to a haunted house. Ha-*ha!* But yeah, there were these weird a█ guys there. I think halloween is the time for the creepers to be the ballers of the month. These guys did a great job at scaring me. Really.

There were these guys saying these weird a█ stuff in my ear and croaking really friggin' loud. Their voices must've been messed up when they got home.

They even had this guy on a string and he would "fly" everywhere around the top of the ceiling, getting really close to us. He was screaming and hollering and I was laughing at how scared I got. Everywhere you looked around, it was epic!

This one guy said to me, "Look at *you!*" His eyes got big, ink and make-up all over his face to resemble some kind of weird zombie. "Agh! My! oh *my!* I would take you home and eat you up. Look at that a▇!" and I told him to shut up. And he just laughed at me.

Then the chainsaw guys part of the house. It was walls full of these guys carrying chainsaws. Like wood walls. Super scary! Int*ense* in fact. They had these chainsaws with these creepy masks on and they would turn the chainsaws on and chase you and your group. One of them caught me, and I fell. Oh man, if I was chased by a guy like that, I would die. Seriously. I would. But the guy came close to me with the saw and that was it. I looked at it and there were no chains.

Then he chases someone else.

It's all a great act! I love it! But yeah, I went back to my group and Tessa and Josh were laughing at me.

By the way, Josh was actually screaming louder than anyone I ever saw. I think he truly was scared. Me and Tessa laughed at him the *entire time!* It was awesome.

I had a blast. But I need some sleep. I'll write when I can. Lots of things are coming up lately. I feel like things are getting better for me. The eye of the storm, though, is coming over Florida—my life. Metaphorically speaking, of course. Tee-*hee!*

October, 31st, 10:10 p.m.

It was Halloween today! Oh my! What was crazy, basically I had to work late because everyone and their kids were wanting to take the day off, so if anyone needed the extra hours (which that means *me)* then you could do it. I took the extra cash flow out, busted it out, and worked my A off. A lot of people, though, that had to work, they stayed and had their husbands come in and bring their kids. Oh my God! These kids were too stinkin' cute! They had their little customs on, dress like Batman, a football player, Spiderman, Superman, everything you could think of. Princesses, mimes, gorillas, ghosts, zombies, even the one guy on Duck Dynasty. These kids got creative.

Sherry's husband, Jeff, he came in with their daughter, Samantha. I met her a while back. Gosh she's the cutest.

"Hey, Sally!" she said running toward me. "Hey! How are *you!*"

I grinned. "Why, I'm doing fine. Yourself?"

She nodded. "Swell!" Too stinkin' adorable!

"What are you dressed like?" I really didn't know. It was a black wig, and she had this poka-dot shirt on or something.

She curtseyed, and said, "A witch! *RAWR!*"

I went, "Oh *my!*"—my eyes all being big—"you're *terr*ifying, Sam!"

"Can I have some candy?" She pouted. "Pretty please!"

I go, "Sure," and went through my desk and got her out a Snickers bar that I was going to eat when I got out of work.

She was too adorable to not give anything to.

"I love you, Sally!" Sam said. Then she gave me a hug.

Before she ran off to go hustle some more candy by being so gosh-darn cute, she held me tight, stopped, looked into my eyes, made me melt, and kissed me on the lips. What a sweet girl! Jeff saw and told her not to do that anymore. But she turned around and smiled at me. *Again,* what a sweet, sweet little girl!

I had a good halloween. It was the best. Just FYI, the kiss was~~n't anything~~ pretty crazy. It wasn't a romantic kiss. She was just being affectionate, is all. I love her. I hope she does well in life.

November, 1st, 1:33 p.m.

I don't know how I can describe what I'm feeling right now. It feels like my mind is going in and out of reality. I don't know how I can describe that. Ever since the day I smoked weed, I get really weird. My hands are losing control of themselves sometimes. Like my hands feel numb. I keep realizing how my brain produces signals to them and I'm realizing this so much so that they aren't happening properly. I feel like I'm losing my mind. I think I need sleep. But every time I turn the lights off, making everything pitch black, I keep thinking that the blackness is death. My mind is playing tricks on me. I feel like I'm just a life-form and that's it.

My senses are just senses. My thoughts are just thoughts. I'm losing control of this body. It's like a vessel. I don't know. I can't describe it. It's odd. Maybe I need sleep.

I'll treat you like my own personal therapist, Journal. Just let me speak, and you just listen. Okay. I have nobody else to talk to but you, really. What's bothering me is my sister. When she left Disney, she added me to her phone plan because her friend had an extra line and she knew I needed a new phone or something. But she told me to pay her. But I haven't been. She got really nasty with me, so basically I am going to put the phone in a bag, and the charger, and the SIM card, and I'm going to write a letter to her to let her know how I feel. Here's what I'm basically going to say:

Dear ███████ ███████,

I just wanted you to know how much you hurt me. I want you to know that I think highly of you, but I'm also rather disappointed because you know my situation and finances, fully.

I want you to know that I truly feel like I shouldn't have ties with you anymore. You're a lovely person, but enough is enough.

I know I never call you often like I should but frankly, I don't give a hoot. There's things in my life that cause me to make my choices. Depression is one of them.

Majority of the time, when I'm not calling to say hi, I am not saying hi to anyone else either. So don't feel special. I hate everyone when I'm depressed. It's bad sometimes.

I hope you understand.

I just wish I was more like you: a happy camper. My life is absolutely dreadful in every way. I wake up and the first thing I do every morning is sigh at how I have to wake up and live like everyone else. I so deeply wish I could not be like everyone else.

Again, I hope you understand this.

I have given you the phone, charger, and a check for $100,

> just to somehow make up for the damage caused.
> Hope you understand.
>
> P.S. If you need to reach me, my email is enclosed:
> Partyg███7███@gmail.com
>
> Love always,
Sally Fairfax

I'm going to mail it out tomorrow at lunch. Going to the post office, whatever. Hope that's not weird.

November, 4th, 6:13 p.m.

I'm trying to clean my house but I feel like it's too late or something. My rugs feel like you spilt honey and glue and you're stepping and everything you do makes the pads of your feet stick with hair. I don't really know how the hair got there—I don't have a cat—but nevertheless, it's there!

Anywho, besides, I don't want to get into all that garbage (quite literally—I mean, I actually *took out* the garbage!), but I want to tell you that at work the big boss man, the big-time CEO, he had a meeting with *all* the supervisors on the floor[30], up to and including Sherr-bear. They came back, whatever, and told us that there's this new competition[31] on

---

[30] — Not sure why I'm putting this note here, but I want to say that the floor is full of rows of cubicles. Like pretty much you walk in and its an open floor, but there's a main row that leads down other rows of desk, and at the ends of the groups of rows are the supervisors. So they are watching all the time. They even have a thing call "Artiva" that monitors you if you've been on a call too long, and then they yell at you. It's kind of scary. They are like God, or something. They also have statistics called KPIs that tell you how long, how many contacts, how many calls, the time you're clocked in, all that, on the phone. It's creepy! Getting off topic.

[31] — They hold comps because these jokers here really do get into it. They give these weird prizes out and these jokers flaunt it like it means something. But yeah, I could be pessimistic, but that's just me. I think a job is a job, no matter what.

the floor. "Capture the Flag." How original. They were given these straw cut-out tarps that we have the decorate (just like how kids do) and we pretty much have ours at the supervisor's desk, and she (or he[32]) takes a payment; and if—and only if—the payment is over 300$, you take another groups flag on the floor. It's silly, but you just watch! It becomes havoc!

Aside from that, I bought a new iTouch! *and* a new Acer computer laptop! Not too much, either. It came out to be about 350 dollars. On sale. I got iTunes on it and started to make me a new "Feel Good" playlist. (I titled it that!) Here's what's on it so far (in its exact order):

- MAGIC! - "Rude"
- Ingrid Michaelson - "Girls Chase Boys"
- The B-52's - "Love Shack"
- Tame Impala - "Feels Like We Only Go Backwards"
- Madonna - "Music"
- Kayne West and Jay-Z - "H.A.M."
- The Police - "Every Breath You Take"
- Envy - "Am I Wrong?"
- Of Monsters and Men - "Little Talks"
- Edward Sharpe and The Magnetic Zeros - "Om Nashi Me"
- Calvin Harris - "Summer"
- F.U.N. - "We Are Young"
- Nu Shooz - "I Can't Wait"
- Michael Frani and Spearhead - "Say Hey (I Love You)"
- Aly and AJ - "Walking On Sunshine"
- Ed Sheeran - "The A-team"

That's it so far. If you—whoever is reading this—ever gets the chance, check out *all* those songs. Every single one makes me happy and makes me smile. I'm trying to be more positive, if you couldn't tell!

;-)

---

[32] — Not many "he" supervisors. . . . *Ha!*

November, 6th, 5:57 p.m.

Today was my birthday. I got lot of compliments on this new sundress I bought. It wasn't dress-code appropriate so I had to take a pin (which is like getting a "referral" in elementary school) and I got really mad about it because, look, it's my birthday and I should do whatever the F I want to! They didn't buy it. Oh well. But hey! it's all gravy because the group bought me a cake and we all sliced it and passed everything out. All the other groups were jealous and got mad at me because I wouldn't give them any. The problem, there wasn't enough slices. Heck! there wasn't enough slices even for the dang group! I know, I know. Maybe I'm evil. I try not to be, but I guess I am. But anyways, I got a bunch of Starbucks gift cards within my birthday cards from all the other girls in our group. I thought they hated me but apparently, they don't; if maybe, if possible, they are just being nice for the sake of being nice so that way if spit goes sour, they have something to fall back on in the possible argument. So lame. The boys, they were all hyped and kept joking about me being 15 because my voice is so weeny-whinny and small like a little kid's. They are so lame. They all are lame, actually. But yeah, I'm 23 now so I got to be more forgiving and responsible and be the better woman in the group. Gosh I hope things get cooler in my life. I have no direction. Oh yeah, and my dad mailed me some cute shorts for presents, which I thought was sweet!

November, 10th, 12:13 p.m.

This contest is pissing me off. The people here are so dumb! Especially Russell. He's the worst one.

Okay, so. Basically he shouts "Dats ri'!" after every single payment he gets because we are starting to make alliances.

Yes. I really did just write "Alliances." We are all adults, with adult-like jobs, and this contest has made all the groups, including the supervisors, make teams and deals with each other, left and right.

I heard a supervisor say to another supervisor, "Okay, here's what I'm offering: If you and I team up, you can't take our flag. You have to take team (a)'s flag, but not us, team (b). Got it?" and the supervisor really nods. And not a laugh-laugh nod, it was a serious one.

It's like we're all kids again.

And what's crazy is that it's the holiday season and people are paying off their bills. Also, apparently insurance process claims in quarters, or "clusters." They pay them in bulk so everything is being paid in all of our insurance routes.

Thank God! The only thing, the payments from insurance don't count toward taking another team's flag. So yeah, people are pissed and working harder than ever.

The people are being insanely aggressive on the phone.

They yell, "Paying? . . . No? . . . Okay, thank you. Bye!" hang up and go to the next call, where hopefully this strategy will work.

There's some accounts that you know aren't going to pay. Like people from Alabama, I just don't get it; they never, ever pay. Ever. They re*fuse*. But what's weird is that they verify[33] themselves almost every. Single. Time. So it's like you have to continue with the call. So I guess that's why people use this strategy to sift through the crap accounts.

So basically, me telling you this, Future Sally, you got to know that Russell is a straight up A-hole. This guy's desk is right next to another group's desks, and he provokes everything.

"You guys are goin' down! Take our flags, *oOooo-Oooo!* you betta not!"

And then he truly gets back at them after they take our group's flag. He pays the other supervisors to make other collectors make sure that that group who took our flag gets nothing left at the end of the day.

It's really that serious.

Russell straight up *threatened* another collector because he was laughing at how into it Russell was at getting back at their group.

Russell goes, "Next time you take our flags, I'm seein' *you* at the parking lot, boy," and he all points at the kid.

The kid put his hands up and basically said F it because it's not even

---

[33] — You have to verify each person (Responsible Party) a.k.a., the "RP," on the phone, by law, or else you get canned.

worth it to actually get into a fight with Russell about this, and plus, the kid was 30 and had kids and he didn't have time for all that mess considering his wife picks him up in the parking lot after work.

Russell is a punk. I'm so glad he's not in my life. What was I thinking? I know. I wasn't thinking, is what it was.

November, 12th, 1:43 a.m.

I can't sleep. ~~I'm being bothered by~~ ■■■■ ~~that keep telling me to~~ ■■ a g■ a■ k■■■ ■■■■■■■.

It tells me ~~that, hey, if it was you as a terrorist, wouldn't you blow up the world? and I say yes out loud. It's really strange. I always try to think about something else because~~ I would never, ever actually hurt another human being. I think it's just lack of sleep. My dreams carrying into my waking life, or something.

I thought about my hair, just after that. I think that women worrying about hair, it's all a joke. Basically it's thought that having great hair is what makes or breaks a woman's beauty. I hate the idea of that. A girl is beautiful no matter what. Women's bodies are probably the greatest invention in human history.

Also, I thought about the flag contest at work. Basically they have a new twist: after lunch, for every payment you get, divide the payment by $300 and that's how many flags you get.

Russell went ham.

I hate Russell.

Basically it's a madhouse after lunch but my bonus check next month is going to be something like two thousand bucks. All my insurance is paying.

Speaking of insurance, the insurance lady with the super big balance account called in and said that she got the medical records and she just faxed over all of it to her insurance. She said it's up to me now.

I literally clapped for joy. I was too, *too* excited. The kind of excitement you should write about in a journal and remember later on in life. I hope it pays soon. I could really use the cash.

November, 14th, 6:13 p.m.

Once in a blue moon (Blue Moon is my fav!—aside from Jack) I lie my heart out—which inclines you to think I lied about the whole razzle-dazzle Blue Moon favorite beverage thingamabobber in parenthesis.

That said, I've been, well (and a big "*Well*" on that!), a nuisance at work. I've been not listening, not doing this, not doing that, or that (that, that, that!) and it's catching on in the management spectrum of the blasted office.

The office is all hush-hush sometimes because I like to do things my very, very, most very own way. Like the keys on my keyboard—F10, F11—I've taken the liberty of removing the buttons entirely, for the higher likeliness of catching the throws[34], with the other buttons not being in the way and all.

F9 is the "Catch The Throw" button, and yeah (also a big, big *Yeah)*, my boss, Sherry, was ordering me to put the keys back in their proper place, accusing me afterward that it's damaging company property and I shouldn't ever, ever do that.

I told her she was wrong.

I told her she was dead wrong. I told her that the keys were just keys and they could be put back, because they could, considering the keys were in my desk drawer.

"Forget it," Sherry said, "go home."

But I quickly laughed it off and did it, the putting back of keys, because I was in the middle of a payment (and money talks!) so she perked on up and then went on to say, with her index and thumb and inch apart, "You are *this close* to getting a write-up." So I think I'm going to be fired soon. I may have to find a new job. Sherry hates me.

---

[34] — A "throw" is a term used for call centers. It means to transfer a call. It's slang, I think.

November, 14th, 9:46 p.m.

Just came back from Walmart. I'm noticing a couple of things: (1) if society was led toward chaos, the type that makes civilization crumble, everyone would become savage; (2) if those savages are fighting against one another for food, water, shelter, sex, drugs, rock'n'roll (the things people in this Walmart, in particular, are buying, needing, wanting), creating a modern-day civil war, in essence, constant casualties would be among us—leading into people not going over the age of twenty in, say, a decade of this chaos-like void of un-comfortability—; (3) and therefore, considering the previous 1 and 2, then there mustn't be God because God would bless Life with His Love (whatever the kind of love you're perceiving) and this cannot, will not, happen, for the simple fact that (a) Humans want to be on top, be greedy, be the "Chosen One," and (b) With as little effort, little say from others, and in as little time possible—and that, Humble Journal, is the very reason why I had gotten so depressed that I bought a six-pack of Blue Moon, an orange, all from Walmart, and sat my happy A-hole down on my bed and wrote about this piece of crap idea I'm having. I'm all alone . . . Well, not entirely: I have my beer with me. I named him Bobby. He's tasty, and *cute!*

November, 17th, 9:46 p.m.

The director of our building told us that the prize is for your entire group to have lunch with him, your supervisor, the CEO, the president of the company, and also his wife, if your group gets pulled in the drawing. Basically all the times the groups have played this whole month, the end group with the most flags got a ticket that went into some bin, and that's how they do the "drawing." Our group has won the most, so it's a bit of a no-brainer that we'll win this. The lunch'll be entirely free, too.

And another thing: I found out how Russell makes so much money.

He goes into the Cell-Phone Pool[35], accesses an account, and then doesn't call it because he looks to see if the person has either (a) Already paid, or (b) Has insurance.

I want to write down all the account numbers because it's actually sort of unfair. You're not suppose to do that! He's pretty much taking potential money from the group, see. That's why it's F'ed. Everyone has to call every account they access, by policy. So yeah, I'm sort of ticked.

I also hate Russell because basically I'm realizing that I do actually hate him and how I actually dated him. So it's nice to get him back, for a change. I hope he doesn't freak out. I'll try to be anonymous.

Also, this guy in the break-room, the one that always stares at me, is now reading books at his table and he always sits facing be from afar, so I know he *stares* at me everyday!

He's in my group and it's really annoying. His name is Kevin. What a weirdo Kevin is.

November, 25th, 9:46 p.m.

I've been straight slackin' on these entries. Mostly because I'm too tired all the time to write, and because, well, work is a drag. I'm trying to stay positive but it's just too much sometimes. Our group has been busting butts, though, and I hope it pays off, and another thought: Anything I want in life—and I mean *any*thing—always has a price. That is all.

November, 26th, 10:46 p.m.

So I compiled a bunch of account numbers on a huge piece of paper of all the accounts Russell has been skipping over in the Cell-Phone Pool. I

---

[35] — There's two pools: the Cell-Phone Pool, and the Dialing Pool. The Dialing Pool dials out on house phones and skip-trace numbers. The Cell-Phone Pool is a pool where the collector manually dials. This is because it's illegal to have someone's cell phone on an automatic dialer without their permission. So if we call, verify them, all that, we ask, at the very end of the call, if they would like us to call them back, or if their cell is a "good number." If they say yes, *great!* they are now in the Dialing Pool!

gave the list to Sherry and she was furious! I explained to her what the big man was doing and she totally agreed that it wasn't fair. So she brings him up to her desk—Now, realize this, I sit next to Sherry's desk so I can hear everything that goes on. So she brings Russell up, has one of the many accounts up that he skipped on her screen, and proceeds to explain to him that what he's doing is against company policy, so she goes ahead and tells him he's on "probation." He starts hooting and hollering and, at first, he was saying how, "*Oh!* all those *other* groups always skip accounts, so *they* rat on *me?*" and he all truly thought that the *other* group beside us wrote the accounts down to rat him out, when in fact it was I! Ha, *ha!* I'm evil. He didn't even know it! So yeah, funny funny. But he goes to his desk, all saying, "I don't care what a *collector* says," carrying on, and he goes and sits his happy butt down, probation commencing and all. Revenge is awesome. That is it.

December, 1st, 12:12 p.m.

I brought my journal in today because the president of the company said that he was doing the drawing for the company lunch that everyone has been all carried away about. I thought it might be interesting, so I brought good ole Journal, and girl, was *that* a good call!

Okay, so. Our team got picked. YES! We did! I swear! I know that sounds like a load of crap but I'm totally foreal. Yesterday was the last day to collect for the month of November and today, Mr. President draws *our* group! We all cheered like mad, crazy, wild. It was real exciting. I was real happy.

The day we go is on the 18th or something. It's at lunch time and we can go for as long as we want, with pay. This is awesome! Our group gets to pick, as well.

Books[36] haven't closed yet, so I'm keeping my fingers crossed on closing out at 300%. I closed out at 261%, and I'm getting close to a

---

[36] — "Books" are the company's monthly end numbers. Like the numbers to determine how much of a bonus they have to give an employee.

3,000 dollar bonus check. I'm very excited! This Christmas is going to be awesome!

December, 4th, 9:30 p.m.

Today was a normal day. Very plain. Very lame. I just worked and made a few calls and didn't bother too many people. It was pretty standard.

Until I found out about a little s__t-talker, Russell.

Gosh, I hate him so. Know what he did? Get *this:* he finds out that it was me who "ratted" him out on the Cell-Phone Pool. ~~The guy just won't quit.~~

He was talking hella spit—and I know this because one of the girls in my group that sits near him was telling me that he was saying stuff to not only our group but the group *next* to us, too. He's lame as heck.

He was like oh, I F'ed her F'ing brains out when we dated and she was a screamer and how I'm a find piece of a__ and a s__t and everyone has had a piece of me. Blah, blah, blah, I'm a little b__ch type of s__t he was spewing out of his lame mouth.

I told Sherry about it after work.

"Hey, Sherry. Could I see you by my car?"

"Yeah, sure." It was the end of the day, that's why I told her to meet me there in private.

We left out the doors, walked around the building, and got to my car, which just so happened to be kind of close to Sherry's car.

"Listen," I told her, "Russell is bothering me."

"How you mean?"

"The guy is talkin' smack!"

"Really?"

"Yeah!" I said, and I was surprised she already didn't know because everyone at our job tattletales on people.

"What's she—I mean *he*—saying?" she asked. "Sorry. My mind was on something else. Didn't get much sleep."

"I understand. Well, I'm hearing from people that he's saying things about me: like that I'm a slut or whatever. We used to date, so he's pulling all sorts of cards out."

"Sally, I'm going to have a word with Russell. This is totally unfair. I don't want you to be harassed."

"That's the thing. I didn't even know he was doing it or saying anything."

"Oh."

"Yeah, and he found out it was me who left those accounts on your desk and told on him."

"How in the world would he know that?" Sherry was pissed, you could tell. "He's so petty."

"I know!" I said. "He used to be in jail, so he knows how to do that sort of thing."

"Yeah, he probably narrowed it down to you. . . . Gosh. I'll talk to him." She was wiping her face, touching her eyes. "He probably narrowed it down to you—but hey, Sally, I gotta get on home. I'm very tired. I'll talk to him."

"Thanks, Sherry. I really appreciate it."

She left and I drove on home. I hate Russell. He'll get what's coming to him soon enough. At least I hope.

Gosh, I hate exs. Don't you?

December, 5th, 5:11 p.m.

I've never been so happy in my life! Oh my God! Wow! The insurance payment paid! I repeat: The. Insurance. Payment. *Paid!* I'm *so* damn excited. It posted right in the morning time. Sherry announced it during pre-shift. Oh my God! I cried! Not to be a big baby, but yeah, I cried, hard! It's because my bonus check is going to be something like twelve grand! and today was literally the last day for books to close. I'm so excited! This Christmas is going to rock my socks off! I'm going to celebrate. Probably this weekend! Shelby congratulated the heck out of me. Life is getting gold!

December, 7th, 12:03 a.m.

Most of the people at work—Sherry, Shelby, et cetera—couldn't make it to the planned dinner date for yesterday, so I had to reschedule for today, tonight, whatever. I told them to dress up in something awesome. I'll explain here, in chat:

Shelby was, of course, dazzling, and she brought her boyfriend, who I think is rather cute. Sherry, looking oddly okay—wearing a sundress that doesn't match her red high-heels—brought her hubby, too, like Shelby, and Jeff is doing okay, he says to me, in passing, when I asked him how everything was.

I told them, as I sat down after coming back from the bathroom, that the entire thing is on me.

"No, no, nonsense!" goes Sherry. "I insis—"

"*No,*" I interrupted her, "*I'm* the one that insists. My treat. Honestly."

"Did you just say, 'Incest'?" Shelby's boyfriend went.

We all just stared at him like a retard.

"Oh, I was just kidding"—and I was tempted to slap him for saying anything at all.

"Anywho!" I announce, "it really is my treat because I'm going to run into some money."

"That you are, that you are, Sally," Shelby puts in her two cents. "I'm truly happy for you."

"Aw. Thanks, Shelly!"

"No problem!"

"Hey, everyone," a voice says. "Can I take your order?"

We all looked over and . . . and, *and, gosh!* You won't believe it!

"John!" I go. "You work here now?!"

"Yeah. My mom and I didn't get along" (his mom is Dora) "but I'm doing better, though."

"That's great! So. Applebee's, huh?"

"Just a job, Sally"—and, changing the subject quickly, he looks around—"What can I get'cha guys? Salad? Dos Equis? Beer? Anything?" and Déjà vu rushes over me because I used that same line before when I worked the food industry.

"I'll take a Corona," goes Sherry, "and he"—she thumb points to Jeff—"um, he'll take one, too. I also just want steaks for both of us."

"Medium or rare?" John asked.

"Rare as the smiles on these chicks' faces," Shelby's boyfriend is at it again.

And again, we stare at his dumb self. But before Shelby passively says the old "You're embarrassing me in front of my friends" spiel, Jeff answers John's question, saying, "Medium."

"Fine choice, sir," John said. Then he looks at Shelby. "And you?"

"Steak. Rare. Two Jack'n'Cokes. Doubles." She hands John the menu, quick as day.

" 'Kay," he said, taking it. "And you, Sally?"

"I want *you!*" I said, and everyone busted out laughing.

"Oh Sally! *Oh*—you're just making me blush . . ." he purposefully mimics me, and I'm the only one that catches it at the table.

My anger subsided. "Steak. Water."

"All steaks!" John says. "Who's buyin'?"

"That's none of your concern, John." I hand him my menu; and Sherry, God rest her lovely soul, hands over hers and Jeff's menus, too—passing them to me to give.

So John, struggling, has them all, saying, "Be right back with everything" —he almost drops the menus—"woah, Nelly! Woah!" and ~~she~~ he turns to leave.

"Mhm, you do that . . ." I go.

There's no silence; everyone is spewing out nonsense, in unison, almost. Talking about work and drugs and sex and rock'n'roll, and I almost regret coming here.

"Sally?"

"Yes." I look around.

"Sally"—finger-snapping—"over here."

It was Shelby talking.

"Yeah, Shelly?"

"How'd you do it?"

"Do what? The account?"

"Mhm. I wanna know."

"Well . . . let's just say a birdie told me," and I look over at Sherry,

who, adjusting her top, is flirting with Jeff, not noticing I'm staring at her.
"But," I say, "it's no thang."

"Bull! Sherry totally gave it to you!"

"She did not!" I was caught. "And plus, Shelby, I earned it. It's no biggie. Be happy for me," I pleaded.

"I *am* happy for you. I never said I wasn't, Miss. Rollin'-in-the-Benjamins now!"

"Oh hush," I said. "Hey, Sherry."

She looks over at me. " 'Ello!"

"Did you give me that one big insurance account?"

"Yeah . . . ? Why?"

"Shelby wanted to know," I said.

"No I didn't!" Shelby seemed mad. "I was just laying stuff on the table."

"Look, girls," Sherry said. "If you guys don't quit it I'll"—she was raising her fist, messing around—"knock ya out, sistas!" and me and Shelly just laughed.

"Still. I'm getting a *five*-grand bonus," Shelby said.

"Gosh, this night can't get no better," I said, clapping: "Can't—get—*no*—better!"

"It can!" said good ole Shelby; "check it out!" and she showed me her phone.

What was on her screen was an Applebee's coupon for buy-one-get-one-free steaks. Unlimited usage!

"Yay!" I said, then, under my breath, "Not sure why."

December, 19th, 1:48 p.m.

Um . . . Most embarrassing thing happened. To start, the group lunch was today, not yesterday. I made a mistake. Oh well.

So I go into work and they tell me that it was today. Now, look, I'm pissed because usually I'm good with these types of things: a lunch, free food. Not bad, not the worst thing that could happen. But I was mad.

So I'm waiting, waiting, waiting, calling accounts, doing the usual, and then I get this idea, see, so I turn to Sherry.

"I can't go."

"Why?" says she.

"If Russell goes, I'm not going."

"Well, that's unfair, Sal."

"Unfair my butt. I'm not going. He'll start something."

"How do you know?"

"I just do," I said.

Then Sherry sort of tells me that everything is going to be okay and that Russell won't actually do anything rash. He can't, she said. He'll face the consequences.

So my stupid self listens, and goes with the group. We all drove in each others cars. Sherry told me to ride along in her Cadillac (that I'm sure she just recently purchased, the weirdo that she is), so yeah, I totally did because I like the old-timey *verrrrum verrrum* the engine makes.

Coming out of the building, I had a bad feeling. A really bad feeling. Can't describe it.

But maybe it was my period. Who knows?

We get into Sherry's car and it wasn't the type of Caddy I envisioned, but whatever.

I told Sherry, "I have something embarrassing to ask," before Shelby found her way into the ride, way outside.

"What? Russell isn't coming in. Quit your worrying."

"No. Not that."

"Then what, Sal?"

"I forgot my pads at home."

"Oh that's no big deal. Here," and she rummaged through her purse and got me one. It was the smaller ones, "but it'll do," I thought.

"Thanks," I said.

"Don't mention it," good ole Sherry said.

And simultaneously, Shelby gets into the car and Sherry starts it.

As we came up to "Tokyo," the hibachi grill restaurant that my group picked, we were blasting a song that was on my "Feel Good" list: MAGIC! - "Rude."

We were singing along and getting all carried away . . . Well, at least *I* was anyway.

Then we got out.

The place was hella nice on the inside. The classic Oriental-style stuff—you know the kind.

"Feel the atmosphere," Shelby said.

"I'll give you somethin' to FEEL!" I said. Then I shoved Shelly playfully.

"Knock it off, you two," Sherry said. "Behave. I'm not your dang mother." And we all three just laughed.

So we get there, and Shelby and I sit but Sherry sits on the other side, away from us. I guess there just weren't the usual amount of seats. The entire group was there before us.

Two grills. Two groups made from our one group. Circled around both the grills, they were. I was already missin' Sherry.

I was sitting next to the director, the CEO, the assistant director, and I asked the maître d', "I need a drink menu," but when it came out I was misconstrued wrongly because I was looking for the soda-type drinks, not alcohol, and the director of the company says to me, "Just stop, Sally."

By the time the maître d', the little bugga-boy, came back, I was over it. Completely.

I wanted to leave!

After 40 minutes of hearing others talk about their lives, their kids, their husbands and wives, their friends getting married, the new cars they bought, the colleges they're about to go to, the loves, everything, the two chiefs came out.

Ours was awesome! Basically he did a bunch of tricks. Like, he said, "You guys ever seen a Japanese butterfly?" and we shake our heads no and he actually threw butter in the air and onto the grill! Too *cute!*

Then he was asking each of us how we wanted our food cooked and he separated everything surprisingly even. Then he did everything all happy and perfect. He was about to——Ah, sh█! I'm doing it again: Getting all off topic. Dang it.

Here's the part where it gets embarrassing. Never mind the perfectly, happily happy chief-guy.

We had a good time, okay? We all did. Pretty much. Except I glanced once or twice across the grills and saw, vaguely, Mr. Crabby-pants with his eyes dead at me. Yeah, Russell. You guessed it.

I hate talking about him so much in my diary.

But anyway, we get all done, the bosses pay the bill, tip people, shake a few hands, all that, and me and Sherry decide to go to the bathroom.

Now, I'm PMS-ing, so you could bet I was getting real irritated. Sherry could tell.

"Use the pad I gave you," she said. "Just lighten up."

"Okay," I said. Then I went in the stall while Sherry was "powdering her nose." Tee-*hee!*

Sherry left, okay? She did. She left me in the dust! I'm not happy that she did or else this would have never happened.

So after I put the old red waterfall stopper on, I got out of the stally stall, with my handy hands, blow-dry themy them, and open the bathroom's door, on my way out.

Russell was . . . right . . . F'ing . . . *there!*

Talking spit . . .

"You lucky those supervisors ain't here; you lucky. They ain't here to protect your ol' h■-a■, mark-a■, trick-a■, b■ch! H■-a■. I f■■d yo' a■ up, b■ch. I'll do it again. I'll do it again, huh. Yeah. Yeah, yeah . . ." and he's saying this next to me as we walked straight from the bathroom to the friggin' front *doors.*

The maître d' just rolled his eyes.

Tell me about it, I was thinking. He just won't quit.

So we get out the door, and finally, enough was enough.

"Shut *up,*" I said to Russell.

He's just talking and talking until finally, "What?" he says. "What did you say to me?" and he's all walking all up near me and everything. I wasn't scared. Honest.

"Shut *up!*" I repeated. "Please *shut the F up.* You're stupid as heck! Get over yourself, buddy."

I guess he couldn't believe his ears. "What the f**k did you just f**king say, b**ch? I'll knock your f**king teeth in, you b**ch."

"Then do it, a**hole," I said. Calmly.

(Sorry for all the cursing. It's what actually happened, is all.)

So that really riled him all up. But by the time that happened, God bless it, we were already in the parking lot, where our group was; excluding Sherry, for some odd reason, I don't know.

"I'll throw my food at your f**king face!" Russell told me, holding up his to-go box full of Chicken and Steak.

"Do it," I said. "Get it out of you."

And he sort of snickered in some "off" type of way. Then he held it up, started coming up close to me, Shelby in the passenger seat of Sherry's car behind me, and Russell stops. He huffed and puffed, then he set his box on some person's car hood. He turns around and . . .

"What the f**k, b**ch! What the f**k did you just say! You motherf**ker!" Russell was hooting and hollering, and then, get this: he picks me up by my shirt. A man! A man picks up a woman up by her *shirt!* holding a fist up to her friggin' temple, trying to frighten the living daylights out of her; and I was calm as rain, thank you very much.

Everyone was saying stop this and stop that and Russell you're making a huge mistake and he probably got some justification out of it, I reckon, but hey, I stood my ground.

So Sherry comes out and is pissed as heck! She was telling Russell to get on to the office and Russell, telling me out the side of his window that I'm a "h**-a**," drove off.

So I get inside Sherry's ride and I'm pretty much silent the whole time. But Sherry was asking me questions so I had to answer them.

"What happened, exactly, Sal?"

"The guy was talking smack as I was coming out of the bathroom, and it lead to the parking lot, so I said enough is enough and told Russell to 'shut up.' He thought I wouldn't stick up for myself, so he got pissed and picked me up by my shirt—And I'm leaving! F this. I'm gone for today."

"Why, Sal? We'll figure this out."

"No. That's what you said before we left."

"Just wait until we get to the director's office. We'll get this taken care of."

" 'Kay," I said.

And yeah, we got to the office parking lot, came out of the car, walked up, parted ways with Shelby; and yeah, all after, though, me and Sherry went to the director's office, like Sherry said.

If you think Sherry was pissed, you should have seen the director. Oh wow. Heated! He was raving about how Russell should have never done that and he was asking me all kinds of questions. I laid it on him simple.

"He picked me up by my shirt. That's it. No punches."

And the director pretty much told me that he'll take care of this.

"But that's not going to do anything," I told him. "Look. Russell knows he makes this company the most money out of anyone in the entire floor. He knows this. That's why when I ratted him out he felt like I was 'intervening' in his glory. That's what I mean.

"So. What you got to do, really, is you got to let him know that the s##t he's doing is not acceptable. Because other people follow his lead. I mean he's a *lead* for God's sake.

"I just either want two things to happen: One, I go home today because I'm going to be bombarded with questions until the end of time, and two, if you don't fire him, I want to move to a different group—this is *insane*."

So the director and Sherry agreed and sent me home, with pay. . . . Nice people. My weekend is complete, I guess.

Russell, come to find out after I chilled at home for about an hour and received a phone call from Sherry, Russell got fired, for good. Done. Nice to know you, sucker. (And this is why I was inspired to write this journal entry, right after mine and Sherry's phone call.)

I actually didn't agree with it, the firing, to be honest. It's not like he actually hit me. He just sort of rough-housed me, is all. I tried to tell Sherry that, but she said it's not fair and it needed to be done. I guess it was a choice that was beyond me. I didn't provoke anything. I swear my life on it.

I just hope Russell does okay.

December, 22nd, 5:40 p.m.

I came into work today and nobody really spoke about Russell and I's little fight we had. I guess nobody wanted to provoke it or something. What I heard from Shelby, though, was that everyone was almost saying "good riddance," in favor to the idea that Russell was fired. I sort of laughed! I know that's wrong of me, but truly, come on! You know it's funny when a guy you hate so completely is hated by others, too! It sort of makes you feel good, huh? I know I'm bad. I wish him the best. My weekend was really nice. I bought me a new sofa, a new 60 inch 4K plasma TV, and a bunch of movies: *A Clockwork Orange*, *Fight Club*, *Jersey Girl*, *Clerks*, *Clerks II*, *Dallas Buyers Club*, *Enemy*, *Donnie Darko* (my favorite!), *Goodfellas*, *Her*, *Milk*, *Peter Pan*, *Star Wars* I-VI, *Trainspotting*, *Less Than Zero*, *Pulp Fiction* (the collector's edition!), *Walk The Line*, *Wedding Crashers*, and so much more! All Blu-rays! I'm a movie buff/fanatic, in case you don't know . . . or something. I love you, Future Sally. Don't forget me, please. Thank *you*! and Christmas is so close, too!

December, 23rd, 10:36 p.m.

Something has been on my mind. To start, I've always wondered why I haven't been too much into makeup and things like that.

Yes, I do like to dress up, do all things of the sort, but—and a big "but" at that—I feel like it's unnecessary.

All women are beautiful, no matter what anyone says. You could look directly in the eyes of the ugliest woman in the world, and, assuming life hasn't crapped on her, she may be a non-bitter, open individual, and hecka sweet, too!

Sometimes I do look in the mirror and I feel okay with my body, but at times, frankly, I'm just another individual. I'm no different. Yes, you could say it's easy for me to say because I *am* beautiful, but that's not my intent.

Master the art of letting go. If a person is telling you this—that you're something that you know, in fact, you are not—and you know it's this—not correct—then why beat yourself up with the idea? Let go of all the thoughts of others, even though it's not easy. Let go of the trials, the issues, the affairs, because they are no better off than you.

All things suffer. I want to talk about a time I was in elementary school. You see, I was always the sensitive type. I would always look at others and think, Wow, that's not me—or, That's not what *is*. It was weird to think that at that age, I know, but it lead me into being alienated from others. I remember my kindergarden teach, Mrs. Silva, she would say, "Time for story time, kids!" and everyone would cheer. But I would stay and continue to play "House" with myself.

You know the game "House"? You remember. You'd have a person be the mom or be the dad or b be the kid. Then you all would just play "House." It's acting. But I think it teaches children to learn what responsibility is. But yeah, I really enjoyed it.

Anyway, I would play House and Mrs. Silva would always come up to me, look down at me, and say, "Sally, it's story time. Why don't we sit down with some of the others and read along, huh? It'll be fun."

I'd always shake my head because I didn't want to hear anyone else's story but mine. Mine was the only one that mattered to me.

So I'd sleep. I would go to the back of the group, and sleep. I just didn't think it was necessary to conform with the lesson of the day, and this carried on and on throughout middle school, high school, and in my workplace/adulthood. I'm starting to think it's my personality. Sometimes I hate my personality.

The point is is that makeup isn't needed. High heels are cool. Sometimes you got to just go natty[37] and be yourself. Forget everyone's story. You probably will be disappointed in the end, anyway, regardless if you're listening to your story and theirs.

---

[37] — "Natty" just means: Natural.

December, 24th, 10:00 p.m.

It's Christmas Eve and 10 o'clock and I'm thinking about going over to Shelby's but her boyfriend is there and I don't really like him so I'm staying home and getting some shut-eye and possibly watching some movies but I'm scared because I feel like it's a cop-out so I have to go over Shelby's and feel better about not doing anything here right now.

December, 24th, 11:42 p.m.

I think Shelby is the sweetest girl. The moment I walked in they all gave me hugs. By "they" I mean all of Shelby's friends who I haven't met. I like them. They are all pretty and all wearing really nice clothes, and I show up with an American Apparel black jacket, Chuck Taylor's, blue jeans, and no make up with my hair up in a bun. The good ole hair-tucking-behind-the-ear bashfulness. Shelby's friend, Terra, was talking to me on Shelby's living room couch about how she loves my blonde hair. I don't even know my natural hair color any more, I told her, but I appreciated it anyway.

She just told me that it's okay because she doesn't know her hair color neither, but she was wondering where I worked. So I told her, and she made the connection, and, *voilà!* her and I were acquaintances.

So I left her in the dust and went over to Shelby's Christmas tree and looked through it, almost *into* it, and decided that trees are the weirdest things in the world. I thought that we spend all year—well, scratch that, *they,* the trees, spend all year—growing, just to be cut down, dressed up with decorations, and then burned or thrown to the side of the road when we're all done with them. It's pretty tragic.

I got depressed and sort of tried to find Shelby.

"Where is she?" I asked a guest.

"Over there!—and I love your *hair!* it's *cute!*"

I had my hoodie up, but I said thanks anyway.

So then I found Shelby and by the time I got over to her, she sort of put her arms around me and said, "Sally!" whilst she was holding a wine glass.

I was assuming it wasn't her first drink so I just laughed at how drunk she was but she just told me, "I'm not drunk, Sal. This is apple cider," and I said, "Oh," and she goes, "A toast!" and spins me around and lifts her wine glass and announces, "Everyone, meet Sally!" and everyone turns around and I got scared and lost and whatever. Then Shelby announces, "She successfully got the biggest insurance payment in all of the company!" and I was noticing that most of the guests were people from my job.

Everyone was all congratulating, and then, Shelby goes, "Being her lead, I'd say this was a successful year since I, too, get a piece of that insurance pie!" And everyone laughs. Then she goes, "Where's everyone's gifts, Sal? Got that cash and no gifts! Shame on you!" and I got scared but everyone was laughing at me.

The rest of the time was pretty okay and I felt fine but this bugged me the whole time coming back from the event prematurely. I felt like I wasn't really with them because they were celebrating and I was just there, being a person, and nobody saw what was coming when I left. They asked me to stay and get drunk but I wasn't interested because it was too much for my brain.

So I'm home now and it just turned 12 o'clock which means it's Christmas and I'm excited about that. Like insanely excited! It's Christmas, it's Christmas, it's CHRISTMAS! But I don't really have that Christmas-y feeling you get of together-ness. I guess I did that to myself.

I also don't have a tree with presents under them and this makes me sad but I probably also did that, too, to myself, considering I feel like a Christmas tree's life is unfair.

February, 3rd, 3:13 p.m.

I'm in ICU right now, and I can't stop crying. Some things are hard to remember, but I'll try.

Okay, so. The first thing I remember: It's Christmas Day and I'm watching the movie *Taxi Driver* and being totally into it, when suddenly, I heard a knock at my apartment's door. So I get up, wonder who is knocking, don't sweat it much, and look into my door's peep-hole. What I saw scared the living daylights out of me! It was Russell, grinning, his hands behind his back.

What could *he* want? I thought. Maybe he's here to hurt me! So as I thought this, of course I got scared crap-less. I started yelling so he could hear me from outside the door.

"What, Russ! What do you *need?*"

He grinned even more. "Sally, I came to say I'm sorry."

"*Sorry? Who's* sorry? You? You're *never* sorry."

"I got wine and flowers," he said, and then he pulled out those very two things from behind himself.

"That's sweet but I still don't trust you!" I shouted. "Go away!"

"Sal, what can I do to make you not look at me like I'm some *enemy* or something? I'm a human-being, Sal. Not just some *guy*. Jesus. I was your freakin' first kiss for crying out loud. Come on! Give me a break. Five minutes. Just. Five. F'ing. Minutes. *Please!*"

So I thought about it. He was right about one thing: he was my first kiss, my first love, my first everything with a guy. He had a point. I thought he was okay, and plus, he did bring my favorite wine. Rose of Ivanhoe. It's sweet but tangy. Try it.

I opened the door, still pretty wry of Russ, and he goes, "Hi!" with a friendly smile. "Trust me?" and he puts out the flowers in front of him. They were my favorite. Daisies.

I just love Daisies!

So yeah, of course I smiled. "Yeah," I said. "I trust you. Come on in."

Biggest mistake.

"Okay," he said.

The first thing he did when he walked in was say how hot it was inside the place, and I reminded him, yet again, that my fans don't work, and he just laughed and said, "Some things never change." Then he sat down on my living room couch.

"You like *Taxi Driver?*" I asked him. "Been getting into Martin Scorsese. Terrific director. I want to buy *Wolf of Wall Street* next. I hear it's good."

"It is, Sal. It's sort of guy-ish, though. But anyways, sit, sit. I wanted to talk to you."

So I did. I crossed my legs and sort of looked over at the bat that was at the front door, in case he tried anything rash or crazy.

"Okay. Look," Russell started off, "we have our baggage, but who doesn't? I don't hate you for telling on me at work. That's not my intentions to hate you. Yeah, sure, I *resented* you, initially, but, um, I'll have to get over that—and I have . . . Wine?"

"Sure," I said. "Is that Rose of Ivanhoe?"

"Your favorite."

"You're so sweet!"

"Thanks, babe," he said, and then he popped open the cork. I look back at it now and I should have known something was odd because when he popped the cork it didn't sound like the normal *pop*. It didn't have that sizzle type of opening. It was more of a *clunk*. It was as if the bottle was already opened, even though, somehow, the package was still intact, or *looked* intact at the time, and I just didn't bother to look. But yeah, the sound was off-ish.

I didn't pay any attention to it like I should have. "I'll get glasses," I said, and got up.

"You do that," Russell said. "I'll be here."

So I went into the kitchen, got some wine glasses, and then came back to the living room couch. He smiled in a way I hadn't seen him smile before. That, too, I should have taken as a sign that something was odd.

I set the glasses down on the coffee table in front of us. Then I looked at the flowers sitting on the table. "Where did you get these?" I asked. "I swear they look like the ones by the garden that's down the street."

"They aren't," Russell said. "I got them from this guy selling them at the intersection over there"—and he pointed. Either he was lying and in fact got them from my neighbor down the street, or the guy at the intersection did. Either way, they looked just like the flowers I said. That was a third sign that something was odd. Russell poured the glasses. "I know you like this stuff," he said, "so I'll put a lil' more in yours."

"Thanks." I didn't really care for more, but I guess it was whatever.

So we got to talking and I was sipping my drink but Russell wasn't even touching his. He was explaining something about me, but it's hard to remember what. I'll put it here what he said.

"Sally, you're the most beautiful girl I've ever known. I think you're just the s■t. That's why I decided that even though I got fired I, um, should at least come over and say I was sorry, in person.

"We've always butted heads and always done this or that [I, Sally, am omitting here] but I want you to know that you were my first love, too.

"You've inspired me in some ways to be more honest with myself. I shouldn't have taken the money from those people in the group, so to speak. I should have been honest about business. It's just that, well, I'm going through some stuff with lawyers and probation and everything, so I really need that money.

"I'm glad you got that big insurance payment—" (lucky for me, I keep all my money on a debit card with a PIN, or else I would have lost all that money, too, along with . . . oh . . . well, you'll see in a sec) "and I want to let you know, Sally, that I'm truly proud of you.

"You're the smartest, the most kind, the most polite-est, *the must this, the most that, the most this, the most that, the most this, the* . . ." and the rest is something of a blur.

According to the police report, Russell, this guy that is pouring his heart out to me, this guy I used to love, hate, all that bull . . . well, he roofied me.

My face is beyond repair. I don't remember pretty much anything after that because I went into a coma. Russell—oh *God,* I'm crying right now while I'm writing this (okay, okay, get it together, Sally)—Russell roofied me, got my car keys off the little hanger thingy by my door, seatbelted me inside my car, poured gasoline on the inside and outside of my car, and set me on fire with matches (while I'm still inside the car!).

I'm lucky I'm still alive. But my face is literally mangled (or going to be). You know that one girl in that one movie with Angelina Jolie or something—I think it's called *Girl, Interrupted*—well, in that movie this one character, Polly Clark, A.K.A. "Torch (awful name!)," is a burn victim.

Her face is completely jacked up. Oh man. My eyes are watering so bad! ——I look like Torch! My face is all bandaged up and everything and they say it'll take *months* before I can even take the bandages off.

I went into a coma because Russell put too much Rohypnol in the wine bottle than people normally do. Right now he's on the run, but I guess he got what he wanted. He took away everything from me. I feel sick to my stomach.

There's a part in the police report I refused to read because it's too much for me. Basically I have a hunch that Russell also raped me before he burned me alive inside my car without me pretty much being conscious to do anything. I'm not a virgin anymore. This is so upsetting to me that I can't even think. I can't believe this monster! I HATE HIM!

So now I have to deal with these cops and everything and I got out of a three-day coma and then had all these pain medications and everything. I told them one request: *I wanted my journal.* It's all I thought about. I couldn't help it. I wanted to write this down immediately. I even saw on the police report that my neighbor, Jerry (never talked about him before, in this, because I see him very briefly, in passing, when I go to work in the mornings), was the one who called the cops.

Jerry said he didn't hear anything outside until Russell set everything on fire. Jerry didn't even hear the gasoline being poured. I guess Russell did it very slightly all over the place.

These hospital bills are going to be through the roof, but I think it's being paid for by Crime Victims. I hope. I really hope I don't have to lose all the money I collected. Because, again, Russell would get what he wanted.

So Russell got his revenge (a), took my virginity (b), burned my F'ing face off and pretty much mangled my entire body so pretty much nobody will want me after all this is over (c) (with probably intent to murder), and he's on the run like a coward. I guess no matter what way you spin it he got his revenge. . . . Incidentally, I asked one of the police officers about if it's a misdemeanor to burn a car or house down as long as no living inhabitants are around, and the officer said, "Just get some rest." I guess I was probably wrong. But then again, I *was* a living inhabitant inside the thing Russell burned. I hope, hope, hope they find him and throw him in jail forever! I hate Russell, and I missed New Years because of all this.

February, 4th, 12:01 p.m.

I forgot to mention that Shelby and Sherry were the ones that brought me my journal to the hospital. They came in this morning and were crying like how I have been. Sherry told me to not worry about my job because this is grounds for me to keep my job after all this is done. She told me not to spend my money, though, and to get better.

Shelby just cries the entire time and it makes me cry, too, more so than I'm already doing. I did tell her about what I'm going through. Like how my bandages have this silver or whatever to prevent infections and things like that. And how I'm probably going to get skin grafts on my face and major seeable parts of my body. It's crazy, I told her, because a skin graft is pretty much taking a piece of skin from another part of your body and then making it into these cross-hatching rows and stapling them to the majorly damaged area. It's pretty cool when you think about it.

My butt is going to pretty much be entirely cut to make all those skin grafts. You see, when I was in my car during the fire, I was sitting down in my driver's seat. Russell locked the doors when he left. So when help came (meaning Jerry) he smashed the driver-side window, unlocked the door, and dragged my body out of the car and poured a bunch of buckets of water on me. The problem was that he didn't do it fast enough from the time Russell first lit the car on fire to the time when my body was saved.

Anyway, why I'm saying this is because my butt skin is almost intact because I was sitting down the whole time, and I have leather seats so it's a little bit harder, I guess, for them to burn. So they are going to take all the skin grafts on my butt and put them on my face and arms and parts of my legs. So yeah, I'm going to have butt skin on my face.

Isn't that just peachy/grand?

So I'm telling Shelby this and she can't really handle it, the poor girl. Imagine my shoes, I told her. Imagine going back into work looking like hell. Imagine sinning.

Sinning? I don't know why I wrote that just now. I guess I could cross it out ... but I don't really feel like it.

And before Shelby left, I told her one thing: "Wait. Can you wait a moment?" and she did. "I want to write something in my book here, real quick," I said, and that something was this very entry. I'm about to tell her, "Take this journal back to my apartment; I don't want to see it again; I don't want to write in it and be reminded of being at a gosh-darn hospital and being miserable. I want this memory to somehow fade away."

February, 18th, 10:20 a.m.

Finally out of that hell-hole—excuse my French. The bandages are still on, but I'll all be right. Nothing newsworthy. I don't want to talk about being at that place. It was awful. I pretty much have to take it easy from now on and rest, and yeah, at least I'm getting FMLA while I wait to be all healed up. I have to put on this cream all over my body and take all these crazy painkillers and everything. I'm in pain at the moment, so I'm going to cut this entry short. ~~I really can't write while I'm high on pills~~.

February, 20th, 11:11 a.m.

I checked my mail today and this is what I got:

> Dear Sally,
> I haven't told Dad because I didn't want you to freak out. Me and my husband feel so sorry for what happened. I hope you get better. That a█hole! I wish he could be found. I know about all this because your boss called me. I hope she didn't call Dad. He would be going apes█t over this. Trust me. Dad would murder. I just want you to be okay because you're my baby sister. Work has been way too hectic and I don't have anymore time off or else I would visit you while you're going through this. I just wanted to write this because I know you probably didn't bring your phone to

> the ER when it happened because I tried to call and text you. I want you to know, Sal, that I love you so so so much! I want you to be okay. I'm repeating myself now and I'm sorry.
>
> PS: Please get rest.
>
> Love,
>
> ███ ███

Copied it verbatim. Thanks, sis. Thanks for not coming down because your work is "hectic." I almost died over here and my life is pretty much ruined and I need someone to be here and to talk to and you're over there having your life being all "hectic." Wow. I'm jealous of you, sis. A█hole. What a joke. Hectic my a█!

February, 27th, 6:11 a.m.

Been reading lots, been doing lots of drugs. I've bought a lot of weird psychedelics and I'm seeing all types of weird things. Maybe I'm depressed with myself. All I know is is that I'm over all of this. I'm so sick of waking up and looking in the mirror. It's like it's not even me. It's like I'm trapped inside this fake body and—Oh crap. I just flinched with anxiety just from writing this. I need to take it easy.

I've always wondered why I feel the way I've felt. I'm thinking that before this life I was somewhere else. I keep feeling like it might be possible to be a spirit of some kind in a previous life. Sometimes I feel like I was forced into my own body and I don't have control over it.

I hope this isn't weird to think. I probably should stop doing the drugs; they make me queasy. But on a side note, I'm trying to take up some hobbies that I've always wanted to do. I've actually always wanted to be a writer, I'm finding out. I think I always was a writer—I just never read anything and never put my thoughts down on paper. Sometimes they freak me out, sometimes they help me.

But as far as freaking out goes . . . it's happening frequently, and I don't think I can stop it. I think I want to quit my job at the collection agency. So what I'll do, I'll just ride this FMLA out, and when it *does* run out, sayonara!

March, 1st, 10:43 a.m.

Woke up this morning and decided to close my phone service I got a couple weeks back. I just don't want to speak to anybody because they all annoy me with all the sorrys. What are they saying sorry for? They didn't do this to me. It makes me mad and upset. STOP IT. Please, people. Leave me in PEACE. So I'm shutting everything off and I'm just going to be alone and sulk. I've been sulking a lot and it feels good. But I may have to leave the house soon, and oh yeah, I'm writing short stories now. I'm making this short story about these two aliens. One is black and one is white. It's about them coming down to Earth and touring with a suicidal man. Only, the ending is this: Blackey is Satan, and Whitey, well, he's God Himself. I think it's going okay. I may turn it into a novel. We'll see. I don't know if I'm any good. I've always wanted to write a novel. Imagine going up to someone and saying, "Hey! I wrote a book!" But yeah, most likely people'll just say, "Oh cool!" and then go about their business. Writing is, like, the lowest paying thing in the world, and oh yeah, another thing: I think I like money because it's proof you're doing something right. But the actual *object* of money, well, I don't like it's purpose, that's it.

March, 3rd, 3:04 p.m.

I'm so upset right at this moment. *Ugh!* So I start my day off pretty well, see. I wake up and I'm actually not in that much pain, and so I look out my window and I could hear birds chirping and everything. Like I never really notice such a thing, but today I did. So I opened the window and you know what, I closed my eyes, took in a breath of that fresh Florida air. Aside from the fact that cars are surrounding the front of my house, and I didn't really see the birds.

But anyways, I actually was feeling sort of positive. I didn't look in the mirror, which is a good thing. I've actually got rid of most of the mirrors inside my apartment. It just makes me upset, and I don't want to be upset anymore. I also haven't been checking my mail, lately, so I may get evicted soon or something, but I'm not too sure, anyway.

But whatever, I got on my pants and a shirt, no bra, and put on this really baggy hoodie I got when I was in high school and never wore. It smelled really funny, but hey, it conceals, which is what I was going for!

I got outside and decided that, hey, I want to buy a book or something. So I walked over to Hastings, this crazy book store, and got over there and yeah.

Even when I got out there it *smelled* lovely in the air.

So I walk up to the store doors and—Wait. I have to say this: I haven't left my house pretty much ever since coming back from the hospital. Maybe here and there for food or whatever, but nothing too major, I think. So yeah, anyways, I walked up and a bum decides to look over at me and he makes a blow-out *pfft* noise, as if I'm garbage or something. So I got ticked off and said to him, "Take a picture; it'll last longer."

And he goes, "I'd burn that picture . . . Just like your face." Total MEANIE! I felt like crying when he said that! I pretty much found out that I couldn't speak up to anyone anymore and be my sassy self. So I didn't say anything back to the bum and went on into the store.

I immediately go in and they didn't really greet me like all the other times I go in. The people there are all teenagers in high school and don't give a dang about their jobs, but their bosses always make them say hi. This time, I saw one of them snicker and whisper to another kid in his ear, and I just *knew* they were talking about me, and it made me sad.

I tried not to care. I went down passed the registers and into the book section, and I saw this really weird author on display. His name was Kurt Vonnegut. He had a red book with a picture of a skull on it. I flipped through it and it actually seemed kind of cool. So I put it under the old armpit, just because, you know, why not?!

Then I started going from shelf to shelf. Nobody was around, at first. Usually nobody's ever around the book section. They usually rent movies and buy music over on the other side of the store. The book side is pretty much for the book-buyers that rarely come in—on account of the fact that Hastings is too expensive for books—or the people that steal stuff within the store—because there's no cameras on the book side, stupidly.

I pretty much only picked up the stuff with cool artwork on it. There was this one guy name Chuck Palahnuik, and it turns out he's the guy that made *Fight Club*! I got all giddy. So I grabbed that. Then I looked at another one of his books. It had this picture of a girl and then you flip it over and it's a old guy. I read the back (same thing on the front!), and then I got out my phone and read on it. It's about a girl who shoots herself in the jaw so she could be ugly. I could relate. So I picked it up.

Then I started to walk more down the aisle and I saw a guy start to come down, too, and then look up at me. I smiled at him but then his eyes got all wide and he turned the other way. Then I frowned. It doesn't feel good to not have anyone look at you special anymore.

I went to the classics side and I saw so many different things there. Stuff I read in school, see. I picked up all the Salinger's, all the Faulkner's, all the Shakespeare's, all the Rand's, all the big novels, ever! I got all giddy. But it was too many books to hold. So I set them all down on the ground and walked back to the cash registers, and I tried my hardest to not be scared of getting laughed at.

I got me a buggy and when I turned around, this lady asked me if I needed any help, her having a big, wide smile. She was the manager, I think.

"No I don't need help," I said. "Thank you."

She leaned in and whispered all close to me, "I respect people like you. If you need anything, let me know, okay?" and she smiled again.

I just smiled and walked away, for obvious reasons . . .

When I came back to my books on the ground, I saw an associate picking them up off the ground and putting them back, away, all that mess.

So I go, "Those are mine. I'm buying them."

The guy goes, "Woah, woah, whatever you want," and he stands up, hands up, and walks away.

So I picked up the books and put them all in the buggy.

Then I decided I did enough shopping, so I went on over to the Hardback Café. The lady there was really nice. She helped me ring up some things and she told me some sales and if I wanted a coffee and I smiled and said yes. She made me a caramel frappe. It was delicious! It tasted better than Starbucks, in my opinion.

Then the lady at the register told me, "Hey, I see you bought a lot of books and stuff. Here. I'll get you extra bags. I want you to know that you could read here any time if you'd like. Look around. It's dead. I'm totally bored. You could read here and keep me company."

"How old are you?" I asked her.

"Eighteen. You?"

"Twenty-three. Just turned, kind of . . ."

"Lucky *you*," she said. "But yeah, I think you ought to come here more. My boss tells me to say this to people, but I think you'd actually be really fun to talk to."

"Why's that?" I asked. "Because of my face?"

The chick got all weirded out. "No, no, no! Nothing like that! I don't judge people. But I do think you're sweet. I saw that you picked up Kurt Vonnegut's stuff and J. D. Salinger and I thought, 'What the hey . . .' so I thought you'd come here more."

"Okay," I said. "That'll be nice. I'll stop by tomorrow, though. I got to put these books away back home."

"I hear ya. My books get all messed up if I buy a lot of 'em. There's a book club here, too, by the way. I'm leader of it. We have about three people; me included. Me and two other old ladies. It sucks because nobody's interested."

"I know," I sighed. "Well, I'll just, you know, think about it."

The chick looked funny. "What's your name, friend?"

"Sally. Yours?"

"Ashley," she said. "You can call me 'Ash,' though."

"Ash Ketchum!"

"Oh hush! You're silly, Sally!"

"Call me 'Sal,' if you don't mind."

" 'Kay, Sal. Have a nice day!"

"You too!" I said, and I left.

At least Ashley was one good thing today, besides all the haters drinking Haterade.

March, 4th, 11:30 a.m.

I miss my hair. I miss having the type of hair to just touch and feel. That's one thing I hate about all of this. I just wish, you know, I had my hair again, so I could be happier. I miss brushing it. The cool thing about no hair, though, is that I threw out most of my hair-product stuff. It actually made my bathroom seem less cluttered, which I liked.

At 9 o'clock, I woke up, got dressed, and decided to take Ashley's offer and go down to Hastings to read, maybe write . . . Or whatever, just *something*, you know?

Ashley was there. Ashley is such a sweetie pie. Her and I sat down and had some coffee. Occasionally she had to get up and make something for customers, but only occasionally. The thing about Ashley, she told me all the places she's ever worked. She said she worked at CVS, Blockbuster, a gas station, et cetera, before she wound up at this joint called Hastings. She's not the café manager or anything, but she likes to handle all the product. She likes to tell customers about stuff and everything. She said she's perfectly satisfied with her job she's at. She says she smiles everyday.

I asked her what it's like to genuinely smile. She smiled and told me that it's the best feeling in the world. I told her that I don't think I've ever genuinely smiled a day in my life. She said sure I have. I had to've had at least one time I smiled. I told her not genuinely, and she said, "Pity," and then tickled my armpit and I laughed. She stopped, though, because I said my skin hurt. She said sorry.

I like Ashley but I don't think I'll go to her book club. I think it's weird to say things about a book that are meaningful to you. . . . After all, it's just you and the book and nobody else. If the book speaks to you, don't go blabbing about how it makes you *feel* to everybody else. Let it get kept inside and just try to genuinely smile about it, I guess.

That's what I'm going to try and do.

March, 5th, 3:20 p.m.

I want to spend these next few days just reading. I think it's better that way. I'm just blazing through these novels like cake.

March, 8th, 4:57 a.m.

March, 12th, 6:01 p.m.

Something made me cry tears of joy today. I can't wait to write it. I'm going to spend a long time on this entry because I actually accomplished my first *genuine* smile!

So I'm at Hastings, talking to Ashley, sipping a decaf mocha frappe, and then, get this: Ashley goes, "Oh my . . . *God*. Don't look. Okay. There's this guy I used to know that worked here. His name is Kevin. He's really crazy and funny. He's really hot."

"Where is he?" I said.

"Over there. He's checking out the books."

So I lift up my head and then—

"Sally! Don't be a creeper! Sit. Gosh," Ashley said. "He comes over here no matter what. I used to talk with him all the time and flirt with him."

"Oh yeah, Ash?"

"Ooooh *yeah!*"

I started to laugh.

"What?" Ash said to me. "What's the joke?"

"You're all giddy. I'm happy for you."

"No. Not just yet, missy. He's also sort of weird, too."

"Weird?"

"He never makes moves. He'll sort of flirt and everything and the second you think he's cute, he pretty much gets all nervous and weird and he'll walk away."

"Really?"

"Mhm."

"Wow," I said.

"I know!" Ash said. "I once got close to him, and him and I were flirting and I sort of looked into his big, big eyes and smiled. But then he started talking about some other girl he liked. It really screwed me up."

"I hate when guys do that."

"Oh Sally!—that's the thing!—he's not like other guys. The thing of it is is that he sort of puts up a huge fake, I sort of think. Like he talks about taking girls out, doing sweet things, but the moment you like him, he'll shoo you away. I think he has some issues or something. He once said he's going to see a psychiatrist."

"I had to see one of those for awhile—it's not weird."

"I think you should. From what you tell me, people are reacting to you differently from what you were used to. Those pictures of you on your Facebook and on your phone, *wow!* you were really gorgeous!"

"It makes me sad, Ash. Really. Sometimes I feel like—"

"Hey, Kevin!" interrupts Ashley (just as *he* walks up), "how you been?!"

"Hey, Ash. Been good."

I wasn't looking up at Kevin; I was too scaredy-cat.

Ash asked him, "How's your job at ▮▮▮▮? Still paying well?"

"S'okay. The season's sort of passed and I'm not hitting budget."

Just then, my brain sort of lit up. "Holy s▮▮t." I said this really wild-like as I looked up at Kevin. "We worked at the same job."

"I'm sorry? Never seen you there," he said. "—Hey, Ashley. Can you make me just a regular hot coffee—black?"

"Sure thing!" she said. "I hope you brought cash, Kevin. Last time you didn't tip me, and you *know* I'm your most favoritest barista in the whole, wide *world!*"

He laughed. "Just make me the coffee, doll-face."

~~Doll-face. That's so cute of him. He was flirting.~~

"*Oh!* Okay!" Ashley said all excited, and then walked off.

Kevin looked at me and said, "So we worked at the same place, huh?"

I nodded. "Mhm."

Kevin sat down in the chair in front of me (where Ash was sitting). "That's cool. What's your name?"

"Sally. . . ."

Then, get this: his eyes pretty much got so big I swear you could see into his *brain!* "Oh . . . my . . . God! Sally! Oh my God, oh my God. *The* Sally?"

"Yes, Kevin." I rolled my eyes. "Weren't you the guy always staring at me in the break room? I was in the same group as you. Sherry's group."

"Oh Jesus. Wow. I remember now. I feel dumb. I used to look over at you in the break room all the time. Wow. So why did you leave?"

"Well . . . look at me . . ."

"I know. But what happened?"

"Remember Russell?"

"Oh yeah. That a▮hole at our job that tried you at the group lunch—yeah, I remember him. What about him?"

"Well, he sort of came over my house, drugged me, and then put my body in my car and set me on fire."

Kevin's eyes got big again. "You're joking...."

"Nope. Not at all, Kev." Then I took a sip of my drink. "I can't believe you didn't hear about it."

"Dude. What a straight up coward. Holy crap. What a straight up coward. I wanna fight that motherf⬛ker. F⬛k that guy. F⬛k him!"

"I try not to think about it."

"Jesus Christ. This is so lame."

"I know," I said, and then I took another sip of my drink.

"The reason I'm upset," Kevin began, "is because I used to, well, have a thing for you."

"Everyone did," I said.

"Yeah. I'm sorry. But not like me."

"What do you mean?"

"It was almost like an obsession, you could say."

I leaned back a bit.

"No!" Kevin laughed. "Sally. Be nice. Come on. No. It's not like that. I more mean that I used to think so fondly of you. I was *really* attracted to you.

"You were the part of my day I looked forward to. Whenever we would have break I always made sure to sit in a place where I could see you. I thought you were perfect."

"Well," I sighed, "I guess those days are gone."

"What do you mean?"

"Look at me. I'm ugly."

"That's not true," Kevin said. "I still think you're really sweet."

I almost wanted to cry right then and there. "Really?" I said to him. "Like, you really mean that? Like you're not just saying that?"

"I swear. I think just from talking to you I just know how cool you are or whatever. I always got mad at myself for—"

I couldn't take it. I stood up and gave him a hug, reaching over the table. You know the ones. A big, big hug!

"You're squeezing my face, Sally," my little bug said. "You're adorable but you're hurting me."

So I stopped and said, "That hurt me, too. I'm still recovering from this. My skin sucks now." Then I sat down again and sort of kept quiet.

". . . I feel bad, Sal," Kevin finally said. "I really do."

"How come you never talked to me, butt-head?" I asked this with a frown. ". . . I'm waiting. Explain!"

"I, uh . . ." he hesitated. "I, um, don't really know why."

"That's selfish of you to not've came up and at least introduced yourself. Even in the group you never spoke to me but you always spoke to the other girls."

"I flirt with everyone. There's that one chick Shelby there, and she—"

"*That's my* best friend, and no, she has a boyfriend."

"Really?" he said, like he was *surprised* or something. "I thought she was cute."

"You know," I said, "you're a d▮k, you know that? I'm sitting here asking you why you didn't talk to me and you're sitting here telling me that you were thinkin' about other girls, when I know *damn well* that's not the case. How about you start all over, like a man, and give me the real truth. Come on. I'll wait."

"Uh . . ." he hesitated like a cute little kid. "Um . . ."

"Come on, Kev. Honestly."

"I think I was scared to talk to you because you're so beautiful. I feel like—"

"HERE!" Ashley interrupts, sarcastically mad at Kevin, setting down his coffee in front of him. "Black. Black as night. Sorry it took so long. I had a few customers, randomly. What are you guys talkin' about?"

"Well, thanks for the coffee but I, um——"

"Can you please give us privacy, Ashley?" I asked her. "Please. Give us 'alone time.' Please."

"*Ooooh!*" Her eyes got all big. "I see. Well . . . toodaloo!" and she walked off, surprisingly no questions asked.

Kevin took a sip of his coffee.

"Well, Kev . . . ?" I held my hand out. "You were saying?"

He licked his lips for a second. "There's only a couple notions that you have to realize, Sally. First, you have to account for the great risk a girl of your stature holds. One thing is for sure: majority of women of your beauty—yes, *still* you are beautiful in my eyes—have been given anything and everything of this world, neck and foot. This makes me upset.

"Two, majority of men, big and small, all ages, pretty much have a universal idea of *physical* beauty: the girls that are under the allotted potential suitor's height—"

"Allotted?" I asked him.

"Yes. Allotted."

"Okay. Go."

"So yeah," he started again, "secondly, as I said, girls that have these traits:—is care-free, is *normal,* for F's sake—they must be under I'd say five foot three inches, et cetera, and they gotta have big breast, birthing hips, all wide-like, in other words, and the chicks got to have 'the lips.'"

"The lips?" I asked.

"Yes."

"Okay. Continue." I was getting sort of mad at him.

And he goes on like, "Third, the girl's are only interested in image, or 'frame,' if you will. The frame is a man's portrayal. If a girl was referred from another girl on a man's appearance, then the man can be viewed from the girl as attractive. The only thing attractive girls like are attractive males. But there's only some of them, like there's only some of hot girls. Tens like tens. Um, what do guys like me do?

"I'm not that good-looking. I do art, and I'm not that good at talking. My job isn't too good of pay, so I look like a last-resort type of suitor for these girls I desire. I stay put. That's what I mean, Sally. I'm trying to say I didn't speak to you because you had no good image of me before I approached."

"But how could I?" I asked. "You can't *like* someone before the approach. You can only find them attractive."

"My point exactly, Sally. My point is right there. You, the hot chick, have to view me as high-value before I approach, or else you shoo me away before the first words I say come out of my mouth.

"Look, Sal. Girls like me only sometimes. When I approach them they already have an idea in their head if they're going to have sex with me or not. It's nature. It's high replication value. The replication value in a male, in our modern society, is him having a good job—one that adequately provides for a women and her future children—and having good looks—for the children must look good for *their* future relationships and survival—and the man has to provide comfort, emotionally, financially, and physically, whether through lying, telling the truth, or his 'awesome personality,' as women sometimes say . . .

"Also, too, Sally, it does help if a man is over five foot eight or ten, which I myself am not. Height also shows power and strength. A hot chick or woman likes to look up at her man and feel safe. It's as if the 'little girl' in her is seeking a father, almost. Yeah. That's right. Like a father, and I'm *far* from father material, Sally, so I couldn't *possibly* approach you because I'm not at that, so to speak, 'father level' of a man. I'm just me."

"But Kev . . ." I said, "you're missing the very point. Humans have to have together-ness. Without it, you're alone. That's what I mean. All this time I'll be alone. That's why it's selfish."

"But I'm alone, too," he said. "And I'm fine with that."

"But I'm not . . ."

"Why? Why must we be together?"

"Because, Kev, 'together-ness' unites us as a civilization. It only kills us to be hermits, which you're being."

"No I'm not!"

"Yes. You. Are!"

"Prove it."

"Okay, I'll prove it," I began . . . "Firstly, like you said, it's not all about looks, it's about the *indivi*dual. What you're looking at is the potential survival methods of the individual.

"Of course if you're in the jungle, and hungry, with no food to eat, then yes, you *will* choose the suitor that best fits *those* needs. If a person is happy, they won't be hungry no more. They will feel complete.

"Now, I know what you're thinking: 'But I'm not happy,' and that's okay, because I'm not either. But what if, say, we talked—like we are now—and bonded—like are now—and we end up really falling for one another, we could feel a sense of together-ness that we wouldn't possibly achieve without the 'other half'?

"It's crazy to think, huh, Kevin? That there's people that are happy, and people that are not. But most of all, there's unhappy people looking to seek something: and that something is—you guessed it—love. God is love. People being together is love. But yeah, I'm being a hypocrite because I, too, am not so-called 'together-ful.' I'm just, well, you know, *whatever*."

"You're not 'whatever,' Sal."

"I feel that way."

"I feel that way, too. But I see what you mean. The bottom line is that basically now I'm realizing that we are the same person, in regards to, you know, ideals . . ."

I nodded. "Yup, yup."

"—but I do have a question, Sal," he said . . . "um, did Ashley say anything to you about me, prior to me walking up?"

I go, "Yes, but . . ." before Kevin said, "Ah-*ha!* See. Told ya!"

And I just smiled. "That's not fair!" I said.

"It is! My point was proven."

"You're a butt-head!"

"That I am," lil' Kevy Kev Kev said. "Say, I do want to ask something."

"Shoot," I said. "All ears, baby."

"How come you never would really talk or associate with the group much? Even, like, when Sherry or Shelby and you would eat lunch, you'd still be sort of not into everything."

"Wow! You *really* watched me!"

"I was a creeper, I guess!" he laughed. "Just tell me, please!"

"I've just been depressed my entire life. In some ways I'm thinking about just up and leaving this place."

"Up and leaving?"

"Yeah. Just going."

"Why?" Kevin asked.

"Because I'm tired of it. It's like all of us are just doing things for ours and other people's perceptions. We aren't doing things that are natural.

Like if I wake up in a bad mood, you'd *still* have to say good morning to people, even though you don't want to."

"I know exactly what you mean," Kev said.

"I just don't really get it, really. I'm putting up a front for people, and it's especially for me, the girl that is good-looking, because, hey, something that looks good has to be pleasant, right? *Right, Kevin?*"

"I guess," he sighed. "But I don't know."

"I don't know either. Maybe I'm just bitter or mean."

"I don't really see why."

"I don't either. But now that I've got a reason, my own life has become clear: I hate it. I don't like the things inside it. Everyone is too selfish for anything, Kevin. Really. And——

"Say, Kev, I want to tell you about this ideal I have. You ready?"

"Okay, yeah," he said.

"Okay. Um . . . basically I have this idea—Can I have a sip of your drink?"

"What?"

"It looks tasty."

"Sure," he laughed passively.

So I grabbed his coffee, sipped it, winced at how black it was, and then said, "Jesus that's *strong*. But yeah, what I was going to say was this ideal I have is about lions."

"Lions?"

"Yeah," I said. "I had this dream this one time about these two girls. One was playing hopscotch and one was drawing pictures with chalk or something, on the ground, and pretty much the drawer chick drew a bunch of lions and tigers and bears, and I didn't really understand it.

"Now I sort of do, Kev . . . I think the lion is Capitalism, in a weird way. Or society, maybe."

"But what does a drawing have to do with Capitalism?" Kevin asked me.

"Let me explain. Basically the drawing chick drew a lion in one of the hopscotch girl's numbers. She got pissed because the lion was in her number-one box. The girl that drew it, though, didn't understand why she was getting mad. The box isn't really even hers to begin with. It's the park's box.

"The hopscotch chick is getting pissed by this because she doesn't want those numbers, those things providing her with such a laughable 'good-time,' in her boxes. So she gets mad. So you could hoot and holler at the hopscotch girl for doing that, but the point is this:

"Life isn't like a box of chocolates, like Forrest Gump says, so to speak. Life is just a box, and if there's a lion inside it, you will shoo it, yell at it, do whatever to it, to get your way. But there's people drawing the lions and people having them be put inside their boxes. There's the winners and the losers, and you know what, *I'm* on the loser-side."

After a pause, "Wow," said Kevin, "holy crap."

"I know," I said.

"Jesus, Sally. That's crazy."

"I know. But it makes me justify . . . you know . . ."

"I understand."

"You *do?*" I said.

"I do," he said. "But think long and hard on what you're doing because it effects people."

"I want to put lions in other people's boxes because all this time *they* have been putting them in *my* boxes, and I'm sick and tired of it. So F it."

"I'd hate to have one of your lions in *my* box!" Kevin laughed. "Just know that if you need anything—and I'm telling you anything at all—just let me know. I don't want you to be this upset."

"Thanks, Kev. . . ."

"No problem," he said. "Say! I'm writing a novel right now. It's called *Biflocka*. It's about drugs or whatever. I want to use you in it somehow. Is that cool?"

"Of course, Kevin! I write too!"

"Yeah?!"

"I write journal entries and stuff, but I don't know, it's whatever."

"I see. That's great! But I do want you to know about it, I guess."

"Show me it whenever you get the chance."

"I will," Kevin told me. "Most def."

And I had my first genuine smile.

But then I said, "I really got to go. . . ."

"Okay," Kevin said. "Be safe."

"I will," I said, and I walked out of the café, where three kids, all in high school, laughed and told me how ugly I was and threw pizza at me, and I thought, "There's not going to be much more of this crap I have to deal with. . . ."

March, 13th, 7:46 a.m.

Happy Anniversary, Mr. Journal. Did you know that today is Friday the 13th? So fitting for the situation at hand. But whatever. I don't care anymore.

Basically I've decided that I should end my life. I want to put that as bluntly as possible, Future Sally, and that would mean that puts an end to you, too. It's okay, though. Because there is some shred of hope left: The hope that I'll be in a better place, *duh!* But I have to plan out a few things, first, to, you know, get my affairs in line.

The first thing I've decided to do is write letters to all my friends and family. I feel like making just one suicide note is dumb. If you don't make notes for each person, I feel like they won't understand, fully, of your intentions. I feel like one note doesn't explain enough. But I suppose this journal does enough explaining on it's own, Future Sally, but I couldn't *possibly* give this to them because it's way too intimate for my taste. I sort of want this to be private, to a degree.

The way I want to die is the fastest way possible. I want to shoot myself in the head, and I don't mean like just sit down and do it—like I've sort of tried to do before—I more mean in the way of actually making it happen.

I'm looking up online of how people kill themselves, and you know what, it's actually the toughest thing in the world! Killing yourself is not easy. Do you know that sometimes kids in high school try to kill themselves and fail, and then they tell themselves, or their haters tell them, "Wow. Can't get anything right? Not even killing yourself . . ."

which causes the person to actually get sadder, et cetera.

I don't want all that. I want it to be quick and simple. So I've decided to perform a double-take type of suicide.

Basically I'll get a rope and hang myself from the ceiling fan—it's new and sturdy and won't break easily. I'll stand on a chair, put my neck into the loop, and then just sort of kick the chair away and drop down. But the thing of it is is that this method leaves room for error. You could break your neck, or not die, or just lose oxygen temporarily and then you're brain-damaged for the remainder of your life, and then, after that, all the hospital people around you try to keep you alive with your crappy brain, as if it's *not* your choice to live or die, regardless of other's thoughts.

So what I'll do in this double-take is while I'm kicking the chair from under me I'll shoot myself in the head at the same time. This way it's pretty much heightening my chances of dying. I'd probably use my father's gun that I still have. The bullets are still in it. But I'm just now thinking that doing this act in my apartment probably isn't a good idea. So I may go to some deep forest and hang from a tree or something. That might be less gruesome for people.

So I got the method and the game plan on these notes, but what about my will?

Basically I'll explain that in the first letter to my dad, and then just go from there. Pretty much I'm going to write down with my pen here of what I'm going to say, and then type it all out or something and print it, mail it. But, like I said, this journal is *not* to be seen by anyone. So let's backtrack:

Here, I'm writing down, with pen, the suicide letters to each person. Then I'll type them. Then I'll make a new letter; and so on. . . . After they are all done, I'm going to mail them out. It's Friday so I should be able to write all of these before the post office closes at 5.

1▇1 Mal▇nch Circle,
West ▇lm Be▇h, FL. 3▇62

Dear Daddy,
 You're the best thing that's ever happened to me, even though

I never showed it. You've always, always been real with me, and I appreciate that. So I've decided to stop being silent toward you and be real as possible, finally. For the sake of because.

I don't know if you know yet but I've been burned and my face is sort of mangled. I'm sure people have told you but I turned my phone off and deleted all my emails and social media stuff and I know I never invited you over to my house, so you don't know where I live. It's F'ed of me to not tell you, but I hope you understand that I don't want to ever see you be sad.

Sometimes I hate the brain I have. It truly sucks. I don't even think laughs or smiles help any. I just want to not have my mind. Lately when I listen to music I always keep thinking about it being played in my funeral and the feeling of leaving my body and listening to that music with my eyes closed as I leave the casket. I think about this now and it makes me sad but also hopeful that all this will eventually stop for me.

Some things are really strange to me. I just want to die, Dad. I just want to finally leave my little body. I'm tired of being trapped inside this vessel full of feelings. They hurt too much, and therefore, I'm unable to function in this life because, on the inside, I'm already dead as far as I'm concerned.

I want you to know that you didn't do anything to make this choice happen. You were always helpful to me. You were always there and I thank you for that. Even all those long talks on the phone we would have when you were away on business trips, I'd get a kick out of that.

But yeah, Dad, my suffering is beyond help because my suffering is being alive. I don't have a connection with anyone. I feel like everyone is separate from me. I don't even approach people anymore because it makes me sick to my stomach. Sometimes I feel like the old saying of "just be yourself" is a load of crap and doesn't really work.

I want you to take care of my affairs for me. I'm granting you my bank account with about 5000$ on it. Hopefully that can pay for me to be cremated. What I want is to have a funeral without a priest or anyone specializing in talking about death. I want music from the USB flash-drive that I'm enclosing in this envelope to be the music that could play in the background. The songs are as follows:

- Sam Smith - "Stay With Me"
- Tom Waits - "It's Over"
- Edward Sharpe and The Magnetic Zeros - "Home"

These are to be played while people pray about themselves or me. I also want people to read their letters they got from me aloud. I want people to know these are not in no way intimate. My debit card is enclosed, too, in this envelope, and it's PIN is ▮▮▮▮▮▮▮. My email is this: Partyg▮▮▮7▮▮▮@gmail.com. My password is w▮▮▮▮▮12

From there, at the funeral party, I want people who know me to say exactly how they felt about me. Good or bad. I want them to. I want them to say anything they want, and any memory they want. I would do the same for them.

I also want anyone wearing black to be kicked out of my funeral. I want everyone to dress in hawaiian shirts. Pretty colors. All of them bright. That way there's no way people will get depressed about my departure.

I want everyone to pray but I want them to have a purpose for their own lives. Let me explain. I don't want them to pray about me but I want them to pray about themselves. I want them to live because it works for them. I want them to know that nothing could be prevented.

I want them to know I envy them.

Also, I want the ceremony to be held at Okeeheelee Park's lake. The one by the golf course. I've never been to that lake and I know it's small, but I always found it to be peaceful. Please sprinkle my ashes in that lake. I would very much like that, if you guys eventually find where my body is.

That's another thing. My body is going to be hidden in a

forest somewhere. Probably the forrest across from the park. So by the time you get this I've already died. Don't feel sad or embarrassed, it's only temporary. I'll be in a cooler place soon. I want you to know that I love you. Oh yeah, one more thing: invite whoever you want to the funeral. Everyone! I want it to be a party!

P.S.: I'm going to give you letters to send out with each of the person's addresses, too, along with the debit card. Make sure you get those letters out. Counting on you.

Love,
Sally Fairfax

10■ J■er■n Way,
Boca R■n, FL. 3■60

Dear Dora,

Sorry for saying all those things about you and John. I'm just sorry, okay? That is all.

Sincerely,
Sally Fairfax

122 Ca■bad Ct.,
West Palm Beach, FL. 3■59

Dear T.N.,

I want you to know that you and D.L. are probably my best friends ever. I want you to know that every single memory that we've ever had together was honestly the funnest, most best-est times of my life. Especially high school when we skated after the "hellhole." I want you to know that I still kept those rollerblades whenever we did skate home. Remember that bridge from Palm Beach Central? You know the one. We would bomb it like some glorious hill! I remember my long blonde hair and your black hair were all flowy in the wind and everything. It's crazy to think about it now. But yeah. I've decided to kill myself, girl. It's not your fault. I'm just sending letters to everyone. I care about you a lot but I think you should contact my father about it. Here: Partyg▮▮7▮▮@gmail.com. Just keep cool. I love you. Be safe. Have the best life ever!

Love,
Sally Fairfax

101 Lion K▮g Rd.,
▮usta, ▮. 4▮05

Dear Sissy Dukes,

 I remember when you worked at Apple and you told me the Steve Jobs story about how there was a kid sitting next to you and he was talking about all the stuff Apple needs to do and whatever, and how Steve Jobs himself was in the cafeteria and taps the guy's shoulder and says to him, "We need more people like you working here," and then spins back around and continues to eat. Classic! I always think about how crazy of a CEO that guy is. Or was. The kid probably freaked!

 I miss little Alex. I want him to make me a drawing. Tell him to and I'll keep it with me forever. I have so much to say to you, Sis, but so little time.

 Anyways, I don't want you to know right away what's going on. Just call Dad. He'll know. Love you. Miss you so much.

Love,
Sally Fairfax

107 N. Gr■d Rd.,
San Antonio, TX. 8■54

Dear D.L.,

Good luck with the company. You know what I'm talking about, and that's all that matters. This company symbolizes me. I hope you know what that entails, too.

Sincerely,
Sally Fairfax

Address?
—Forward to Daddy

Dear Russell,

Thanks for enlightening me. Bye. I hope your life breaks into teeny, tiny pieces.

Hate,
Sally Fairfax

---

267 Fil■ore Dr.,
WPB, FL. 7■16

Dear Josh,

I don't love you to death. I think you're actually really weird. It's messed up to say this now, but it seems real to me. I do want you to attend the funeral. Tell your customers to stop buying your "dank-a■" weed.

Love,
Sally the Beezy!

10■6 Oke■obee Trail,
Lake Worth, FL. 3■06

Dear Sherry,

Hi. I just want you to know that everything is going to be okay. By the time you get this, you may already know what's going on in the city, or life, of Sally Fairfax's whatever. I want you to know you didn't do anything wrong to make me do this. I just want you to know that everything you've done has been great for me, and I love you. I sometimes hate when you make fun of me, but then again I make fun of you, too, at work. I just want you to know that there's no hard feelings with us. I also want you to know that you're beautiful and don't ever forget it. Oh. Also. I want you to know that this has nothing to do with my face. I've been thinking about this for a long time and by the way, when I first met you on the PalmTran, it was really the first time; but, however, it wasn't my first time meeting Jeff. He hit on me when I worked over at Flanigan's. He knew me. That's why it was sort of weird, and that's probably why I left the bus and got anxiety the way I did that day. I love you. No harm done.

P.S.: {read aloud to our group} You all are fake.   Yeah-ly,

Sally Fairfax

Address? —Forward to Daddy

Dear Mom,

I can't believe that you would leave my life the way you did. I needed a mother in my life. It's selfish that you did that. You probably won't ever read this because I still have no clue where you are. I hate you a million times and I hope you feel bad about leaving. Just know that you may have caused me to die. You left me in the dust, so yeah, I'm leaving YOU in the dust. Bye. NOT nice to know you!   Hate,

Sally Fairfax

Done with all the people I wanted to write to. As for that, I'm going to stamp an envelope a separate letter to a person I love, Ms. Not-So-Future Sally Fairfax. I'm going to mail it to the collection agency where my "love-interest" works. Hopefully they don't read the mail. I'll probably put "confidential" on the front of the envelope. Hopefully that does the trick. It's getting close to 5 o'clock so I better hurry before the post office closes! . . . Here:

> Attn. ███ ███ ███
> (Place Of Employment)
> P.O. Box 33█89,
> WPB, FL. 73█15
>
> Dear Kevin K. (Collector #439),
>
> There's a couple things I want you to know. First, I would like to tell you that you were the most brilliant person I ever met. Really. You were. The conversation we had at Hastings Café, on the 12th of March, was amazing. I really connected with you and you made me smile. It's been a long time since I felt anything I felt with you. I want you to know that I love you and not the type of love where someone just says it, I mean the real kind. The kind where I would marry you and live my life with you forever. I hope you don't think that's weird, considering we only talked just once. But whatever.
>
> I want you to know that if you heard about my suicide, don't worry, it's all going to boil over soon. I want you to know that—*shh!* I didn't really die! . . . I'm telling people this so they can let me go. I want them to know that I'm leaving their lives. What I've decided to do, I've decided to go to Africa and travel the world by backpack. I've decided to see the world and explore new things. You have inspired me! I don't really know how, but frankly, I really don't care!
>
> I feel FREE right now. Like a weight has been truly lifted. I

want you to know that you should go to my funeral and laugh at this piece of information that only I'm telling you. I hope you feel special because you should feel special. You're a sweet man, and you deserve to know.

They probably won't find a body in any old forest or something because there is none. At my funeral they may have an empty casket. They may have it closed and everything. I'm having my dad read everything to everyone. I'm having everyone read something about me. So here's what I'm having you do for a mission:

If it's apparent that people need to know my whereabouts, show them this journal. I'm going to enclosed it to you, with all my secret writings. You have permission to open it. I'm granting you that. You have permission to peek inside the mind of Sally Fairfax! You'll know all the reasons and nonsense crap of why I want to do this. I love you.

P.S.: I'm going to watercolor your name on the front of this journal. That way everyone will think it's yours and not mine. I want to be incognito about all of this. I hope you understand. Please also note the dice I'm putting in your envelope. It's my favorite. I'm super into die. I'll put "Author of *Biflocka*," too, on the front of this book! I hope you become famous!

P.S.S.: Distribute it if you find it necessary. If you read it and feel like it could leave an impact on people and their lives, so be it. I'm done with this portion of my life. Also, I want to let you know that on March the 30th, I'm going to probably be at the Miami docks. I may have to go to Cuba to hitch a ride on over to Africa. It's going to be tough to get a passport. I may have to do this the illegal way. Meet me at those docks if you would like to join me or come and see me or something. I have to go. The post office is closing soon. I love you so much! I really do, Kevin. Bye! XOXO!!

Sincere love,
Sally Fairfax

AUTHOR CONTACT INFORMATION

Instagram ——————— **@kevinklix**
X, formally *Twitter* ——— **@kevinklix**
E-mail —— **kevinklix@yahoo.com**
TikTok ——————— **@klitztopher**

PHOTO BY CASEY MILNER-KNOTTS

About the Author:

Kevin Klix lives and works in West Palm Beach, Florida with his girlfriend, Casey. He has written six novels, two self-helps, two non-fiction, and one collection of poetry. He enjoys writing on his typewriter, where he makes frequent poetry posts on his Instagram (@kevinklix). He does ink drawings, digital/film photography, and he plays Blues on his electric guitar when he has free time.

Did you enjoy this book?!

Please, if you would kindly go online to . . .

- ✓ www.goodreads.com
- ✓ www.amazon.com

Search the title of this book and please take a second to post an honest review! Tell other readers what you thought of it!

NOTES

NOTES

NOTES

NOTES

Milton Keynes UK
Ingram Content Group UK Ltd.
UKHW041342141024
449707UK00006B/44